WITHDRAWN

WITHDRAWN

Ready
Aim
MURDER

L.C. BLACKWELL

If life, like an aimed arrow, pulls you back, it can only

mean that you must conquer challenges to meet your

destiny path and target, thus launching your

goals into greatness, or infamy.

Don't ever stop aiming!

FRONT DOOR PRODUCTIONS LLC

This is a work of fiction. The names of people, places, companies, and events mentioned herein are fictitious and are in no way intended to represent any real individual, company, or event unless otherwise noted. They are the product of the author's research and imagination dramatized for this story.

Edition 1, April 2021
Copyrights © L.C. Blackwell
All rights reserved. Published in the United States by L.C. Blackwell & Front Door Productions LLC, Chicago, IL
Version 1

In accordance with the U.S. Copyright Act of 1976, no part of this book may be reproduced in any form by any means. This includes reprints, excerpts, photocopying, or any future means of reproducing text. Scanning, uploading, or sharing electronically without the written permission of the author constitutes unlawful theft of the Author's intellectual property. To seek permission, contact LC@authorblackwell.com.
Cover and Interior Design: Erika Blackwell

ISBN: 978-0-9907115-5-1

Library of Congress Control Number: 2021907730

DEDICATED TO

Erika, Christina,
Jason, and Sylvia

Contents

Cast of Charactors. x
Chapter One. 1
    Hugh Taylor Birch State Park:
    The End Of The Shoot
Chapter Two. 3
    En Route To The Hotel
Chapter Three 5
    Chicago: Peter Dumas Returns
Chapter Four 9
    Susanna's Condo
Chapter Five. 13
    A Body In The Park
Chapter Six 15
    CB Post production Studio: The Edit
Chapter Seven. 19
    The Police At The Park
Chapter Eight 22
    Susanna's Condo
Chapter Nine 25
    The Investigation Process Begins
Chapter Ten 28
    Ryerson, Foot, and Burner Advertising
Chapter Eleven 32
    Peter Dumas Meets Ryerson For A Late Lunch
Chapter Twelve 36
    Whose Body?
Chapter Thirteen 37
    Leven Meets the C of CB Productions
Chapter Fourteen 40
    The ME's Domain
Chapter Fifteen 44
    The Mind of Peter Dumas
Chapter Sixteen 48
    The autopsy

Chapter Seventeen 51
    The Missing Person

Chapter Eighteen 54
    A Panther Does A Move

Chapter Nineteen 55
    Susanna's Condo

Chapter Twenty 57
    A Face Gets A Name

Chapter Twenty-One 60
    News Travels Fast

Chapter Twenty-Two 62
    An Away-Home For a Dead Man

Chapter Twenty-Three 65
    The Suite

Chapter Twenty-Four 68
    The Arrow

Chapter Twenty-Five 71
    To Grandfather's House We Go

Chapter Twenty-Six 75
    Widdicomb Appears At The Agency

Chapter Twenty-Seven 77
    The Limo Arrives

Chapter Twenty-Eight 81
    Leven Packs Warm Clothes

Chapter Twenty-Nine 83
    The Family Grows

Chapter Thirty 85
    A Special Delivery Letter

Chapter Thirty-One 90
    Secrets Revealed

Chapter Thirty-Two 93
    Peter Sees Red...

Chapter Thirty-Three 95
    Leven, Leven Where Art Thou?

Chapter Thirty-Four 97
    Leven Lands in Appleton

Chapter Thirty-Five 99
    Two More Arrows In A Line
Chapter Thirty-Six 102
    The Party's Getting Started
Chapter Thirty-Seven 104
    David Meets Larry Leven
Chapter Thirty-Eight 107
    There's A Killer In The House
Chapter Thirty-Nine 110
    Dinner Is Served
Chapter Forty 114
    Whose Ear Is Missing an Earring?
Chapter Forty-One 117
    No Rest For The Weary
Chapter Forty-Two 120
    Arrows and Earrings…
Chapter Forty-Three 123
    Susanna And David Get The Green Light
Chapter Forty-Four 126
    The Sheriff. No Small Time Lawman Here.
Chapter Forty-Five 130
    News from Florida
Chapter Forty-Six 132
    Chit Chat…Fun, Fibs, And Deathly Facts
Chapter Forty-Seven 136
    Redfeather In The Hot-Seat
Chapter Forty-Eight 141
    Susanna Takes A Break
Chapter Forty-Nine 143
    Redfeather In The Hot-seat – Part 2
Chapter Fifty 146
    Party Hardy
Chapter Fifty-One 149
    Redfeather In The Hot-seat – Part 3
Chapter Fifty-Two 152
    Stranger Danger?

Chapter Fifty-Three 154
    Carol Spirals Out Of Control
Chapter Fifty-Four 156
    Carol Nelson Meets Her Fate
Chapter Fifty-Five. 160
    And Then There Were Seven
Chapter Fifty-Six 163
    Dancing To The Sound Of Music
Chapter Fifty-Seven 166
    Magic And Murder At Christmas
Chapter Fifty-Eight 169
    Who Done It., And Why?
Chapter Fifty-Nine 174
    Hide And Seek
Chapter Sixty 175
    Words From The Dead
Chapter Sixty-One 178
    The Scene Of Chief Blackhawk's Murder
Chapter Sixty-Two 182
    Arthur And Chris Get Some News
Chapter Sixty-Three. 184
    Flo-Kimi-Abigail Speaks Up
Chapter Sixty-Four 189
    The Second Trip To Chilton
Chapter Sixty-Five 193
    Preparations For Sam Blackhawk's Funeral
Chapter Sixty-Six 195
    Back At The Ranch
Chapter Sixty-Seven 199
    Checking The Details
Chapter Sixty-Eight. 201
    The Widdicomb Murder Is Solved.
    Will Justice Be Served?
Chapter Sixty-Nine 206
    Jody Bares Her Soul
Chapter Seventy. 209
    Whose Blind?

Chapter Seventy-One. 212
    The Transgressor's Words Strike The Heart

Chapter Seventy-Two. 214
    Daddy's Girls

Chapter Seventy-Three 218
    Peter Makes a Breakthrough

Chapter Seventy-Four 220
    Blind No More

Chapter Seventy-Five. 222
    On The Road From Chilton: Big Meets Bang

Chapter Seventy-Six 225
    A Family In Crisis

Chapter Seventy-Seven. 228
    The Scene Of The Crash

Chapter Seventy-Eight 232
    Life Continues

Chapter Seventy-Nine 234
    Eeny, Meeny, Miny, Moe
    Will The Killer stay or go?

Chapter Eighty 236
    Show Me The Way To My Home

Chapter Eighty-One 239
    The Skiers Return

Chapter Eighty-Two 241
    The Epiphanies

Chapter Eighty-Three. 245
    Emma Meets A Different Peter

Chapter Eighty-Four 247
    The Family Is Home For Christmas

Chapter Eighty-Five. 249
    Peter Talks Chess

Chapter Eighty-Six 252
    Girls Talk; Boys Plan

Chapter Eighty-Seven. 254
    Dinner Is Served

Chapter Eighty-Eight 259
    A Reveal. An Attack.

Chapter Eighty-Nine 263
    Peter Ignites The Room
Chapter Ninety 270
    The Irony Of It All
The Final Word... 272
ACKNOWLEDGMENTS 274
About the Author 276
Other Books 277
    by L.C. Blackwell

Cast of Charactors

CHICAGO and WISCONSIN
Family and Friends

Arthur Ryerson, Founder— Ryerson, Foot and Burner Advertising (RFB)
Susanna Ryerson, Daughter
Christopher Widdicomb, Grandson
Peter Dumas, family friend; internationally known clairvoyant
David Arnstein, family friend; Chicago P.D., Detective
Mr. and Mrs. Gala, friends of Arthur
Mordecai, Arthur's driver and lake house, manager
Alena, Mordecai's wife and chef extraordinaire
Hezekiah, lake house employee and Mordecai's relative

Chicago
Agency Personnel/family
Hank Redfeather, Commercial Director on contract to RFB agency
Jody Marks, Producer
Carol Nelson, Creative Director
Emma Patric, assistant to Carol Nelson
Charlie Cabot, Creative Director; Christine, his wife
Other

Wisconsin:
Chilton Police, Hospital Personnel, Other
George Tyler Bush, Sheriff
Sam Blackhawk, victim
Flo (Kimi, Abigail), Sam's ward
Dr. Spensor, Chilton Hospital

FORT LAUDERDALE
Crime Scene: Police, Forensics, Witnesses, Consultants

Jason and Justin Weller, 12-year-old twins who discover a body
Larry Leven, Detective-in-charge
Modulsky, Detective
Briggs, Detective
Peterson, PD Sergeant
Officer Catanky, first on scene
Harry Bodimann, Medical Examiner
Sarkis Varzhen, Professor Native American Weaponry

CB Productions
Jerry Cargill, company co-owner
Katie, receptionist
Buddy M, editor
Mike Steel, editor

Aqualina Hotel
Mr. Bouchet, Manager
Jake, Asst. Manager

Tuesday
December 19, 2006

Chapter One

Hugh Taylor Birch State Park:
The End Of The Shoot

FLORIDA

"It's a wrap," he said softly. Three magic words from one man and dozens of others sigh in relief that the shoot is finally over.

Speaking those words: Hank Redfeather, an Irish, German, 6 foot 4 Native American dressed in black cargo pants and black t-shirt. Around his neck, a silver stopwatch dangles from a silk cord. Perched on his head, a red baseball cap, its brim framing a cascade of black curls tied in a careless ponytail.

Releasing muscles tight as corkscrews, Redfeather slowly stretched his lean body until a production assistant interrupted with a steaming cup of coffee. "Cream, no sugar?" he asks. She smiles and nods in agreement.

The rest of the production crew stood alongside the road filling up at a white-covered table resplendent with mountains of sliced bananas, melons, and kiwi, seasoned with sweet, ripe strawberries. Two large silver servers at both ends of the table offered buttery, crisp hash browns and scrambled eggs peppered with thin strips of swiss cheese. And from a high-tech traveling kitchen, smiling caterers delivered baskets of delicate jam-filled pastries and hot cinnamon buttered toast.

Redfeather lit a cigar, his ritual following the wrap of every commercial film shoot he directs; it is the only time he smokes. Feeling the slim Cuban contraband in his fingers seems to add finality to his work, the way a good Cognac punctuates an outstanding meal.

It had been a problematic shoot with child actors, wild animals, and a variety of locations. No dialogue, just action, and voice-over were not particularly his favorites. Redfeather was a "people" director and hated whiny, pouty children, especially when animals were on the set. No doubt, the extra tension contributed to the extra day for a re-shoot of the panther jumps.

Redfeather, relieved it is finally over, leans back against the tree, sipping his coffee and slowly smoking his cigar, drinking in the pure peace of the still chilly, early morning. His smoke infiltrates the yellow and hot pink hibiscus perfumery across the road — potted hibiscus planted haphazardly by the shoot producers to create a more tropical paradise.

Marvin P. Widdicomb hated Redfeather's cigar smoke but was able to ignore it, having quite recently lost his sense of smell. He lay there hidden in the bushes behind the hibiscus, unblinking eyes staring at the sky, hands gripping the arrow that felled him. It appeared as if he froze, struggling to remove it, unfortunately, with no success.

Ignoring thoughts of Widdicomb, Redfeather smokes away until one of the grips calls out, "Hank, we're all packed. You better grab some food before it's all gone. You gonna come back with us to the hotel, or are you heading to the studio?"

"I think I'll head back with you. I'll look at the dailies tonight. Tell Marty I'll ride with him." He draws on his cigar, exhaling ever so slowly, then turns suddenly to join his crew, leaving Mr. Widdicomb in repose at the shoot's final scene.

Chapter Two

En Route To The Hotel

Marty was packing the gear in the Bronco when Redfeather arrived.

"You bout ready?" he asked.

"Almost, Hank. Couple more light filters that wouldn't fit in the van, and we are good to go."

Redfeather nodded, lit a new cigar then climbed into the front seat of the truck. He pulled an iPad from a beat-up satchel he always carried, started it, and began to search his emails. Selecting three, he moved them to a desktop folder labeled Bike Shoot. Redfeather still added every note and suggestion he received into a shot folder before assembling the final takes for an edit.

Marty opened the driver's side door and jumped in, "Got another one of those," he asked, pointing to Redfeather's cigar.

"You betchum, Red Rider," he laughed, reaching in his satchel for another of his favorite Cuban treats.

As Marty lit up, Redfeather leaned back, taking a deep draw on the slim tobacco cylinder held delicately between his fingers. Gently smiling, he let a sliver of smoke slip between his lips in a slow, steady stream infusing the front seat with a heady perfume only a smoker could enjoy.

Marty, following suit, sighed, "This is one mean cigar."

"The only kind," Hank responded.

"Why smoke 'em only after a shoot?"

"It's the only time I need 'em. Did a shoot in Cuba once, and I got hooked. They erased the clients, the account guys, the talent, the producers—all of 'em. They all disappeared in the smoke. Hell, a stiff drink couldn'a made me that mellow."

"Maybe that's why Widdicomb didn't make it," Marty laughed. "He doesn't like to see you mellow. You really piss him off when you smoke these babies. Still, I can't believe he didn't make an appearance if only to tell you how to direct."

"He's told me how to direct for the last time. I told the old man I'm not doing another shoot with Widdicomb. The guy's a frustrated, no-talent ass, and I'm finally done with him."

"Well, the old man likes you. So, maybe he told Widdicomb to stand down, and that's why he didn't show."

"Let's hope he finally got the message."

Marty took the next exit off I95 at Alton Road south to the hotel. "Hank, you heading back to Chicago after the edit, or you planning to stay in Miami for Christmas?"

"I'm leaving after we finish. The old man invited me to his house in Wisconsin for Christmas."

"Woo woo! The old man invited you to his place for Christmas? You have arrived, brother. A guest of the founder of the biggest agency in Chicago, a thorn in the side of WSJ New York! Whoo-wee. You will be rubbing shoulders with some pretty impressive people."

"Just as long as Widdicomb doesn't show up."

Chapter Three

Chicago: Peter Dumas Returns

CHICAGO

The doorman at the Drake Residences rose suddenly from behind the entrance desk when the black limousine entered the building's turnaround—a unique conveyance that rotated vehicles 180 degrees upon entering. It allowed passengers an exit under the dome protected from the elements and provided drivers an exit forward instead of backing out onto East Lake Shore Drive.

A diminutive man with a shock of white hair was the sole occupant of the stretch limo. He wore a chamois-colored, suede shearling jacket baring a crisp white shirt collar at the neck. At the coat's hemline, threadbare jeaned legs ended in a pair of ostrich leather Western-style boots dyed a vibrant shade of purple.

His smile awakened when he saw the doorman approaching. "Charlie, it's good to see you!"

"Welcome home, Mr. Dumas. It's been a while," he said, reaching for the luggage the limo driver removed from the trunk.

"Too long, Charlie. Too long."

"Will you be here for the holidays, Mr. Dumas?"

"Well...part of them. I'm off to Wisconsin, believe it or not, for Christmas."

"They've had a bit of snow up there, so you can be certain it'll be a white one."

"That, I certainly will like. How about you, Charlie? Are you off for Christmas?"

"Yep! Christmas Eve and Christmas Day, but I've got the New Year's shift."

"Well, you get to share a most important holiday with Martha and the girls, Charlie. You cannot beat that. I brought something back from New York for them, so don't let me forget to give it to you before I leave."

"Yes sir, Mr. Dumas," he smiled, opening the door to the resident elevators. "I'll have Bennie bring up your luggage after he gets the mail the office is holding for you."

Peter nodded, waved, and stepped into the elevator where a uniformed operator waited. "Good evening, Mr. Dumas. Nice to see you back in town."

"Good to be back, Larry."

Peter was probably one of the most liked and respected residents in the building. He remembered names, family members, birthdays, anniversaries and always had a smile for the staff, many of whom remembered and admired his mother when she was a resident.

Like his mother, Peter loved having his piece of heaven in Chicago. No matter where he traveled or how long he was gone, this was home. Peter was fortunate to have several pieces of heaven in several cities, hip-hopping between them. However, Chicago held a special place in his heart because of his friends—friends, now family.

Peter tossed his jacket onto the Chesterfield sofa and reached for the phone to dial Susanna's number. After three rings, she answered.

"Peter, you're here! It is Peter, isn't it?"

"Yes, dear Susanna. I am here. It is I. I've just arrived." He was interrupted by the door chime. "Just a moment, Susanna, Bennie's here with my mail and luggage."

He opened the door, thanked Bennie, and pointed to the bedroom as he continued his conversation. "Sorry, Susanna. I am so looking forward to dinner. Now, is David able to join us tonight?"

"Yes, of course, he is. In fact, he just called and said he'd be here in about 15 minutes. How much time do you need?"

"Have a Jack Black waiting for me in about 30 minutes."

"Will do. Can't wait to see you, Peter."

"Lots to tell you, sweets. By the way, is Christmas at the lake house still a go for you?"

"Yes, yes. We'll talk when you get here. Get ready. Goodbye. Goodbye."

Peter retrieved his mail and switched on the black-shaded reading lamp at the desk facing the Oak Street beach. The waves pounded the shore, reducing the beach to a narrow strip of sand under a new moon in a starless sky, black like the cold water beyond the white caps.

He loved the view and often sat at his desk, contemplating Chicago's near north architecture. He secretly called the buildings the Hi-Rise Ladies of North Lake Shore Drive. To him, they stood at attention, ready to grant approval to those entering the brown and grey stoned homes on the streets of the Gold Coast.

Peter grouped them by height. There were 50-story ladies, contemporary with welcoming balconies, 20-story ladies traditionally accessorized with concrete gargoyles and lacy adornments, and grey mansion ladies with smoke spilling chimneys, warm and inviting. The Drive, indeed, was magic to him.

Returning to his favorite city was a jolt to Peter's psyche, one he desperately needed. Spending his supernatural gifts often reduced his energy and his faith in humankind, particularly after a stressful or violent crime scene or victim he was forced to witness. Despite the impact upon him, he rarely refused an invitation to help solve a crime.

He sat quietly in the dark green-walled living room, eyes closed, attempting to give boundaries to an amorphous shape as it began to invade his mind. But nothing materialized, except a chill that seemed to envelop him wholly. Rising suddenly, he shook off the cold and said aloud, "Am I not permitted a peaceful holiday? Is mayhem to follow me here? Can I not be freed of this damned familial curse?"

But the anger he felt dissipated in a flash after an outburst, knowing full well how much his unique gifts could help bring aid or justice for someone.

At the age of four, Peter was anointed with his mother's clairvoyance when he foretold an accident to be suffered by his nanny. His mother, in turn, accepted her gift of premonition and acutely heightened senses from her mother. Generations of daughters were the source of Peter's growing intuitive nature. For the first time in eight generations, the matriarchal gift was bestowed on the firstborn male descendant of Marie Dauphine Sophia Fillibran DeMent.

It was Madame DeMent, in 1789, who convinced her husband Jacques Pierre Phillipe St. Denis DeMent to flee his beloved France. Mere days before the fall of the Bastille, the aristocrat with his wife and two daughters braved an ocean crossing to settle in St. Martinsville, Louisiana.

DeMent prospered in America, advised by his wife. And, when Napoleon and President Jefferson negotiated the Louisiana Purchase, DeMent followed Marie's directive to buy thousands of acres in the territory west of the Mississippi River, thereby positioning himself to become a wealthy and powerful man.

In the early 1900s, Peter's great, great grandfather created a family trust securing remaining family properties for development, thus providing financial freedom for future generations—allowing Peter to follow his heart and nurture his gifts.

Gathering Charlie's family presents, Peter Dumas grabbed his jacket and left to meet Susanna Ryerson and David Arnstein.

Chapter Four

Susanna's Condo

The ten-foot-high glass wall of windows looked out onto the black waters of Lake Michigan, holding back the sound of icy waves crashing over the concrete stretch protecting the parade of cars as they approached the treacherous Oak Street curve.

Susanna Ryerson sat at the piano, her back to the cold night. Playing the keys softly, she fingered a soulful tune. "It's hard to believe a year has passed since the murders, isn't it, David?"

Arnstein nodded, "Yes, it is. Time felt as though it would never move forward, and yet, twelve months have passed."

"Letitia Goode's conviction still haunts Peter," Susanna added. "He may be mollified. Her appeal has been successful. The appellate court granted a full remand with instructions after hearing oral arguments. Peter certainly contributed to that decision. His suggestions to Goode's attorney played a major role. And because of his direction, Harry, Mac, and I were able to uncover new evidence after the original trial."

"Well, whatever happens, my healing began when you, Mac and Harry, made the arrest. I'm finally beginning to feel normal again."

The phone rang, and Susanna smiled, saying, "Peter's here. I told the doorman to ring once when he arrived. Will you get the door? I'll get his Jack Daniels."

David stepped into the hall just as the elevator doors opened. He walked toward Peter, his smile growing. "You are a sight for sore eyes, my friend."

They met and embraced in a brotherly hug. Two close friends. Two distinct opposites. David Arnstein, 6-foot 3 towering over Peter's five-foot-six lithe frame. An Armani power suit and Cole Hahn loafers standing in friendly opposition to Peter's well-worn jeans and purple cowboy boots. David's black, black hair spiced with grey framing a tanned complexion marked by a jagged scar, from the inside corner of his right eye to his right ear; Peter, in contrast, boasting an unruly thatch of longish white hair crowning a fair face with skin soft as a baby's bottom.

David, a former attorney now a police detective, mind-married to a clairvoyant.

≈ ≈ ≈

Susanna waited at the door, her face filled with joy, arms open wide in welcome. "Oh Peter, I have missed you so," she called out, embracing him.

Arnstein watched still in disbelief that violent crime brought these two wonderful people into his life. A life he closed to friendship, love, and passion. A life in limbo after surviving a deadly crash that killed his wife and three-month-old son.

Comfortably settled, the trio exchanged news in a flurry of questions.

"Peter, tell us what happened—in detail," chimed Susanna. "Your brief phone conversations only gave hints."

"First, I must imbibe my spirit of preference, Susanna," he smiled at her, reaching for his Jack Daniels. Taking a sip, he continued, "It was a simple case of abduction but perpetrated by a uniquely clever abductor who strove to punish the parents mercilessly. He continually moved the child, offering complex clues to the locations, each more dangerous for her than the last. But his choice of locale began to suggest a pattern, upon which I was able to fix. Fortunately, it enabled the police to secure the final location before the villain communicated the last of his clues."

"Something tells me it was final in more ways than one," David suggested.

"Indeed. It was at a bridge one mile from the child's home. A rope attached to the railing with a noose at its end, waiting for her to wear. But she is safe, and the governor is free to complete his term in office knowing that some critics can and will stop at nothing to embrace an opposition agenda."

"Oh, Peter," Susanna cried. "What a horrid thing to do. That poor child."

"She will be fine, Susanna. She has loving and caring parents. They will be the real key to survival. But enough criminality. David, will you be able to join Susanna and me for Christmas, unfortunately not in Connecticut, but in the heart of Wisconsin?"

David laughed, "How can I resist? You and Susanna. An old-fashioned family Christmas in a country home. My only hesitation is not knowing the host."

"The only thing you need to know is that it's my father's home," Susanna explained. "And most of the guests are not family. Dad loves tradition, and to experience it, he fills the house with friends and acquaintances, both business and personal. You'll love it."

"David, you will love it. Arthur enjoys bringing differences together for stimulating conversation and thoughts. Conservatives and Liberals, priests and rabbis, young and old. It will be a weekend of wonders and filled surprisingly with the joy and wonder of the holiday. Now let us leave. Dinner beckons. We can talk more as we begin the evening with a wonderful appetizer, preferably mussels in a simple white wine sauce."

*Wednesday,
December 20, 2006*

Chapter Five

A Body In The Park

Florida

It was around 10 a.m. when Jason and Justin, the Weller twins, cut through to the Hugh Taylor Birch State Park. They preferred to conquer the ridged, pocked trail with their dirt bikes instead of the paved road that circled the park. There was something magical about the silence and the lush tropical growth. Banyan tree branches reaching out to incredible lengths and the aerial vines springing from them to root in the ground for support and nourishment; tall pine trees fanned by super-sized palmettos with long green lizards and more, hiding beneath.

And peeking through it all were wonderfully bright wildflowers like yellow joyweed and ocean-blue morning glories. And of course, a December-appropriate, native flora: the Wild Poinsettia, an orange-red leafed plant— aptly named Fire-on-the-mountain.

But the silence of the boys' magic world began to buzz, causing the boys to pause and listen. "What's that noise," Jason called to Justin.

"I don't know, but it's coming from around those pink and yellow flowers over there."

"Why don't you check it out?"

"Why don't you check it out? It could be bees. You know I'm allergic to bees."

"You're always allergic to somethin' when you're fraid or don't want to do it."

"Am not."

"Are so."

"Let's flip a coin," Justin offered.

"I don't have any coins. Do you?"

"Nope."

"Then why'd ya say, let's flip 'em."

"Seemed like a good idea."

"If you weren't my brother…."

"Maybe we should just go."

"No! I never heard anything like that buzzing sound here before. And it stinks, too." Jason added

"Maybe it's a dead crocodile."

"There aren't any crocodiles here. At least I don't think so."

"Aww, let's go."

"No, I want to check it out."

"Ok, Ok. Let's do it together, but fast."

Dropping their bikes, Jason and Justin inched slowly toward the buzzing bushes. They bent down and cautiously spread the dark green growth until they saw big black flies flitting on puffy-pillowed hands holding a feathered arrow. Their eyes grew wide, and wider still, when they realized the arrow was buried in a body with a face of flies and a swollen tongue protruding from swollen lips.

Justin jumped up and began to vomit. Jason just ran screaming to his bike.

Chapter Six

CB Post production Studio: The Edit

FORT LAUDERDALE

Redfeather walked into the low-lit edit suite, battered satchel in hand, dressed once again all in black with his dark curls pulled into a careless ponytail under his always present red baseball cap. He chose to drop his satchel next to one of the three high-back swivel executive chairs, waiting for occupants behind a room-wide table facing a wall of editing screens.

A slightly raised ledge at the table's end held a platter of sweet rolls and bagels and a silver bowl with an assortment of cut-up fresh fruit alongside a coffee service. Grabbing a cup from a coaster-sized depression in the desktop, Redfeather began to pour the steaming liquid. After a careful sip, he planted his six-foot-four frame into the plush leather seat to wait for the editors.

≈≈≈

Jody Marks, the producer from Ryerson, Foot, and Burner Advertising, walked into the suite just as Redfeather retrieved copies of the 30-second script, scene list, and notes from his satchel.

"Hey, guy, you were lucky to miss the recording yesterday," Jody announced as she took a bite of a mini strawberry-topped cheesecake from the platter before settling in the chair next to Redfeather.

'Trouble?" he asked.

"Nope, a breeze!" she answered between bites, "We finished before you wrapped. Fifteen minutes. I couldn't believe it."

"That is something. Who was there from creative?"

"The writer, appropriately named Lulu Wright," she laughed.

"She's great. Smart girl, and talented. When'll she get here?'

"She won't," Jody said. "She told me she expects nothing but greatness from us. Besides," she added in a surprisingly tuneful voice after a quick gulp of water, "she's over the river, and through the woods, to grandmother's house, she goes. Her horse knows the way but needs all today for white and swirling snow."

"The lady sings, and with a mouth full of cheesecake," laughed Redfeather. "Jody, I've worked with you on over a hundred shoots. How do you do it?"

"How do I do what?"

"Devour cheesecake, pizza, chicken, ribs, pasta, everything under the sun they serve at shoots and edits and look at you. You can't weigh more than 115 pounds soaking wet. Hell, that mop of red hair on your head most likely weighs more than the rest of you."

"Sweetie, it's all in the genes. That's G-E-N-E-S," she spelled out emphatically, "and a little Taekwondo. Now just so we're on the same page, you get the bagels; the sweet stuff is mine."

"And I was dreaming about those blueberry muffins."

"Dream all you want, big guy; they're still mine. By the way, Widdicomb was a no-show at the recording. Thank God for small miracles. He would have asked the talent to emote, to put soul into the reading, and of course, tell Lulu Wright how the words she wrote should really sound. We'd probably still be there."

"I know what you mean. Widdicomb's gone after me, too. Too many times."

"What's his problem? He puts his two cents everywhere. No one listens to it, and no one wants it."

Redfeather nodded in agreement, "I told old man Ryerson, this was my last shoot with Widdicomb."

"Maybe the old man had a little chat with his ex-son-in-law. Your lighting guy, Marty, told me Widdicomb didn't show up yesterday either."

Redfeather thought for a moment, took a swallow of coffee, then said, "Thank God he isn't here today. It wouldn't be a pretty sight."

Before she could ask what he meant, the editors walked in. Jody and Redfeather had never worked with Buddy M and Mike Steel but heard great comments about their speed, creativity, and instinct. After introductions and some small talk, the work began in earnest.

The two editors sat before a dizzying array of knobs and switches below super-sized screens that suddenly went live, coruscating fast-moving images into color and lights that turned the small room into a discotheque minus music and dance.

"Earlier this morning, I put all the keepers in one digital file,"

Buddy M announced. "Thought we could look through them and ace the ones that you chose and see if they work best."

"Timings were pretty close when I checked," added Mike. "We've got a couple'a frames, in and out to play with against the audio."

When the images came to rest, a boy of twelve sat atop the Black Beauty dirt bike, the lead product set to hit the airways in the post-holiday ad schedule for Cycles, Inc — the world's leading manufacturer of trikes and bikes.

"This kid can ride," Buddy whistled.

Redfeather agreed. "You should have seen him in real-time cruising over stumps, sliding under low tree branches, and weaving through banyan tree vines. He was incredible. I wish I could say the same for the other kids."

"Hank Redfeather!' Jody admonished. "You know perfectly well those other kids were riding the competition's bike. They didn't have a chance."

"Jody, it's OK. The client isn't here."

"Oh, when you're right, you're right. Those kids were embarrassing."

Buddy M laughed, along with his partner and Redfeather, then asked, "Where did you find that kid, Jody?"

"Well," she said breathy, "your very own producer extraordinaire just visited all the dirt bike trails in Chicago. Easy peasy. I watched these kids perform at the Garden Dirt Bike Jumps on the North Side, the trail in Highland Park, and the Major Taylor Trail off 83rd and the Ryan. You have to see them to believe how amazing they are."

"Why didn't you just shoot in Chicago between snowfalls?" Mike asked.

"The bike jump, when it dissolves into the panther making his jump! We had to have a tropical environment so that the panther was in a natural habitat. Florida made the cut, and Jody found us the perfect setting, along with finding you guys, of course." Redfeather added.

They continued checking scene after scene: how the light filtered through the pines; how the logo would play on close-up turns and jumps; how the arc of the panther's leap mimicked the bike's jump; and how the audio married the visuals.

"Your scene pics duplicated mine, Hank, except for the main jump. But you're right. That shaft of sunlight sure does amplify the panther dissolve," Jody admitted.

"That's why I like working with you, Jody. You know the right stuff when you see it. So, I'm outa here. Everything looks good, in fact, great. I trust you and the boys to dot the I's and cross the T's. You gonna add the music in Chicago?" he asked while collecting his gear.

"Yep. I'll send a cut of the spot to Bill so he can play with the sound levels. We should have the final rough cut by noon or one o'clock tomorrow."

"Great. I'm off to the airport. Mike, Buddy, it's been a pleasure."

"Yo guy. Ditto. You've got a winning spot here. Nice to play a part in it."

Hank waved and opened the door, almost colliding with a food delivery. He looked at Jody, laughing. "And another lunch bites the dust."

≈≈≈

Mike and Buddy M cleaned up frames between cuts and short dissolves while Jody paused to chow down on sweet and smoky barbecue ribs. I am so glad Widdicomb won't be here, she whispered, licking her lips to catch every drop of the tangy sauce.

Thirty minutes later, she collected the master bike spot, thanked the editors, and headed back to the hotel.

Chapter Seven

The Police At The Park

FLORIDA

Birch Creek Park, 11:30 AM
After finding the dead man on his road to decay atop a lush green bed, the boys cycled away as fast as they could to get help and to distance themselves from the flies, the smell, and the ugly, inflated image now cemented in their minds.

Exiting the park, they saw a policeman at a Starbucks parking lot returning to a car where another officer sat waiting. It didn't take long to blurt out their story.

Directed to the back of the patrol car, Jason and Justin sat quietly, their young bodies still taut with shock. In moments, they were watching the roadside as the patrol car slowly moved to find a body the boys didn't want to believe they had seen.

"There. That's the place." Justin tearfully whispered. "Behind those yellow and pink flowers."

"Yup. That's where it is," Jason confirmed, determined not to cry.

One of the officers left the car to investigate. A curtain of green, a scrim to a still life scene of a feathered arrow piercing the chest of a bloated man, greeted him. The arrow's red and blue colored shaft was all that was visible; the arrowhead was buried beneath the body's dark green shirt. After a few moments, he turned and nodded to his partner.

"Are your parents at home, boys?"

They both nodded yes.

"I'm going to take you for a snack and contact your parents. Then we'll wait here for a detective. It won't be too long. He needs to ask you a few questions, and then you can go home with your folks," the officer in the car announced.

"Yes sir," they both answered.

"And don't worry about your bikes. We'll take care of 'em," he said reassuringly.

"Yes sir," they said, responding once again with voices as dead as the body in the bushes.

As his partner drove off with Justin and Jason to the Starbucks at the park entrance, Officer Catanky notified his Sergeant at the Fort Lauderdale Police Department. He described the body and identified the location as being one-quarter mile north of the southeast entrance to Hugh Taylor Birch State Park.

And the process begins. The case number is assigned, the Homicide Division notified, the ME and Crime Scene Investigators alerted, and the investigative team assembled.

Catanky was securing the crime scene just as his partner returned with the Weller boys.

While they waited in the patrol car, Catanky made notes for his Offense Incident Report (OIR). He indicated his original location at the Starbucks parking lot across from the park at the corner of Sunrise and E Atlantic. He noted the time when witnesses Jason and Justin Weller, twin brothers, approached to say they had discovered a body with an arrow in it.

He further indicated that Witness #1, Jason Weller, reported: "big flies were all over his body, and his hands looked like a bunch of marshmallows holding the arrow in his chest." He added that Witness #2, Justin Weller, described the victim's tongue as 'puffy' and said, "the lips looked like the big red candy lips I get at the Dollar Store."

He mapped out the approximate scene location and the exact time he and his partner arrived. He stated that his partner remained in the patrol car with the boys as he alone checked their claims.

Catanky was a 3rd-year officer who often had been sent to crime scenes after an initial call was registered. He knew the importance of taking notes, indicating initial observations, and knew absolutely, positively, to touch nothing.

Catanky's notes registered what he saw:
Date: Wednesday, December 20, 2006
Time: 11:21 AM   Temperature; 78 degrees F

There are no distinguishable footprints within a small dirt and graveled area roughly ten feet from the victim's body. Hibiscus plants and bushes between four and five feet high separate the body from the graveled area. The hibiscus isn't planted in the ground; plants are in pots set into areas dug out at the bushes' front edge. A partially smoked cigar rests next to a pine tree about fifteen feet south of the flowers and bushes hiding the body. I cannot see the body from the graveled area or the cigar location — my height six foot two. The body appears exactly the way witnesses described: slightly swollen tongue protruding from swollen lips. Additionally, there is seepage around the eyes. Hands are clutching an arrow. They may be in Cadaveric Spasm or beginning the end of full Rigor. Blowflies are still on the body. The body is fully clothed: dark slacks (black or dark blue) and a dark green shirt (possibly silk) opened at the neck. The victim is not wearing a jacket, and no jacket is visible in the immediate area. There are no socks on the Vic's feet, just black, loafer-style shoes with tassels. The victim appears to be about six foot one. Muscular build. Weight between 190 to 220 pounds. He has a full head of dark hair with gray at the temples. The arrow in the vic's chest has feathers and blue and red markings at the top of the shaft.

Catanky took several pictures of the area with his new 3G Sony Ericsson K800i. He bought it because Internet gurus heralded it as one of the best camera phones in 2006. He didn't like the size, but he was keen on making detective and figured his initiative would be another plus on the sergeant's annual assessment report.

He was clicking away when the ME's van and three cars arrived.

Chapter Eight

Susanna's Condo

CHICAGO

It was just past noon when a familiar Reggae sound woke Susanna. She reached for the off button to silence the clock radio, but when Bob Marley began his One Love, her hand stopped, her lips parted in a sensual smile. She took a long deep breath remembering the soft breezes kissing her skin while the sun peaked through that thatched roof. There is something magical about Marley, the way he can turn off the world and take you back to another place where time pauses, and every moment seems to last a lifetime

The music stopped; she opened her eyes. One Love was over.

It's amazing how a sound can trigger an emotional response that refuses to leave yet does, again to hide in your memories from a lost love or unrequited one. Or perhaps an unfinished dream, a goal unfulfilled. A wish unsatisfied.

She kicked back the covers and walked to her shower, humming, perhaps hoping to bring that feeling back from its hiding place in her mind. Maybe it would help her discover what was missing in her life.

Susanna was successful, talented, a mother fulfilled, an ex-wife without a husband but happy, moderately so. Something was missing, and she couldn't find it. She didn't know where to look because she didn't know what to look for.

Still humming, she stepped from the shower just as When the saints come marching in played to announce a call from her son.

"Hello, pumpkin," she answered.

"Oh, Mom! I'm not a pumpkin anymore. I'm twenty-three years old."

"You'll always be my pumpkin, sweetheart. Are you calling to say you will be coming to the lake house for Christmas, I hope?"

"Looks like it. I don't wanna drive, though. I checked the weather. It looks like northern Illinois, and much of Wisconsin might get a lot of snow. I'm thinking of taking a train. If I do, can someone pick me up at the station?"

"I don't think it'll be a problem, Chris. You know Gramps. When there's an event or party, he prepares for everything, especially at Christmas time. I haven't spoken to him, but I wouldn't be surprised if he calls to say he arranged for a car to pick us up in the city. You can certainly go up with Peter and me. David Arnstein is joining us, too."

"Oh, nice. I like David. When do you think you'll leave?"

"I'm thinking Thursday or Friday. You could do some cross-country skiing, Chris."

"Hmm, let me check. I think our office holiday party is tonight so that works. I'll get back to you later. If I can't go with you, will you take my skis?"

"Definitely. Love you, pumpkin."

"Ditto, Mom, sans the pumpkin."

Susanna was thrilled that Chris would be coming to the lake house. It had been over three years since her father planned a Christmas there. She knew how much he loved the place, and more importantly, the memories that hid behind every photograph, every decoration, every ornament they placed on the tree.

The Ryerson lake house was not a simple get-out-of-the-city getaway. Old Man Ryerson bought the eighty-five-acre compound when Susanna was five years old. As she grew and changed, the topography of the land changed with her. Newly planted trees now tower skyward. Planned trails now twist and turn between thickets of tall pines, occasionally bordered by berms, before disappearing into the forest beyond. And apple and peach trees now dot the land near the main house.

So much change in the last thirty-some years, yet so much to remember. The 9500 square foot home now welcomes a family of guest houses, a tennis court, a boathouse, a new pier, plus a new barn for an assemblage of horses. At the back of the property sits a 100-year-old stone caretaker's house alongside a three-acre plot where vegetables are planted and harvested for family, friends, and neighbors — and have been since the day the Ryerson's moved in.

It's Annie's Place. At least that's what Ryerson calls his home and the land where it sits. A piece of heaven is what Annie called it in those years before she died. He often walks the trails where Annie walked. He picks the fruit the way she did, filling the baskets in the old, red truck. He keeps that Ford truck in the original barn and visits when he wants to talk to Annie, his beloved wife.

Susanna was twenty-eight when Annie died; her son Chris was ten. She and Chris and her father grieved as one. Annie's love bound them together and still does.

It will be a wonderful Christmas, she thought, the three of us together sharing Annie's Place, sharing it with Peter and David and a house filled with friends.

Chapter Nine

The Investigation Process Begins

FLORIDA
Hugh Taylor Birch Park

The ME van pulled up to the yellow police tape that secured the crime scene with a radius of some twenty-five feet from the body.

A short, round man looking much like a giant green pepper exited from the drivers' s side — his clear, plastic raincoat-covered green scrubs that fit snugly across his generously bellied body. Catanky recognized him immediately as Harry Bodimann, the infamous Green Pepper from the Broward County Medical Examiner's Office.

At the same time, a jeans-clad man wearing almond-sized glasses and a windbreaker identifying him as part of the Fort Lauderdale Police Department stepped from a BMW 745i. He waved to the ME, then beamed in on Officer Catanky. "I'm Detective Larry Leven."

"Catanky, here," the officer said, reaching out to shake his hand and grab his card. "We got a real winner."

"Witnesses?" Leven asked as Catanky directed him to the Vic's body.

"Nope. Just twelve-year-old twins who found the body. They're pretty shook up — my partner's with 'em over there," he said, pointing to the patrol car outside the perimeter tape. "I did a visual — no jacket, no wallet, no briefcase, at least not visible. I identified one cigar stub at that marker over there. Figured the techs would prefer to bag it."

"Good job. Would you email me all your notes and your OIR.?"

"Sure thing. I took some pictures of the surrounding area, too. I'll send those with my notes."

Leven nodded, then asked, "Are there any cameras in the park?"

"Just at the entrances and exits. There's a camera at Starbucks. Might get another angle there, but I don't know how often they roll over."

Leven slipped on some gloves and moved vines and greenery to inspect more of the body. "Those kids really got an eyeful."

"I don't think they're gonna forget it," Catanky said as he started to walk away. "Good luck, Detective. You've got your work cut out for you. We'll wait with the twins till you're ready to talk to them."

≈≈≈

The Crime Scene Investigators began to process the scene as Leven finished his initial observations.

They moved like a well-oiled machine, systematically checking the secured area, looking in the brush for evidence near the body or hidden some distance away: articles of clothing, personal items, anything that could relate to the victim or his killer

Two techs examined the body, grasping almost invisible hairs and threads with long thin tweezers depositing them in individual plastic containers that they labeled. As they continued to search, a photographer captured their finds as well as the bloated body.

When they gave the all-clear signal, Bodimann began his inspection, working with complete concentration, oblivious of any other techs performing their specific functions. Leven watched as the ME checked the body, replacing gloves occasionally to avoid transference of any trace evidence.

Bodimann measured the arrow's shaft from its penetration point to the bottom of the feathers, then from penetration to the shaft's top. He also measured the upward angle of entry into the body, aware there might be some movement when the body gets transferred to the morgue. When he came to the wound created by the arrowhead, he nodded to the photography tech, indicating the need for an extreme close-up. The tech obliged shooting the area and cuts at the entry point from several angles.

They worked quickly in deadly silence. It was a little like watching ants traversing a hill with designated duties and goals until the ME called for the removal of the body. A team of techs covered it, arrow intact, and placed it in the body wagon.

Leven watched, then walked over and asked when the autopsy would begin.

"I might get to it by 3 PM, or it'll be tomorrow," Bodimann replied. "Call me around 4:30. We should have complete x-rays by then.

All I can say now is that the arrow most likely penetrated his lung and heart. Based on rigor, I'm guessing he died Tuesday, early morning. I'll have a better fix after the autopsy."

Leven nodded, waved goodbye, and headed to the patrol car to question each of the boys.

Chapter Ten

Ryerson, Foot, and Burner Advertising

CHICAGO

Michigan Avenue was ten abreast with shoppers, sightseers, and vacationers from the Chicago suburbs to cities worldwide. Children clutching hands with mom or dad, eyes wide, staring at twinkling lights on all the trees. Teenagers wearing every costume possible: preppies afoot with Uggs, maxi skirts and tailored coats; cowgirls with skinny jeans, puffy jackets, and western boots; and a host of teens yet to find themselves—labeled with brands and characters like Nike on sweats, Disney on jackets, Dr. Seuss on scarves. Arm in arm, they walk, singing and laughing, catching snowflakes on their tongues as they march hurriedly to the Magnificent Mile's magnificent shops.

But not everyone was bent on shopping.

A short walk east on Huron Street, at a building ablaze with lights, creatives and account types were preparing to burn the midnight oil to prime advertising campaigns for presentation after Christmas. More than fifty employees got a decidedly delicious incentive: Wrap up the creative by Thursday afternoon, and everyone is off till January 2nd with full pay. They didn't need to be asked twice.

Next to the entrance, a small brass plaque identified the five-story structure as Ryerson, Foot, and Burner Advertising. Arthur Ryerson liked his company's current location and the extra space but sorely missed the handsome stone mansion, just west of Michigan Ave., where his company began and grew. An elegant statement of status and stability less than a block away. It prepared future clients for the Ryerson style of solid thinking, strong creative, imaginative marketing, and an old-fashioned work ethic. What's more, nothing diminished its effect, not the insufficient heat, knocking pipes, uneven floors, or oddly shaped offices.

Ryerson became deeply saddened when forced to move o see another hi-rise glass box bound to eliminate sunlight and blue skies, erase a piece of Chicago history. He knew he was self-serving to think his history was more important than the city's progress, but that didn't stop him from holding onto memories.

The mansion had its own history, according to advertising old-timers. The six-foot-high fenced courtyard with its cobblestone walkway was touted as the entrance to the second home of Chicago's first gentleman's key club. No, not Hugh Hefner's Playboy Club. The Gaslight Club: the inspiration coincidently of another ad man, Burton Browne, in the1940s. It was the club with the New York Room, the Speakeasy, the Longhorn, and more, where talented Gaslight girls sang, danced, and waited tables wearing scanty costumes or flapper dresses with Radio City legs, long and lean.

Clients were intrigued by the mansion's history and the memorabilia tucked into the agency's current office corners. Ryerson re-imagined one of the favorite Gaslight attractions in the new building's dining room — the 5-cent sandwich lunch bar. Both clients and creatives did not find it hard to miss the mansion since its essence was alive and living in Ryerson's new location.

≈≈≈

"Does anyone know where the hell Widdicomb is," Ryerson asked the two people seated at the conference table?

Carol Nelson, one of the agency's Creative Directors, looked up and answered. "We talked Friday morning before he left for Florida, Arthur. But this morning, when I talked to Redfeather about the bike edit, he said Marvin was a no-show at the shoot on Monday and Tuesday."

"I've called his cell and the hotel where his secretary said he was staying. Nothing. That man's going to give me a heart attack," Ryerson snarled.

"He and Redfeather aren't on the best of terms. Maybe he just wanted to choose his time for a confrontation," Charlie Cabot chimed. "It won't be the first time our illustrious V.P. shows up after everything's over to add his negative two-cents on spots ready to air."

Cabot, the other Creative Director present, was very familiar with Widdicomb's critique habits. His group's recent string of commercials featuring an animated lion for a successful national bank chain nearly collapsed after Widdicomb delivered a stream of cursed comments to the client. Fortunately for Cabot, the bank's CEO was tight with Arthur Ryerson and thoroughly in love with the lion before and after the spots were produced.

"Well, enough is enough. I'm making changes after the New Year. Right now, we have two major campaign presentations scheduled right after the 1st. Let's take yours first, Carol. Where are we?"

"We came through the Creative Review Committee with flying colors. We had a double win, so we're prepping both campaigns and recommending they be tied to separate brand groups under Smith Shoe's umbrella theme: Fashion Plus. We're inserting a headline feature next to the theme line.

"For teens to young adults, a new writer delivered this fantastic concept that accurately homes in on the 12 to 24 target. It incorporates high-style fashion illustration with a photo identifier of a typical buyer image hitching on the logo line, and super headlines give the shoe personality — for example.

Here's the copywriter's rough.

Logo at top with line extension; ID target image hitched onto logo line

Eyebrow headline: Fashion Plus...

Headline: Red that goes POW

Fashion Illustration: Red high heels on four sticks of dynamite

Short copy block and brand logo

The concept art is outstanding—red on red for this one--with eye-catching props.

For the more mature female target, we're going high-fashion demonstration photography with headlines that stress the comfort features: Fashion Plus... Pillow soft soles."

"Are you using photos to identify the target buyer as well?"

"Yes. The layouts are slightly different for each brand, but logo placement and tagline, plus the identity photos, marry all the brands to the Smith Shoe Company."

Ryerson nodded his head, "Can't wait to see them. How about you, Charlie? What's on the agenda for Anderson Investments?"

"Well, the CR Committee gave the green light to a campaign that identifies successful people with their habits and possessions. The theme line is "people who know, know Anderson. We use full-page photography with bubble quotes. An example is a 40-plus-foot sailboat in Lake Michigan. Think full-page Tribune. The image is mostly water. The boat is about 2 inches in size out on the lake. Three bubble quotes sit above the boat: 'I'm looking at a 9% return this year.' "Huh!! My broker has me 2% down!" "You need Anderson."

"Other ads and TV spots include two skiers in the distance on a mountain top with three bubbles. Three bubbles above a rickshaw in Japan."

"I love it! Do we all get to go on those shoots, Charlie?" Ryerson laughed, then asked, "Think we can have everything spot ready by tomorrow at 4 PM? Charlie? Carol?"

They both chimed, "Definitely." Carol then added, "Redfeather should be back this evening. And Jody sent copies of the bike spots for the music, so we'll be able to see them tonight."

"Great work, you two."

The pair left, leaving Arthur Ryerson to contemplate how he would explain Widdicomb's sudden departure from the agency…permanently. And if the agency would survive.

Chapter Eleven

Peter Dumas Meets Ryerson For A Late Lunch

    Peter and Arthur agreed to meet at the Rosebud Steakhouse on Walton. It was particularly convenient for Peter, who only had to cut through the garage from his East Lake Shore Drive co-op and exit at Walton. The restaurant was a few steps east.
    The Steakhouse was Alex Dana's newer addition to his successful chain of Italian eateries. The original Rosebud in Little Italy on Taylor Street set the tone and quality for those to follow. Amazingly three of his restaurants were just a few blocks from each other in the city's Near North area, each of them drawing from crowds in long wait-lines.
    Peter preferred the Walton location. He felt it far more elegant and sedate than the Rosebud on Rush with its tourists and late-night diners, or Dana's other Rush Street crowd-pleaser, Carmine's, which noisily appealed to families, daters, and pure pasta lovers. Not surprisingly, he wasn't that fond of Carmine's location simply because it bordered the Viagra Triangle, a small area infamous for an over-forty crowd looking for love.

    Arthur Ryerson walked up to the table just as Peter put down the menu. "What looks good, Peter?"
    "Pretty much everything, Arthur," Peter answered, rising to shake his hand. "So good to see you, old friend, but…I sense something serious is on your mind."
    "I should know better than to think I can hide anything from you," he smiled, seating himself as though a weight pushed down on his shoulders.
    "Let's order, and then we can talk." Ryerson nodded to a waiter who promptly took their order.
    Peter opted for the mussels with Chardonnay sauce and Caesar salad, while Ryerson chose Fettuccine Alfredo with King Crab.
    They were seated in a quiet corner at the restaurant's back,

where Arthur often entertained clients, friends, and family.

"If you prefer white wine, please choose, Peter. However. if you'd like to join me in a terrific Merlot, I'll order a bottle."

"I'm game. Let's go for the Merlot."

"You will not be disappointed. I've ordered several cases for Wisconsin." He nodded to the server, "Bring us a bottle of the Nickel and Nickel Merlot."

"Great choice, sir," he said with a smile.

"Now, Arthur, what is going on?"

"It's complicated. And the cause is a case of gross misjudgment on my part."

"It's Widdicomb, isn't it?"

"Again, Peter, there are no secrets from you. Yes, it's Marvin. His behavior has been appalling to clients and colleagues alike, causing major issues at the agency. I've lost good people because of him; he's been accused of slander, sexual assault, discrimination—you name it. I could be in for a load of lawsuits."

"You know I've never been a Marvin fan, but I had no idea he was releasing his venom on you and the company. Isn't he a shareholder?"

"Yes, that was my mistake, a major one. When Marvin and Susanna married, I was overwhelmed with happiness for her. He was charming. Smart. And he impressed me with his love and devotion to Susanna. At that point, I gave him and my daughter fifty percent of the agency. Fortunately, my attorneys added a clause in my wedding gift contract: in the event of death or divorce, Marvin's ownership would be, in effect, rescinded and assigned to any descendants resulting from the marriage to my daughter. Further, the clause specified that control of progeny shares would be transferred to Susanna until the child or children reached thirty years of age. If there were no births, Susanna would hold ownership to all fifty percent.

"He so convinced me of his sincerity, I almost stopped the attorney from adding the clause, but Bill was a stickler. It stayed. Thank goodness."

Two waiters appeared with their entrees and a bottle of Arthur's favorite Merlot, which he quickly tasted, announcing "Perfecto."

Wine glasses filled, Peter made a toast, "To a perfect Christmas filled with love and caring and only perfect solutions."

"Here, here," Arthur agreed, sipped his wine, and continued his story.

"Marvin was an asset to the firm from day one, Peter. After the divorce, our business relationship was still stable, so I frankly ignored the clause--until about three months ago when he suddenly changed, presenting a list of ridiculous demands. At the same time, his expenses quadrupled, causing our accountant to investigate, which led him to a host of inconsistencies. Finally, charm was no longer an appropriate description of Marvin's demeanor. He became the person most complained about in the office. Hated. Avoided.

"I started proceedings to change the share assignment legally, and he sued me. He and his attorney used any argument to prolong the process — custody precedents, work contributions, client additions. Even the judge was getting fed up.

"Marvin didn't have a legal leg to stand on, but I agreed to a bonus as somewhat of a gesture for his agency contributions. That's when he went berserk, delivering one threat after another. My life. Susanna's life. Even Chris's life. I didn't believe he would do anything to hurt us, but hurting the Agency is another matter.

"Earlier this week, Bill prepared a letter defining Marvin's firing from the agency and the financial buyout for his employment contract, plus a substantial bonus for his contributions to our business. His services after tomorrow are officially ended. And he was made aware that the agency would not reimburse him for any expenses incurred after Sunday. Bill also included a letter of recommendation citing Marvin's contributions.

"He signed for the FedEx on Saturday the 16th, so we know he received it. However, no one's heard from him. According to one of our Creative Directors, Carol Nelson, who spoke with him before he left for the shoot, he never showed up.

"I'm on pins and needles. Now, I am concerned about Susanna and Chris—he may blame them. And I'm concerned about the agency; he just may try to take us down somehow to punish me."

"Enough, Arthur. It is my turn to speak and yours to eat. That fettuccine is getting cold. By the way, the Merlot is outstanding.

"Now, Widdicomb. First, Marvin may be a narcissist, but he does not have homicidal tendencies. He would never chance to do anything that would put his person in danger of being arrested, or for that matter, going to jail. I am more inclined to think something physical is at the crux of his behavioral change. You said there was a sudden onset of extraordinary actions. Anger, aggressiveness, aberrant promiscuity, bullying—that's not the Marvin I know. Granted, he cheated on Susanna, but that's a long way from sexual assault. And yes, he can be obnoxious and demanding. But no, I do not think Widdicomb has a violent streak; I think he has a personal problem that may be serious."

"You don't think he's a psychopath, then?"

Peter laughed. "No, Arthur, I do not believe he is a psychopath. I understand your concerns for Chris and Susanna, as well as your concern for the business. My god, you have put your life on hold to make it a success. Even a distant thought of losing loved ones or having someone threaten personal achievements or your reputation can be a frightening experience. But it can be an experience that clouds your thinking.

"Something or someone targeted a change in Marvin, and unfortunately, we must see him to learn what it is. Will he be coming to Wisconsin?" Peter asked.

"Oh, no. Marvin would never show up uninvited to any event, especially if the group included Susanna or Chris. But…showing up at the agency tomorrow to create a scene? Nothing would surprise me, Peter."

"I will join you tomorrow, Arthur. Now, let us cease speaking of Marvin. Let us enjoy lunch and this most extraordinary Merlot."

Chapter Twelve

Whose Body?

FLORIDA

Larry Leven had his feet crossed and resting on the corner of his desk at the Homicide Bureau when his sergeant came in to ask about the Birch Creek body. "Any ID yet?" Peterson asked.

"Nothin' on the body. But folks in the Starbucks at the park entrance said there'd been a lot of activity the last few days. A film crew was working in the park. We're checking permits to see who it was and if they know anything. Other than that, we've got bupkis. No name, no identification, just indications this guy wasn't some nobody. His clothes and shoes were expensive, so was his watch. Haircut, nails, professionally done. Capped teeth, gold fillings. He had money.

"The Pepper's doing the autopsy most likely tomorrow morning. Meanwhile, everything we bagged is at the crime lab. And photographs should be available soon. Briggs and Modulsky are checking CCTV near the park entrance; they're also contacting area hotels to see if anyone has missed a checkout time. I'm waiting to hear about permits."

"Keep me in the loop, Leven. This is a popular park, and we want to clear this murder ASAP."

"You got it, Sarge."

As Peterson left, the phone rang.

"Leven, here," he answered. "Yeah. That's right, Hugh Taylor Birch Park. When were the permits issued? Can you fax me a copy? Telephone number on the form? Great. Thanks for gettin' back to me so fast. You have a great holiday, too."

≈≈≈

Before heading out, Leven made several calls, the first to the CB Production Group. Next, he left a message at the University of Florida.

Chapter Thirteen

Leven Meets the C of CB Productions

Only a skeleton crew was working at the Studio when Leven arrived at CB Productions. Most everyone was taking time out for Christmas shopping before the 8 P.M. holiday office party. Two editors were playing Frisbee outside the entrance, while inside, a cute 18-year-old-trying-to-be-20-something receptionist was painting her nails blood red. Leven knocked a sharp knock on the entry desk, and Goldilocks looked up angrily. "Now I have to do this nail all over again," she cried.

"Look chickee, nail interruptus doesn't call for a hissy fit. I need to see a grown-up." He flashed his shield and gave her the meanest look he could conjure up while trying to hide the grin dancing in his eyes.

With trembling lips, she looked up at him, "I don't think you are very nice."

"Yeah, yeah. Now, where's the manager? I got questions about a murder."

Her mouth opened, her eyes wide, staring blankly at him. He knocked sharply once again on the desk, and she jumped, hitting the intercom like a bullet. "Mr. Cargill, Mr. Cargill. Help. It's Katie at the desk. The police are here about a murder." With that, she grabbed her nail polish and ran.

Leven wasn't always so ready to pounce, but sometimes the attitude of entitled kids helped make his day.

He didn't have to wait long for Cargill. An athletic, 30-something man in jeans and a t-shirt emblazoned with "Let's shoot something together" was barreling down the steps from the upper level.

Leven walked to meet him, shield in hand. "Detective Larry Leven," he said, and without pausing, "your company crew was shooting footage at Hugh Taylor Park on Tuesday. I need to know if anyone who worked that shoot is missing. And I need the names and numbers of the clients who were involved."

"Of course, let's go to my office. I'm Jerry Cargill, co-owner of CB Productions. So, are you saying that someone from the shoot is dead?" he asked, looking somewhat in disbelief while guiding Leven to a corner office on the second floor.

"Someone's definitely dead. Whether the victim worked for this company or is one of your clients is the reason I'm here. This oughta help." Leven showed Cargill a close-up shot of the victim's face the techs had given him.

Cargill held his breath and studied the image, "Not anyone who works here, thank God. But I have no idea if he's one of the client group. When did he die?"

"We don't have a firm time of death yet, but most likely, it was early morning on the 19th."

"Let me check the roster. We had three production shoots on Tuesday." Cargill turned to a computer on a black enameled credenza matching the oversized desk facing Leven.

I could play ping pong on this mother, Leven thought, his eyes looking end to end at the gleaming desktop, interrupted only by a green banker's lamp, and an antique double brass inkwell with an extended tray, and a black enameled pen resting on it. Leven had never seen one like it. Intricate and colorful leaves and flowers were etched on both pen and cap. And the gold pen clip was formed by vertical letters spelling the name NAMIKI. Probably an old ink pen worth a bundle. *Where do these kids find these things and the money to pay for them,* he asked himself?

Cargill turned and said, "The shoot at Hugh Taylor was for a Chicago ad agency's client, Cycles, Inc., a bike manufacturer." When he saw Leven beginning to jot notes in his black pocket notebook, Cargill offered to print a copy or email the information, but the detective responded, "I prefer taking notes."

Cargill continued, "The client didn't send anyone here, but RFB, sorry, Ryerson, Foot and Burner had four people scheduled: Hank Redfeather, the director; Marty Coons, his lighting guy; Jody Marks, the producer and our primary contact; and lastly, Marvin P. Widdicomb, an account supervisor. I don't know if Jody was at the location that morning or in a recording session. According to the roster, they were just doing two re-shoots. As to Widdicomb, I haven't got a clue."

Cargill gave him the RFB number in Chicago and volunteered his company's help. Leven offered his card and said one of the other detectives would follow up to interview members of the CB crew or any support personnel present at the Tuesday shoot. "Would you email me a list and phone numbers for the follow-up, please?" Leven asked as they shook hands.

Cargill nodded, his eyes watching the detective.

Leven had a way of making himself look every bit the man one should never underestimate. Despite his casual yet frequently brusque demeanor, one could not miss sensing the confidence spewing from every fiber in his body.

In the short walk to the parking lot, all Leven could think of was an arrow and a man named Hank Redfeather. "This cannot be this easy," he said aloud. "I gotta get that arrow."

Chapter Fourteen

The ME's Domain

Instead of calling Bodimann, Leven decided to shoot down I-95 south; he was only fifteen minutes from the ME's offices, and traffic was surprisingly light for 4:30 in the afternoon.

I guess everyone's at the mall getting last-minute Christmas gifts, he said aloud as he turned on the radio to Don't Be Late with Alvin and the Chipmunks. Their chirpy, mini voices, always full volume, brought an instant smile to Leven's lips. He knew all the words. And he usually sang along, at full volume no less. He wondered how many kids today knew the words or even what a hula hoop was. He'd have to ask Emily's kids.

He loved the holidays but missed not having any children. Sure, he had terrific nieces and nephews — his sister Emily's kids — but they weren't his kids. Kids he could take to the zoo without making an appointment, or read stories to any night of the week, or share the traditions he and his sister had shared growing up. If only Cary stuck it out for more than six months, he often said to Emily, but no, that first murder investigation she lived through turned her against the work that Leven loved. He was good at his job and refused to quit when Cary demanded it be her or his work. There was no compromise. She packed up and left.

He'd met a few women since that he liked, but no one rang the bell the way Cary had. Maybe, he would often say to himself, there's someone out there who's gonna ring that bell and blow it to smithereens. Yeah, maybe she's looking for me to ring a bell, too.

He pulled into the parking lot and headed to the ME stations. "The Pepper?" Leven asked the guard, who instantly chuckled while pointing to one of the autopsy rooms.

Bodimann was looking at large pieces of film when Leven walked in, "I was expecting your call, Larry, but I'm glad you popped by instead. Just got the x-rays — full body and dental. No implants, no surgeries. No previous fractures, no bone abnormalities. Not a damn thing.

"After x-rays, I removed the clothes, dried, and bagged them. Found a few hairs, one long red one— human, and one brown, possibly from a dog. The techs found a few hairs as well. We'll check 'em all for DNA.

"I did a full external exam. One tattoo. An "S" on his right shoulder. No injuries or scars. The guy's a clean, healthy Caucasian, with brown eyes and dark brown hair with gray at the temples. Hair's been recently cut and styled by someone who knows what they're doing, most likely the night before he died. A few hairs were on his neck. His height is six-foot-one-and-three quarters; his weight, 218 pounds; his age, I'm guesstimating at 42-44; athletic, muscular.

"I've taken samples of blood and under nail matter. We've got mouth swabs and fingerprints. Also got eye fluids to check potassium levels to see how they agree with our Time of Death (TOD).

"As I suspected, the arrowhead did extensive damage. It was a close, solid, and a sudden upward thrust, not an arrow shot from a bow at a distance. He was not expecting to be attacked, let alone murdered. But the arrow damage did not kill him." Pointing to the sternum in the film, he continued. "The arrowhead broke the xiphoid process at the base of the sternum. See the bone fragments? They punctured the lung and liver. The liver laceration caused severe hemorrhaging. Most likely, the shock of the sudden attack and possibly, the shock of who attacked him caused him to grab and try to remove the arrow, thus creating a cadaveric spasm —a type of rigor. He fell backward like a tree being cut down. BAM! That's when his head hit a flat stone. The first impact broke his skull."

"The first impact?" Leven asked.

"Yep. Someone repeatedly smashed his head against the stone. That's what killed him. He died holding the arrow at its entry point… but his brain died first. This act was no stranger danger. This was up close and personal.

"His killer was approximately five-foot-six to five-foot-eight."

Leven, frantically jotting pertinent notes, looked up suddenly. and asked: "How the hell do you estimate the killer's height?"

"The angle of arrow entry. Of course, I'm assuming the killer was very close to the victim, or he would have protected himself. So, the arrow had to be held mid-shaft to get that momentum and thrust upward without being seen. Based on the angle degree, the killer must be under five-foot-ten. On the other hand, the killer could be taller if he/she bent down slightly."

"So, the killer could be short or tall. Great! What about the arrow?"

"First and foremost, no prints. But…it's an interesting weapon. I'm pretty sure this is a replica of a Comanche warrior arrow I once saw at the Smithsonian. It could be a big clue. I don't know if the arrowhead belongs with the shaft, but the barbs on it are killers."

"Can I take it?"

"Yep, just sign the paperwork, and she's yours."

"What about time of death?"

"Based on rigor, external night and day temperatures, body temp—I'm still looking at 7-9 AM. Most likely 7:30 to 8 AM. But…I want to see those potassium levels. They may confirm, and they may not.

"We'll open him up tomorrow morning, Larry, around 9 AM. I'll autopsy his brain as well. Be prompt and bring coffee and donuts. Extra cream, please. No sugar." And with that, the Pepper snapped off his latex gloves with a flourish.

Leven saluted him, smiled, and left.

Thursday
December 21, 2006

Chapter Fifteen

The Mind of Peter Dumas

CHICAGO

Peter Dumas spent the night seeing flashes of Marvin Widdicomb in a sea of color— yellows and pinks on a curtain of green. The figure faded, strengthened, and faded again. Translucent. His body rigid. Lips closed. Hands folded across his chest as in rest. It gave Peter pause.

His clairvoyant mind knew that something was more than amiss with Marvin P. Widdicomb. Should I tell Arthur, he thought, or should I avoid the subject until I speak with Arnstein? He wrestled with those thoughts as he prepared to walk to the Ryerson Agency per Arthur's invitation the day before.

The sun was shining, and the sky, a vivid blue. Unfortunately, the temperature was brutal, but it was a crisp cold, the kind of cold Peter loves because it sharpens senses, awakening those grey cells defined by his favorite fictional character, Poirot.

Although mystery fills Peter's entire life, he is not considered a mystery book buff. However, he is and has been in absolute awe of Agatha Christie and Dorothy Sayers' creative genius. Their characters were so unique, so visually memorable with uncanny minds that ensorcelled their readers.

What makes one so creative, I often ask. What spark bends an individual's thoughts to create truculent acts, puzzles that defy solution, and red herrings that masquerade so authentically as truth?

Peter's clairvoyance is the direct reverse of those authors; he reveals the inconsistencies, dissects the lies, uncovers hidden agendas, and peels away the layers of deception—often before the deception has been announced or even conceived.

And because of this very nature that is Peter Dumas, he spent the night seeing those nebulous flashes of Marvin P. Widdicomb.

Peter doesn't know Widdicomb very well. He met him a few

times before the divorce from Susanna, certainly enough time to form an impression. And afterward, there is no mention of him except when Peter pays an occasional visit to Ryerson at the agency. But before Peter would discuss his thoughts with Arthur Ryerson, he would speak to David.

After a quick conversation, David Arnstein agreed to meet. The receptionist showed Peter to a conference room where he could wait. She explained that Mr. Ryerson would be alerted when his meeting was over.

Pacing as he waited, Peter imagined how difficult and emotional a situation this could be for Arthur, the business, and indeed for Susanna and Chris.

When David arrived, he was surprised to see Peter's agitation. In a sea of chaos, Peter would be the calm, yet now apprehension registers on his face, rigidity wraps his person.

"David," Peter called as he walked to shake his hand. "I need your help."

"What can I do, my friend?"

Peter continued to pace as he spoke. "First, a little history. You do know that Arthur Ryerson is Susanna's father, Chris's grandfather. You may not be aware that Susanna's ex, Marvin Widdicomb, is an integral part of this agency. It's a complicated relationship, David."

"You can say that again!"

"We may speak more of that in the future, David. But let me continue. In the last three months, Widdicomb has been creating difficulties for Arthur, which will, of course, affect Susanna.

"Last weekend Widdicomb was due at a commercial shoot for a major client. According to the director and the producer, he failed to appear. He could be avoiding some legal problems certain to arise shortly, or he may be planning something against Arthur, who fired him a few days ago. I don't believe either of those choices is viable. I think Widdicomb has met with disaster."

"What kind of disaster, Peter?" he asked.

"Murder, David. My mind continues to play an imaginary film, and he is behind the curtain. Translucent. Immobile. It does not look good, and I don't want to conflict Arthur. I must be absolute. David, would you contact the police in Florida?

"I'll be happy to do that, but I'll need a photo and details. I know a few people with the Miami Dade Sheriff's office."

"Let's talk to Arthur. I won't mention my visions, but perhaps he can fill in the details about Widdicomb."

The receptionist led Peter and David to the conference room, where the Creative meeting was about to conclude. Arthur invited them in. "Peter, David, come see our new spot for Cycle, Inc." He nodded to Jody Marks, who replayed the spot.

Peter watched, suddenly aware that the pink and yellow hibiscus in one of the scenes mimicked his translucent visions of Widdicomb. He focused hard on the bicycle to keep from transposing Widdicomb into the spot. "Arthur, the bicycle emanating from that panther's leap is incredible. The footage is stunning, and that dissolve is exceptional, technically and visually perfect."

"It is, isn't it? I can't praise Redfeather enough. He did a brilliant job. And Jody and the editors outdid themselves," Arthur raved. "I'd love to show you some of our other campaigns, but I promised our crew if we finished all the layouts and spot scripts, their Christmas holiday would begin today and end on January 2nd. I don't want to keep them any longer than need be. I'm closing the agency until after the New Year."

"A very nice holiday," Peter acknowledged. "Does that mean you'll be leaving for Wisconsin today?"

"Most likely, Peter… give me a few moments to go over some other details with the group, and we can go over the schedule for you, David and Susanna."

"David and I will wait in your office."

When Arthur Ryerson joined the two men, Peter asked if anyone at the agency had heard from Widdicomb. Ryerson nodded 'no' and said, "I'm getting a little concerned. It's not like Marvin to ignore all attempts we've made to contact him. And frankly, he's not the kind of man to walk away quietly."

"Which is exactly my reaction, Arthur. I was telling David a little of the situation, and he suggested he call a few friends in Miami who can make some discreet inquiries."

Ryerson turned to Arnstein with a look of relief, "It would be much appreciated, David. I'm sure everything is fine, but I would love some corroboration."

"I'll just need a few details, Arthur, and a photo."

"No problem. Let me introduce you to Amanda Birkey; she's Widdicomb's secretary, she'll have everything you need. And Peter, as to Wisconsin, I'm off in the next couple of hours, but I have scheduled my driver, Mordecai, to take all of you to the lake house tomorrow. He'll check with Susanna about the time. Looks like snow is coming to the Illinois border and north, so I expect an early start would be best."

"I agree, Arthur, so let us not detain you any more than necessary."

The men shook hands and left to collect information from Amanda Birkey.

Chapter Sixteen

The autopsy

FLORIDA

Leven stopped at a Dunkin Donuts a block away from the ME's domain and loaded up on coffee, donuts, cream, and sugar. His phone rang just as he paid the cashier, "Leven," he answered.

"Hey guy, do I have to come in, or can you manage without me?"

The gravelly voice of Saul Marengo brought a smile to Leven's lips. "Hey partner, how's it hanging? Enjoying your Christmas break?"

"Yes. Yes. Yes. The kids are going non-stop. We've hit every Santa Claus from Lauderdale to Miami Beach. They figure all these guys are Santa's helpers, so they want to make sure the man in red gets their message, again, and again, and again. Larry, you don't know what you're missin'."

"Oh, yes I do," he laughed. "But to answer your question. Enjoy your break. I'm heading to the Pepper's for the autopsy. I don't expect any surprises. It's pretty cut and dried."

"Still no ID.?'

"Naw, but I have a few leads. It could be a member of a Chicago ad agency that was shootin' a commercial at Hugh Taylor. Or, it just could be some dude on holiday who happened to get killed in the park. Modulsky and Briggs will be interviewing the production crew today. I'd like to know if any of 'em can ID the Vic before I start a long-distance investigation in Chicago."

"Any luck with the hotels?"

"Not yet. But somethin'll crack. Signed for the arrow yesterday, and I'm doing a check with the university this afternoon. The Pepper says it looks to him like a Comanche warrior arrow he saw at the Smithsonian. And, guess what the commercial director's name happens to be?"

"Tonto?"

"Funny! It could be just a strange coincidence, but his name is Hank Redfeather."

"Maybe it'll be a slam dunk."

"From your lips to God's ears, Saul. Me? I think our work's cut out for us. I'll give you a head's up after the interviews with the crew. Gotta run."

It took just a few minutes to park his car at the ME's.

The Pepper and his tech were pulling the body from the cooler when Leven walked in. "Aw, you brought the coffee. Good show, Leven. I believe Dunkin coffee is a far better choice than that rocket fuel they parade as coffee at Starbucks. Too strong for my system."

Leven laughed, "Oh, and I heard you were an original investor!"

"I was," the Pepper said sheepishly, "but that doesn't mean I have to drink it."

As the two men discussed the merits of branded coffees, the tech prepped the rubber block under the corpse's torso, extending the body's arch to give the Pepper better access to the chest and abdomen.

The death smells of the autopsy room always made Leven gag, but as the Pepper once told him, "Stick it out for about 3 minutes and your olfactory receptors get numb, you won't smell it anymore." But those 3 minutes felt like hours to Leven.

The Pepper was an experienced forensic pathologist, so his Y incision was quick and precise. His first step was removing the sternum. Before he did, he pointed out to Leven the damage he identified on the x-rays: the arrowhead's destruction to the xiphoid process and the fragments' tears in the lung and liver. "The arrowhead hit it right on the nose."

"Would have to be a helluva hit, wouldn't it?" asked Leven.

"Depends. The xiphoid process may start as cartilage, but it ossifies as you age. Even doing CPR on someone could damage it if you push hard enough. Several different accidents could cause a break, too."

Step by step, the Pepper examined organs, removing and weighing each one and securing samples, and placing them in formalin.

Everything looked normal, at least until he autopsied the brain.

He showed Leven the jigsaw puzzle cracks that covered the skull. "That's what your head looks like when someone uses it to smash a rock repeatedly. This is after he fell to the ground…still alive. In simple terms, a hemorrhage created a hematoma that shoved portions of the brain into the brainstem. The compression stopped the heart and respiration. This is all while the lung and liver are bleeding out. Not a nice way to go."

"Someone really didn't like this guy," Leven said, watching the Pepper direct his tech to replace the bagged organs into the chest cavity and baseball stitch the Y incision,

"There is one positive result of the head blows; we may have the killer's DNA. I retrieved a lot of skin cells on the victim's clothing and hair."

"All we need is to find someone to match it to if it is the killer's DNA," Leven offered.

The Pepper snapped off his latex gloves and confirmed he would send the report as soon as he received the Tox recap and DNA findings.

Leven said his goodbyes and left. It was time to learn all about the arrow.

Chapter Seventeen

The Missing Person

CHICAGO

At 3 P.M., shortly after Peter checked with Susanna on travel times for Friday morning, David Arnstein dropped him off at the Drake Residences. Before heading inside, Peter recapped instructions.

"David, we should be at your townhome around 8:30. I will call when Susanna arrives here. Remember to pack black-tie; Arthur insists on formality at Christmas."

Arnstein responded with a laugh, "Peter, are you saying that you will substitute an actual tux for those jeans you always wear?"

"Yes. However, I will not be wearing the expected evening wear. Instead of traditional trousers, mine will blend holiday fabrics in a patchwork pattern with a formal jacket. And of course, my holiday footwear, ostrich boots in a Christmas red."

"This I have to see. I'll be ready at 8:30," Arnstein laughed. "Meanwhile, I'll give my friend in Florida a call when I get home. Let's hope we can locate your Mr. Widdicomb."

≈≈

Arnstein's townhome was a little north of North Avenue in Chicago's Old Town neighborhood. When he moved there several years earlier, his family was just beginning to thrive — his beautiful wife and his precious three-month-old son. The psychiatrist he saw after the accident that killed Andie and David Jr. encouraged him to sell the condo and start anew so that he could begin to bury the past. But he couldn't. He needed the connection.

The glazed chocolate-brown walls and the dark walnut floors were pure Andie. She loved the backdrop they created, topped and bottomed with sparkling white cove and baseboard moldings — the perfect framing for overstuffed Chesterfield sofas in soft butterscotch leather. Black and buttery brown striped armchairs faced an antique table with the chessboard still set near end game — the king anticipating checkmate from the last time they played.

Andie's face was beginning to fade in his mind, but the memories would peak through when Arnstein least expected.

He shook his head to clear his thoughts as he looked for Lee Cowart's number at the Miami Dade Police Department.

After a few rings, a voice answered, "Lee Cowart."

"Hi Lee, it's David Arnstein."

"Well, I'll be damned. I was thinking 'bout you a couple days back. That Realtor® killer you caught was in the news online."

"Yep, there's going to be a retrial. But if Letitia Goody earns a pass, she'll be charged with murdering her husband's first wife," Arnstein added.

"Now, if only we could do that to every other guilty creep that a retrial sets free. But I have a feeling your call is about more than retrials. What do you need, David?"

"A close friend is worried about an executive who was a no-show at a commercial shoot that began last Friday. His name is Marvin P. Widdicomb. Hasn't checked out of his hotel, and last anyone saw him was Tuesday heading out to breakfast. No one remembers seeing him after that. I'm calling to see if your grapevine is looking to ID any unknown accident victims?"

"Did your friend file a missing person report?"

"No. The lack of contact is now causing some concern. Widdicomb was fired but scheduled to remain on the company roster until the Sunday before Christmas. At first, they figured he was P.O.'d and just not responding. He's kind of an odd duck."

"Seems to me, I read something on an inter-department memo. Lemme check."

After a minute, Cowart returned to say, "an unidentified body in Hugh Taylor Birch Park is the only one in the area. A guy was found with an arrow in his chest on Wednesday. No ID. Early to middle forties."

"Age is about right. Who's the detective?" Arnstein asked.

"Larry Leven, Fort Lauderdale PD. I'll text you his number. Meanwhile, I'll check Palm Beach and south. Expect a call if I find anything."

"Thanks, Lee. I owe you one. Have a great Christmas."

"You too, buddy. And get out of that snow. You need some Florida Sunshine Juice."

As soon as the call disconnected, Arnstein dialed Larry Leven.

Chapter Eighteen

A Panther Does A Move

    The basement studio at Ryerson, Foot, and Burner was dark except for the light of a single monitor facing a figure crouched in the swivel chair before it. The shadowed figure had just completed an edit to the Cycle, Inc commercial: a 10-frame upload cut in just before the scene with the black panther beginning its jump. Instead of the panther dissolving into the Black Beauty bike, it partially dissolved over the new 10-frame scene then finished the jump dissolving into the bike scene.

    It took a few minutes after the edit to rename the original file, Revision #1, and send it electronically to USA Studios.

    The figure turned off the monitor and left the room.

    Upstairs, the Creative Department was abuzz with assistants and secretaries prepping all the presentation folders for the first week of January. It was almost 5 P.M. Outside, the black sky was afire with the blaze of city lights.

Chapter Nineteen

Susanna's Condo

The third time today, Susanna's mobile phone rang with no one at the other end.

"Probably another sales call," she said aloud. "They are so persistent!" When the phone rang again, she was ready to deliver an ultimatum; instead of silence, a familiar voice spoke, Matthew Stark, a former real estate client who had become a little more than a friend.

"Susanna! It's been weeks since we spoke. How is everything in the new job? Are you still liking it?"

"Very much, Matthew. It beats real estate by a mega-mile. I should never have left. Writing is in my blood. But what about you? Are you moving back to New York?" she asked.

"Unfortunately, yes. In fact, I'm leaving on Christmas Eve. Hence my call. Are you available to join me for dinner on Saturday?"

"Unfortunately, no. We're all going up to our lake house in Wisconsin. In fact, we're leaving tomorrow morning."

"Well, I'm so sorry we can't get together. I'll email you my new address. The mobile will be the same. Perhaps you'll come and visit," he said suggestively.

"Maybe in February," she answered. "I may be working a story on the fashion industry so that it could work out. What are you doing with your condo? Do you need an agent referral?

"No, my replacement will be leasing it from me until I decide what to do. Well, I don't want to keep you, so please have a wonderful Christmas with your family. I'm guessing Peter will probably be joining you?"

"Yes, Peter loves an old-fashioned Christmas, and my father always complies. David Arnstein is coming as well. I hope you have a wonderful holiday, Matthew, and I look forward to seeing you, possibly in February."

When the call ended, Susanna took a deep breath and exhaled.

She was quite taken with Stark when she first met him. He was handsome, tall, erudite, successful—everything a successful independent woman would want. But within a few months, her feelings flipped.

She never dreamed he would be such a narcissist. Glancing at himself in mirrors was just the tip of the iceberg. He consistently managed to convey his superiority with everyone he met, and he knew it. Of course, Susanna could never forgive him for his attitude toward Peter. "Imagine," she told one of her friends, "he was more concerned about being late for a dinner reservation than listening to Peter express why he believed the real murderer was free."

In a world according to Matthew, nothing was more important than Matthew Stark—his life, his thoughts, his concerns. Susanna was glad he was moving. February would have to become a thirty-one-day-month for her ever to visit him in New York.

Stark was the first man Susanna was attracted to after her divorce. She learned a lot from her marriage and more from her Matthew infatuation. She learned what love was not. She came to understand, what is in a man's soul is far more important than his success, the way he looks, or the flattery he delivers.

It was getting late, and Susanna had to finish packing before her son arrived.

The phone rang. She quickly grabbed it, saying, "Hello." Only silence answered her.

Chapter Twenty

A Face Gets A Name

FLORIDA

Modulsky and Briggs waited for Leven to finish his call.

"You got it, Professor. Friday, 9 AM. I'll be here," Leven said, turning to the detectives. "A University authority is gonna check the arrow tomorrow. Maybe we'll get something helpful."

"We better get something quick. I'm beginning to feel as though I'm chasing my tail," Modulsky piped. "First, me and Briggs interviewed the production crew. They never saw the Vic before. If he was from the client-side, it was someone they hadn't met. The director and the lighting guy were their only contacts. Then we checked every hotel in the Fort Lauderdale area north and south of Hugh Taylor Park. The big ones and the fancy B and Bs. No one scheduled to check out is overdue."

Briggs interrupted, "We even checked Housekeeping about occupied rooms where no one slept in the bed for the last twenty-four hours. Found a few. Hotel Management is checkin' em out. And they're showing the vic's pic to the full hotel staff to see if they recognize him. We'll hear somethin' after the night crews start their shifts."

"The hotel gig isn't sparking yet, but the cameras at the Starbucks and the park entrance have a couple of roach motel bits," Modulsky interjected. "Might be something for us. At 7:00, Tuesday morning, a guy in khaki pants and shirt with a yellow vest entered the park, pushing a wheeled trash bin. Can't see his face, but his upper body says gym rat, yet hips down he looks girly."

Leven rolled his eyes, "What do you mean, girly, Modulsky?"

"You know. Most gym rats have big legs, but this guy has legs like a girl, a skinny girl."

"Don't worry about the legs; see if tech can do anything with the face. Anything else? You said a couple of roach motel bits."

"Yeah, at 7:45, the park and Starbucks cameras caught a big guy, all in black with a red baseball cap and a ponytail carrying a big leather bag. A cab dropped him at the park entrance. We got the cab company and the driver, who said he picked up the fare at the Sonesta off the A1A.

"At 8:04, ponytail guy leaves the park—no signs of blood. He hits the Starbucks for coffee, then sits outside before heading back to the park at 8:22.

"At 8:25, the production crew rolls in with two cars and a van," Modulsky continued. "Another van with kids and bikes pulls in fifteen minutes later. And at 9:15, the catering van shows up. A few caterers leave, return, then leave again. They went into Starbucks. Maybe they didn't like the coffee in the van."

"What about our Vic?' asked Leven.

"He came in at 7:15 on Tuesday morning. A limo deposited him at the Starbucks. He paid cash for a coffee then walked to the park. The boys are checking the plates for the limo company. No news yet."

Briggs continued, "We checked the footage up to when you got to the scene on Wednesday. The ponytail guy didn't leave by foot on Tuesday, but he could have been in the caterer's van or a couple of cars that drove out. We got nothing else except families and couples walking in and out. Nothing else till the park closed on Tuesday."

"OK. Get a still of the ponytail guy and take it to the Sonesta. Even if he did check out, management or Housekeeping might give us an ID."

Leven's phone rang, and he told Modulsky and Briggs to wait.

"Leven," he answered. "Yeah, yeah. How is Lee? Haven't seen him since I left Miami PD. What can I do for you?" Leven listened as David Arnstein spelled out his request.

Leven grabbed a pen, jotted some notes in his black notebook, and told Arnstein he would send him a copy of the Vic's photo. When Arnstein explained that Widdicomb didn't show up for the shoot on Monday or Tuesday, Leven said, "If that photo looks like your guy, send me anything you can. I'll need dental records, too, if you can get 'em. Oh, and do you know whether he has any tattoos? Okay! Terrific."

He listened a few moments, said, "You got it," then disconnected the call.

"What was that?" Briggs asked.

"Possibly the answer to our prayers." Turning to Modulsky and Briggs, Leven let a breath escape noisily and said, "A Chicago detective. He may have just given the body a name: Marvin P. Widdicomb, a big shot with a Chicago Ad Agency. He was scheduled to stay at that new Aqualina Hotel on Collins. I'll check it out after I email our photo to this Detective. You two get over to the Senesta and find out what you can about the guy with the ponytail."

Before Leven left for the Aqualina, he briefed Sergeant Peterson on the team's progress.

Chapter Twenty-One

News Travels Fast

CHICAGO

Despite the face being one of death, the resemblance was undeniable when Arnstein compared Leven's victim photo with the image from Amanda Birkey. Marvin P. Widdicomb had indeed met with disaster.

Arnstein called Peter, who volunteered to tell Arthur and Susanna, while he called Amanda Birkey for Widdicomb's dentist and doctor's name.

Luck was on Arnstein's side. In less than an hour, he arranged for dental records to be sent directly to Larry Leven's email address; he also was able to confirm an 'S' tattoo on the right shoulder after a conversation with Widdicomb's internist.

Arnstein was surprised that Susanna's ex would have done something so out of character. He learned nothing about the man that would suggest he would walk into any tattoo parlor, let alone get a tattoo. His mind filled with questions, uppermost, how Widdicomb's death would affect Susanna.

> Did the 'S' signify Susanna? Or did it have another meaning? If it was representative of her, when was it done? After the divorce, or before? Did Susanna know about it? According to Peter, she never spoke of Widdicomb once she learned of his infidelities. How will she feel now that he's dead? Does she still care for him, despite his actions? What about Chris? Did he have a relationship with his father? Will he be saddened at his death? Angry? Neutral? Surprised that someone murdered his dad? How about Arthur? Will he be relieved? Thankful that confrontations and client problems are now mute subjects? And Widdicomb? What about his relationships with colleagues? In

Peter's mind, dislike followed Widdicomb like a cloud. Could their dislike promote murder? Did Widdicomb have a host of enemies? Who killed him? Why? What's the motive for his death? And why with an arrow?

Christmas in Wisconsin may be an extraordinary gathering, he thought as he sent Leven the tattoo confirmation.

Chapter Twenty-Two

An Away-Home For a Dead Man

FLORIDA

Arnstein's text and the dentist's email caught Leven before he left for the Aqualina. He forwarded the dental info to the Pepper for the forensic odontologist and called Modulsky and Briggs to meet him at the Hotel after they finished at the Senesta.

The Aqualina Spa and Resort Hotel is only twenty miles from Hugh Taylor Park and sixteen from the Fort Lauderdale PD. Still, it's a lifetime of luxury away from either location at room rates that could rush past one-thousand-dollars a night in a heartbeat.

Built earlier in the year, it was a natural home-away-from-home for Marvin P. Widdicomb. Elegant. Killer views of the ocean. Private balconies. Champagne waiting in your room after check-in — and good champagne, no less! And, of course, an entrance lineup of Bentley's and Rolls Royce's welcoming your arrival to say you belong.

The car jockey looked askance at Leven's pride and joy: his 745i Beamer. But that didn't faze Leven. Heck, the jockey probably drove a beat-up Ford, ten years and counting. He flashed his shield and said, "Keep it close." The tuxedoed valet rolled his eyes and handed a ticket to Leven, who rewarded him with a five-dollar bill — a drop in the bucket compared to a Bentley's twenty-dollar tip or a fifty from a Rolls.

Leven walked up a grand staircase, approached the first hotel employee he saw, and asked for the manager. His shield put a sudden stop to the young man's suggestion that he might be of help. Instead, he said, "Come with me, please?"

Before introducing the Manager, Leven had to be vetted by the Assistant Manager — just one of the differences, the Detective thought, between a ritzy hotel and a Motel 6.

After passing inspection, Leven was pointed to a pair of double doors, seven feet high, embellished with an engraved brass plate buffed to a glorious gold; it identified Bouchet as Manager. But before the Assistant Manager could announce him, Leven reached for the doorknob. He didn't bother to knock. Enough with this Mickey Mouse formality, he thought.

"I'm Detective Leven, and I'm here about a murder," he announced, walking into the office and placing his ten fingertips on a stylized desk version of a bureau by a French cabinetmaker. It was a simple act meant to demonstrate that he was in control.

It startled Bouchet, who rose quickly from behind the Louis XIV desk, but it did not intimidate him. So, he placed his ten fingertips on the desktop's baize inset, then slowly began to flex them as his dark eyes challenged Leven's control. Bouchet looked far more at home behind the desk than the Detective did. He was petite but not a weak man. He wore a silk suit with narrow lapels, a crisp white shirt with French cuffs, and gold links that incorporated the Aqualina 'A' logo. His trousers were slim and sat perfectly atop glowing black shoes.

"I say!" Bouchet uttered. "Murder?"

'No. I say Murder! You say, how can I help you, Detective?" Leven replied.

Bouchet's gaze cast a critical eye on Leven as he returned to his chair without a word, illustrating why he was the man who managed a hotel of the Aqualina's stature. "I'll be glad to help. I just don't expect someone to walk into my office unannounced without giving me the courtesy of a polite request. Now Detective, before I can help you, I must know how this murder affects the Aqualina?'

Recognizing that his personal opinions of splashy hotels affected his behavior, Leven sat down in one of the high-back chairs at the desk facing the Manager. "You're right, Mr. Bouchet.

This is your office, and you're in charge here. I apologize. I'm sorry for being rude." It was an uncommon act by an uncommon man who rarely apologized for any manner of behavior.

Bouchet smiled, acknowledging to himself that Leven's offer was sincere, then said, "Thank you. I accept your apology, Detective Leven. Please explain how we at the Aqualina can be of service to you."

After a quick briefing, Bouchet acted on his promise with speed and authority. Personnel from Housekeeping and the Front Desk arrived to be questioned and shown a photo of the victim. Recognition was immediate, so Bouchet instructed the Assistant Manager to escort the Detective to Widdicomb's suite. He also cautioned the Front Desk to watch for other Detectives and get them to the suite without disturbing guests.

Leven told Bouchet he would keep him apprised of the situation, thanked him, and shook his hand.

Bouchet nodded, saying, "Till we meet again, Detective Leven. Perhaps when you are a guest at the Aqualina."

Leven laughed, "From your lips to God's ears, Mr. Bouchet."

Chapter Twenty-Three

The Suite

When Jake, the Assistant Manager, unlocked the door to Widdicomb's suite, a vision of white greeted Leven. Chalk white walls with chair rails and wall moldings sized for accent. Some to highlight a piece of art or a super-sized television screen—an architectural backdrop for traditional white wing-back chairs and contemporary white sofas. Teak tables and cabinets introduced a perception of warmth to the room. But the piece de resistance was the gently moving sheers at the windowed wall framing a deep blue to green bed of swaying water as far as the eye could see.

Leven blew a long, low whistle as he stepped out onto the patio. Some people really know how to live, he thought. And this was only the living room.

When he and Jake entered the bathroom, Leven thought he had died and gone to heaven. A gigantic walk-in shower, a spa tub big enough for a party, marble and mirrors, and thick white robes welcomed him. "I could live here," he said to Jake. "It's bigger than the apartment I have."

Jake laughed.

When they came to the bedroom, it was a playground of space surrounding a king-size bed. The real-life watercolor of ocean and sky gave the room an ethereal sensation, as though it were floating gently between puffs of cloud and waves of water.

Leven turned, realizing he was here to search, not to be enthralled with views and furnishings. He began checking the bedside table drawers when he noticed a single gold earring next to the lamp. When he pointed to it, Jake told him that housekeeping must have found it. "They're instructed to place anything found onto the closest piece of furniture and to advise head of housekeeping. A note's left in the guest's mail slot, as well."

"Can you check if there are any other notes or calls left for him?" Leven asked.

A knock at the door interrupted them.

Modulsky and Briggs' arrival saw the three detectives slip on latex gloves and proceed to do a thorough search of the rooms. Leven bagged the earring as well as some of Widdicomb's jewelry and personal care items, including a brush and comb. No identification. No credit cards. No briefcase. No computer or tablet. Just $1000 in cash and a closet full of clothes and Tumi luggage.

The rooms were pretty much a clean sweep due to a Housekeeping team that meant business; every surface was immaculate, the windows sparkled, even the doors had a fresh sheen. The three men wrapped up within an hour.

"What about the coverlet?" Leven asked Jake. "Is it replaced daily?"

"No. Just when a guest checks in, and then every seven days, or at check out. Of course, a guest can request a daily replacement," Jake answered.

"So, when did he check-in?"

"I believe it was Saturday, the 16th, but I have to get that confirmed."

"So, this should be the check-in coverlet? Right?"

"It should be," Jake replied.

"I'll need a big plastic or paper bag, so we can take it to our lab. The blankets, too.'

"I'll call housekeeping."

While they waited, Briggs and Modulsky gave Leven the scoop on the ponytail guy. "His name is Hank Redfeather, and he's a director for Ryerson, Foot and Burner Advertising in Chicago. He checked in on Thursday, December 14th, and checked out on the 20th."

Leven shook his head. "A native American directing a commercial, a hop skip and a jump from our Vic; the weapon of choice — an arrow. It's probably coincidence, but …"

Friday
December 22, 2006

Chapter Twenty-Four

The Arrow

FLORIDA

Leven was in his office by 8:30 AM working through his notes to add to the report. He planned on calling Arnstein after meeting with Professor Varzhen, so he quickly listed questions that he hoped the Chicago Detective could answer.

The Officer at the Desk called, alerting him to the Professor's arrival.

Leven expected to see a sprightly older man with horn-rimmed glasses, leather patches on his jacket, and rounded shoulders. The roughly 35-year-old man wearing John Lennon style specs, a worn aviator jacket, jeans, Nike t-shirt, and flip-flops looked more like a student than a tenured professor.

"Professor…"

"Please, call me Sarkis."

"You bet. First, thanks for coming, Sarkis. No offense, but you look pretty young to be an authority on Native American weapons."

"Oh, I'm a lot older than I look. Good genes."

"What got you interested in early weaponry?"

"An incredible professor at Michigan State got me hooked with Neanderthal cave drawings from Spain. He photographed them for his art history classes. Those drawings reminded me of some Native American art I'd seen. The weapons were similar, so I began researching. I only had two classes with him in the first quarter of my freshman year, yet Dr. Toria changed my life, and most assuredly, many others. He taught you how, why, when, and under what influences shaped the art and the elements. Toria had all the ammunition, pardon my pun," he chuckled.

"Toria was brilliant. Earned a BA at the University of Madrid, a Doctor of Jurisprudence at the University of Zurich, and at Harvard, Masters of Art and Philosophy. And, he put every bit of his background into his art lectures. I know, I know. I'm getting carried away.

I apologize."

"No. No. It's great to hear about a teacher opening minds instead of closing them to different ideas. Are you still in contact?"

"No. Dr. Toria was one of the seventy-one passengers killed in a jet preparing to land in Brussels in the 60s. It was a tragic loss. But enough of ancient history, show me your arrow."

As they walked to the Evidence Room, Leven explained that the ME thought the arrow resembled a Comanche arrow he once saw at the Smithsonian.

"I can easily determine the design for you and if it is an original or a copy," Varzhen offered.

"Comanche bow and arrow skills became more enhanced after they learned the value of horses. The farther they rode, the more buffalo they killed. And, the more they killed, the more they adapted and perfected their weaponry—their arrows were accurate and deadly. In full gallop, the Comanche warrior became a feared hunter of animals and man."

Leven directed Varzhen to a bench outside the evidence locker and gave him white cotton gloves. He put his signature on the evidence envelope along with the sign-out time, then handed the arrow to Varzhen.

"Well, it's not old, but it is handmade. Very nicely done. Definitely Comanche style. First, the shaft. This one is made of dogwood, typical of early Comanche arrows; tapered, so there's less drag— like the nose of a plane. The tapering allows the arrow to penetrate deeper, as well."

He pointed to the arrowhead, saying, "This noch that holds the arrowhead in place is carved by hand, most likely with a flint tool. And, it holds tight with sinew."

"Sinew?" Leven asked.

"Yeah. If you've ever cooked a pork tenderloin, you may remember the whitish kind of skin on some parts. That's sinew. Whoever made this arrow either bought the sinew or processed it themselves, probably from the back leg of a deer — if they're hunters. First, they dry the sinew, then peel off thin strips.

"To keep the arrowhead tight in place, our guy had to chew that sinew to soften it, then wrap it around the arrow and arrowhead. When sinew dries, it shrinks, and it is super tight.

"The painting on the shaft is common with Comanche arrows, as well; the blue color is actually laundry bluing—a gift from the settlers that we still use today. The dried blood color is most likely a red ochre pigment, probably mixed with commercial paint.

"As to the fletching—that's the feathers—they're from a turkey's wing or tail—one of several feather types common with Comanche arrows. Notice that the fletching is also held in place with sinew. No glue.

"The arrow size is correct, too. Comanche arrows are between 24 to 27 inches long. Whoever made this arrow is a hunter, dedicated, and knowledgeable about primitive archery, bows, and arrows.

"I could tell you a lot more, but it might be overkill. Any questions?"

"Where would someone buy this sinew, or a pre-made Comanche arrow?"

"I can probably dig up some names for you. Meanwhile, I'd check "Primitive Archer Magazine". It's a top-notch-publication for competition archers, hunters, Native American bow-makers, etc."

"Sarkis, it's been a pleasure. It's not often I meet an authority who delivers facts combined with real stories—stories that'll make me remember. I'd bet you make every student who listens to you want to listen and learn."

"Thank you, Detective Leven. That's a compliment I'll remember."

After Leven returned the arrow to Evidence, he walked the professor to the exit, deep in thought, wondering if the Pepper could get any DNA off the sinew.

Chapter Twenty-Five

To Grandfather's House We Go

CHICAGO

Mordecai arrived promptly at 8 AM and parked in front of Susanna's co-op building, where she and Chris were waiting in the lobby.

It took a few minutes for Chris to help him pack the luggage and skis. "Long time no see, Mordecai. How have you and your family been, and how is the woman who makes the best chocolate chip cookies I've ever tasted?"

"We're all fine, Christopher. And when my Alena discovered you would be at the big house for Christmas, she baked many batches of the Best-Chocolate-Chip-Cookies-You've-Ever-Tasted," he laughed.

"You and your wife just made my day. No, I take that back. You both made my weekend!"

≈≈≈

Mordecai drove east, then north to East Lake Shore Drive, where he pulled into Peter's co-op turnaround. After giving Mordecai his bags, Peter waved to Chris then joined Susanna in the back of the limo.

Susanna was not her smiling self. Her eyes slightly reddened; she looked pale, drawn. Fragile. It was as if some force was sucking her into the corner of the plush leather seat. Peter could feel her sorrow and see darkness enveloping her. He was surprised at her demeanor. Something connected with the news of Widdicomb's death was crushing her. A connection that did not bode well.

His thoughts were interrupted when the limo stopped, and Arnstein joined him and Susanna in the back seat.

"Welcome, David," Peter said, smiling, hopeful that his arrival would lighten the atmosphere and deliver Susanna from her gloom.

Chris turned from the front passenger seat to give Arnstein a high-five. "I didn't see Mordecai add any cross-country skis to the trunk. Did you forget them? Or are you planning to pass?"

"No pass, buddy. Your granddad offered to take them up for me. I guess he was concerned about all our luggage. I'm planning to give you a run for your money."

"Be careful, David," Susanna offered. "My son is Olympic material when it comes to cross-country skiing."

"Well, Chris, I hate to admit it, but I'm pretty good. How about you, Susanna? Are you Olympic material, too?"

"I'm a Sunday skier. Slow and easy, in love with the snow and out for a bit of exercise."

"Sure, Mom. Don't let her fool you, David. She's competition plus."

"Time out! Time out!" Peter interrupted. "Now that we are officially en route, it is the perfect time to imbibe in some wonderful tidbits that Jana has prepared."

"Jana!" Susanna said with a look of surprise.

"Yes, Susanna. Your incomparable cleaning lady, cook, and baker extraordinaire offered to prepare a host of strawberry delights for a mid-morning refreshment. With coffee, of course."

"Leave it to Peter to satisfy his taste buds in and out of the car," Susanna said with a laugh.

Peter was happy to see her mood brighten. Perhaps, he thought, I may be able to discover the source of her concerns when we arrive at the lake house.

After serving the group, Peter managed to eat a fair number of toasted filo dough wraps filled with strawberries and feta cheese whipped with cream.

"I envy you, Peter. If I had your appetite, I'd be rotund," Arnstein chided.

"I simply have skinny genes!" Peter responded. "Now I must rest, body and mind." He turned, closed his eyes, and quickly fell asleep.

≈≈≈

The snow was falling in earnest by the time Mordecai reached the Illinois/Wisconsin border. We'll never make it there by noon, he thought.

Despite the plows ahead of him, the heavy snow soon covered the tire tracks briefly visible on the macadam. I-41 was getting slippery, and drivers in the caravan of cars slowly began to reduce their speed.

Stockbridge was now a little under 125 miles north.

Peter was fast asleep, Susanna dozed off as well. Mordecai and Chris were listening to the weather report while Arnstein sat silent, wide-awake, watching the snowflakes attack the road and the cars. As far as he could see, the trees were blanketed in white, looking more and more like a Christmas card. However, the magical holiday image failed to erase the photo of Widdicomb in his mind: the pallor of death and the look of sudden stillness on this face.

> *Before his wife's death, David Arnstein practiced criminal law. And he was good. Very good. Although he now is a detective with the Chicago P.D, it doesn't' mean his legal and investigative mind retired with his legal career. Not a chance. Developing alternative killing scenarios and red herrings were part and parcel of his defense methodology for clients charged with criminal acts. It's the way his mind works. Put simply, it's his M.O. No surprise he had an illuminating conversation with himself – after making a list of the obvious: Widdicomb was killed at the shoot location. This was not some wrong-place-wrong-time incident, he told himself. It had to be someone at the shoot or someone who knew about the shoot and knew Widdicomb would be there. Or, Widdicomb knew him well enough to set up a meeting and told him, "Let's meet at the shoot." If Leven has any CCTV, he should be able to isolate anyone who showed up. But why an arrow...to add confusion? Blame someone else? Deliver a message? And how did he bring in the arrow? Hidden under clothing? If it was someone from the shoot, they had to have a connection with Arthur Ryerson. Could someone be trying to destroy the Ryerson Agency? But why? He asks himself, what's the motive?*

While Arnstein attempts to stage the murder in his mind for potential motives and opportunities, Peter, in his relaxed state, begins to uncover hidden actions and agendas from images developing in his subconscious mind:

Arthur disembarking a plane in a sea of yellow; Susanna removing an extra-large hoop earring in a circle colored a brilliant red; two men arguing outside the agency's office – one, a black filled outline, the other, a white cutout.

The secret of Peter's clairvoyance was not merely seeing images; it was his interpretation of each image, peeling away layer after layer of meaning until he reached the image core and its truth.

While Peter's body sleeps, his mind carefully examines each image, questioning every aspect with color playing an important role.

Arthur disembarking a plane? Somewhere warm, hot – yellow? Recently? He asks himself. His clothes are casual. A vacation? Or does he represent someone in his agency family? Susanna, holding a red earring. Is it hers? Does it belong to someone she knows? Does the red indicate blood? Or death? Or is it the color of the earring owner's hair? And the office argument? Are the shapes male or merely an expression of good and evil? Like puzzle pieces, the image parts disengage from the image, floating unattached as Peter watches his subconscious strip the pieces bare, waiting for other images to help him unravel the message.

Chapter Twenty-Six

Widdicomb Appears At The Agency

Ryerson, Foot, and Burner Advertising was locked up tight, but a security guard was stationed at the entry desk when Charlie Cabot rang the bell. After showing his ID., Charlie entered. "Anyone here?" he asked.

"Nope. Quiet as a tomb," the guard answered. "Ms. Nelson was here early this morning for about an hour with her assistant, Emma Patrick. But that's it."

"Well, I won't be long. Did Mr. Ryerson set up security guards for the whole weekend?"

"Yep. We have a list of who can and who can't enter, Mr. Cabot."

Charlie nodded and headed to his office. He wanted to check on all the packets for the presentation the first day after the New Year. Storyboards and ad layouts were stacked neatly against the stainless-steel legs of the Herman Miller credenza. Atop the teak surface sat navy blue folders embellished with silver type identifying RFB Advertising, Anderson Financial, and January 2, 2007.

Flipping through one of the folders, he found copies of the layouts with text, as well as scripts and miniature storyboards. Satisfied that everything was ready, he took the video case labeled Anderson and left his office for the small production studio in the building's lower level.

The room was dark except for low-wattage lights at the corners of the ceiling. One wall was filled with monitors above an editor's station, complete with an assemblage of dials, knobs, and registers for audio and visual controls. At the other end of the room was a small recording studio soundproofed with wedge-shaped black acoustic foam panels. In front of the paneled back wall stood a lone microphone on a tripod stand with a single page resting on a script tray.

Settling in front of the control desk, Charlie slipped the cassette into the slot and watched the 30-second mock-up video of the Anderson TV spot. "Perfect," he said aloud as he pressed eject. While reaching for the video case, he saw another one that was labeled Cycle, Inc.

"Humph," he said aloud. "Must be the new spot." Having heard from Carol Nelson that it was a winner, he decided to play it.

She's right. This spot is dynamite, he thought, before his eye caught something. He rewound the tape and watched again, this time pausing at 15-seconds and 5-frames. A sudden cut in the spot footage brought Widdicomb to the screen. He was holding an arrow stuck in his chest as he fell back. Another quick cut and a leaping panther dissolved into a sleek, black bike.

Chapter Twenty-Seven

The Limo Arrives

WISCONSIN LAKE HOUSE

    The last few miles to the lake house took the limo through the quaint town of Stockbridge. The town and the Indian tribe which came to settle in the area are named after Stockbridge, Massachusetts. The tribe became identified with that eastern city's English name after being forced to emigrate. The members may be known as the Stockbridge Tribe, but they are Mohicans. They are the People of the waters that are never still, and this politically inclined group of Mohicans grew and prospered in Stockbridge and the surrounding towns at the shores of Lake Winnebago.

    Wisconsin's Indian history is what convinced Arthur Ryerson to buy the land to build his retreat. He studied the Mohicans and other Indian tribes and respected their spiritual culture and approach to the land and nature. He was active in Indian affairs and contributed generously to the community in time and money. So too did his wife Annie, who happened to have Mohican DNA through her family's matriarchal side. Hence, Ryerson's love was two-fold. And because of Annie, he particularly denounced James Fenimore Cooper's demise-of-the-Mohican prediction.

> *Annie was proud of her Mohican heritage. She studied the tribe's history, spoke the tongue, and even now, through the family's contributions, her artifact search for all tribes continues. What's more, she did all she could to help historical societies and museums dedicated to Mohican history, particularly the early history at their Housatonic River home between the Hudson and Connecticut River Valleys. She so disliked Cooper's 'Last of the Mohicans' that she was planning to produce a documentary focusing on the Mohican union with England at the onset of war in 1754. Annie died*

before she could complete her project. She watches over Christopher and Susanna, hopeful that mother and son will finish her dream. She directs Peter to help them.

A plow cleared the road directly ahead of the limo, so driving was a little less hazardous despite the onslaught of snow. Arnstein attempted to search for the lake house between the snowflakes, "I can't see a house. Are you certain we're on the right road, Mordecai?" he asked.

"We're on the driveway, Mr. Arnstein. Left the road about a mile back. You'll be able to see it at the next turn," he answered.

"You won't miss it, David. My dad likes to do things in a big way," laughed Susanna.

"A very big way," Chris added.

"Oh, look," Peter chuckled. "It's that house on the corner of Arlington and Lakeview in Chicago."

"Ok, ok, I get it. The lake house is not a log cabin. And, it looks awfully familiar."

"It should, David. It's a copy of the Wrigley Mansion in Lincoln Park," Peter acknowledged.

"And, so it is!" David nodded.

≈≈≈

As Mordecai pulled up to the entrance, Arthur Ryerson stepped through the copycat building's opened doors, more commonly known to the community surrounding it as Annie's place. Like the original, the residence is steel and concrete clad in terra cotta tiles in an Italian Renaissance style, perhaps a style that could be considered the precursor of the prairie school movement. The copper roof is also patinated chemically to achieve the antiqued green color to match the Chicago structure.

But that's where the similarity ends. Inside, Annie's place is only 9,000 square feet, not 13,000-plus. There are no Tiffany windows and certainly no intricate mosaic floors or exotic mahogany. Of course, some of the ceilings are coffered but not gilded or silvered. No walk-in vaults, either.

Having been invited to the Wrigley Mansion for several events, David Arnstein expected a traditional ambiance in the lake house when he entered, possibly with a few Victorian embellishments.

What greeted him was Herman Miller, some Baker, Platner, and Knoll furniture, leather and long-haired shearling rugs covering teak floors, and Schnabel, Kandinsky, and Miro covering the walls.

Before Arnstein could process all he was seeing, Arthur Ryerson hustled him, Peter and Susanna, into a library off the main hall. He suggested that Chris help Mordecai bring in the luggage, then head to the kitchen where Alena was making his favorites for a late lunch. "We'll join you in a few minutes."

Ryerson closed the doors of the 14-foot ceilinged room. It was far different from the other rooms visible on the first floor. Traditional with a capital 'T'. Narrow pilasters separated walnut burled bookshelves edged with carved bands. On the two walls not lined with books, one had matching walnut doors that looked out to a walled courtyard with a stand of birch trees surrounded by clusters of pine and spruce. The opposite wall housed a fireplace, and above it, a glass window and locking mechanism that enclosed a recess. Inside, a glorious 20x30 inch Rouault.

Arnstein joined Susanna and Peter on the enormous contemporary u-shaped sofa with its centered coffee table. Ryerson opted to stand, leaning against the only other piece of furniture in the room— a Sheraton-inspired desk.

"I didn't want Chris to hear what I'm about to say. Not to worry. This room was soundproofed last summer when we had some important meetings at the house," he began.

Peter watched Arthur's face fill with anxiety. He intuited Arthur's words would have a dramatic impact on his daughter and grandson.

"Charlie Cabot called earlier with some terrible news." Glancing at Arnstein, he explained, "Charlie is one of our Creative Directors. He was at the office, double-checking his presentation for January. Charlie's a real buttoned-up creative. He wanted to enjoy his time off, so his philosophy has always been check-now and there will be no surprise problems later. While checking the photo mock-ups of the 30-second spots, he saw a cassette with the Cycles, Inc commercial— the one shot in Florida. He decided to watch it based on our other Creative Director's review: Carol told him it was a winner."

"Widdicomb was in the spot, wasn't he?" Peter offered.

"You got it, Peter. Charlie didn't see it, the first run-through, but he thought something didn't fit. In the second playthrough, he saw it. Roughly 15-seconds and 5-frames from the start, about seven to ten frames are intercut into the footage. It was Marvin holding the arrow in his chest as he fell back."

Susanna's scream echoed in the room. Peter grabbed her arm as she stood up and fainted, falling at Arnstein's feet as her father ran to her.

Arthur helped Arnstein lift her to the sofa. "Peter, there are smelling salts in a first aid box in the cabinet behind the desk. Just press the gargoyle to open the door," Ryerson directed.

Peter did, revealing shelves with glasses, a black onyx sink, and a first aid kit. He grabbed the smelling salts and rushed to administer them to Susanna, who immediately began to cough, frantically waving him away.

"It'll be on every television screen, Chris's father killed with an arrow in a commercial for bicycles," she cried.

"Calm down, sweetheart. It won't be on air. I've contacted USA studios. The electronic distribution schedule doesn't begin until Christmas night. Unfortunately, the spot is dubbed for smaller stations that don't accept electronically…but we stopped the delivery before the UPS pick-up. It'll cost extra, but we still have time to correct, dub, and ship. I'm just grateful that Charlie caught it."

Susanna hugged her father, saying, "Oh Daddy, we've got to tell Chris his father is dead. Murdered. What if Charlie hadn't caught it? What if Chris saw his father murdered on air? He'd never forgive us."

"I know, sweetheart," Arthur whispered. "We'll tell him tonight. Now, Chris is going to be wondering where we are. Thank God I had this room soundproofed when I did. You go and join him for lunch. Tell him I'm briefing Peter and David about the rest of the group that should be arriving late tonight and tomorrow morning."

Susanna nodded and left. Arnstein looked at Arthur and said, "You know it has to be someone connected to the agency."

"I don't want to believe that," Arthur responded.

Peter raised his arm to Arthur's shoulder, "My good friend, not only is someone related to the agency responsible; you are a true target."

Chapter Twenty-Eight

Leven Packs Warm Clothes

FORT LAUDERDALE

Briggs was brave enough to fill his cup with coffee from the Mr. Coffee carafe. It was an older model, not one that turns off automatically. This one just keeps cooking...all day long.

"Modulsky, I want you and Briggs to go through that production crew with a fine-tooth comb, Online and off," Leven barked. "I wanna know what they friggin eat for breakfast, who they sleep with, if they're friendly with anyone from the Ryerson Agency, or the Aqualina staff. If there's a connection, I want to know it. Next, see if anyone from Chicago registered at the Aqualina, anytime during the week before and after Tuesday the 19th."

"You bet, Larry. I think me and Briggs should make nice with all the valets and the bellhops. Maybe this Widdicomb guy had some visitors who weren't staying at his hotel."

"Great, Modulsky."

"How about those leads Professor Varzhen sent? The guys who make arrows and the sinew sellers?" Briggs asked.

"Yes, yes, and yes," Leven replied. "Contact them regarding any orders sent in the last few months to Chicago or Florida from Miami north to Fort Lauderdale.

"And here's some killer news. David Arnstein, that Chicago detective called to say someone shot footage of our Vic holding the arrow in his chest and falling backward— and he intercut it in the TV bike spot shot at the park! An agency guy caught it before USA studios distributed the spot electronically for a December 26 air date."

"Jeez, talk about bragging how you killed some guy," Briggs said, shaking his head.

"Bragging? It's a friggin bike spot! A commercial they put on kids' shows. This guy's a sick puppy," Modulsky piped in.

"That's why you both need to look for anything, no matter how small, that can lead us to this bastard. I'll be interviewing most of the agency people who have any connection with the spot when I get to Wisconsin in the morning," Leven explained.

Modulsky looked up questioningly. "I thought this was a Chicago ad agency."

"It is, but according to Arnstein, the people I need to talk to are spending the Christmas weekend at the owner's lake house in Wisconsin. So, I fly to Chicago then switch to a puddle jumper for an hour trip to Appleton. That's not all. Then I get picked up for an hour trip to Stockbridge, population 622. Of course, if it's snowing, all bets could be off."

Modulsky laughed so hard his belly shook, "Glad it's you and not me! Hell, you could be like that guy on the MTA in that song."

"What MTA song?" asked Briggs.

"From the 60s. It's funny. My mom has an old album by the Kingston Trio. The song is about some guy who gets on a train and never gets off. He doesn't come back; he just keeps riding. Larry, maybe you'll keep going in circles because of the snow."

"Be careful, Modulsky. I could send for you," Leven laughed.

The trio finished the meeting with a round of Merry Christmases, hopeful that a murderer would find his way into their stockings over the weekend.

Leven went home to pack, then headed to his sister's house. He bought Emily's five-year-old a locomotive for the set he gave him last year. Jerry loved trains. Every time he saw a train picture, Jerry would go toot toot, pretending he was the locomotive. This one was special with all-wheel drive and an operating headlight. It was bright yellow and blue, and the best part was that it had authentic sound: three air horns and a bell.

For eight-year-old Erika, Leven splurged on Jess, the 2006 American Girl Doll. He bought two extra outfits so Erika could dress Jess in something other than her embroidered halter top and tie-dye skirt.

Leven, Jack and Emily, and the kids wouldn't spend Christmas together, so tonight was going to be extra special. No murder. No blood. No evidence. Just Frosty and Alvin and the Chipmunks.

Chapter Twenty-Nine

The Family Grows

WISCONSIN

The best-chocolate-chip-cookies-I've-ever-tasted was the main topic of conversation when Peter, Arthur and David joined Susanna and Chris in the kitchen. Mordecai, hands up in defense, politely declined to offer any guess regarding the secret ingredient in his wife's fabulous cookies.

Susanna ventured an idea. "Cereal. That's what it is, but I can't quite decide which one."

"No, mom. It's more exotic than cereal. Maybe chopped Brazil Nuts."

"Maybe it's a secret ingredient that should remain secret," Peter suggested.

"Maybe you're right, Peter," Susanna said with a smile.

"I agree," Alena laughed. "Now, gentlemen, please sit. I will bring your lunch."

In a few minutes, Alena placed a bounty of food on the large circular table: Pasta with fresh green beans and small red potatoes tossed with fresh pesto and imported Parmigiana Reggiano shaved in delicate slivers; On another serving platter, Boeuf Bourguignon in a red wine gravy rested with homemade flat noodles; Crisp Romaine sat in a large wooden bowl with Caesar dressing and cheese baked cubes of sourdough bread; and of course, a large bowl of Susanna's famous black bean soup.

"Alena, you have prepared Susanna's fabulous soup," Peter said excitedly.

"Just for you, Mr. Peter. I promised Susanna."

The group chose a little of everything and began their lunch without speaking a word. Silence prevailed until every plate was naked of food.

≈≈≈

When Mordecai and Alena began to rid the table of serving

pieces and dinnerware, Arthur sat back and said, "Outstanding, Alena. You are a treasure. On behalf of my family and friends, I applaud your remarkable talent."

Alena blushed and said quietly, "I'll bring the coffee, now." Along with the coffee, Alena served a platter of Chris's favorite cookie, then she and Mordecai left. Alena knew her boss and the look in his eye when he needed privacy.

Chris needed no invitation to scoop a handful of his favorite cookies. As he did, Susanna looked at her father, who nodded and said, "Chris, we have something to tell you."

"I know. I know all about it," he said quietly.

Peter interrupted, "Who told you about your father's murder?"

Arnstein watched Susanna close her eyes and lower her head as Arthur Ryerson stared at Chris, holding his breath.

"My step-sister told me," Chris announced.

Chapter Thirty

A Special Delivery Letter

It was about 3:30 when Mordecai opened the door to find the postman, a vision of white wearing enormous black galoshes. He quickly invited Henry B into the entry. "Didn't expect to see you, Henry."

"Special Delivery for Mr. Ryerson. And what looks like last-minute Christmas cards. You gotta sign, Mordecai."

"Of course. Can we get you something hot to drink?"

"Nope. But thank you anyway. I just want to get home before this snow gets any deeper. Our branch won't be open tomorrow, so I got a long weekend. Don't expect any mail till Tuesday."

Mordecai signed for the Special Delivery letter and said, "Mr. Ryerson is in a family meeting, but he has something for you." He walked to the hall credenza and searched through a stack of envelopes. Grabbing one, he took one of the packages on the bottom shelf, as well, and handed them to Henry. "Merry Christmas, Henry, from the Ryersons and from Alena and me."

"I sure hope that box is full of the cookies your wife makes!"

Mordecai laughed. "You can open it before Christmas, Henry. Enjoy."

"Thank you, Mordecai. Give my best to Alena and all the Ryersons. Tell 'em Henry B of the USPS wishes them a very Merry Christmas."

Mordecai smiled, waved goodbye, and headed to the kitchen where Peter was carrying a coffee and cream tray. "I'll take that for you, Mr. Peter. Are you going to the library?"

"Yes, I am. We are consoling Chris. Unfortunately, his father's death was not the only surprise news today."

Mordecai nodded, his eyes filled with sadness. "Despite his on-again, off-again appearances, Mr. Widdicomb had a deep affection for his son. You could feel it when they were together. They often met here when Mr. Ryerson was out of town."

"I was not aware that Chris and Marvin had any relationship,"

Peter said as they reached the library doors.

"Oh, yes. Chris asked Alena and me not to make mention of it. He didn't want Miss Susanna to think he was disloyal to her."

"The unfortunate intricacies of divorce," Peter acknowledged.

"Yes, sir. Oh, I almost forgot. A Special Delivery letter arrived for Mr. Ryerson."

"I will give it to him, Mordecai," Peter said, taking the letter and the tray. "And please make certain we are not disturbed."

"Yes, Mr. Peter," he said as he opened the door.

David came to Peter's aid, glad to have something to do.

Susanna stood in front of the French doors at the courtyard entrance, a cascade of falling snow masking the trees behind as though a curtain of white had been drawn closed for the night. She held Chris in her arms, a current of tears streaming from her eyes. Why hadn't he told me, she thought. I would have understood.

The news that Chris had a loving relationship with his dad was a shock to both Susanna and her father. Susanna particularly did not forgive Widdicomb for abandoning their son, but then to discover that he hadn't...buried terrible guilt within her.

Aware of the distrust and dislike between his divorced parents, Chris could not share the loyalties he felt to either of them and hid the guilt within his heart. Knowing his father had hurt his mother deeply, he kept their relationship secret.

Peter poured some coffee for Arthur then joined him on the sofa. David did the same for Susanna and Chris, urging them to join the others.

Peter took the stage. "We cannot enter the future without shedding the trials and guilt of the past. And to do that, we must understand how we arrived in the present. Marvin is dead. To discover how he arrived at this crisis, we have much to learn.

"Each of us knew a different Marvin. And together, we can rediscover the man and thus solve his murder.

"Chris, you knew a father. A man who dearly loved you, not noisily, but privately. A man who shared thoughts and ideas, likes, and dislikes.

"Arthur, you knew a brilliant creative force. A man who could present your agency's creativity as nirvana for clients. A purveyor of magic and mystery. Bright. Believable. Trusted.

"Susanna, you knew two Marvins. A first love who became husband and father. And a man who sought uncontrolled love and approval in the arms of others.

"The Marvin I knew was created with bits and pieces of conversation, a collection of the judgments of others, a persona of brands and possessions. He was a man of a thousand faces without soul or reality. A shape that morphed into identities required of him.

"And so, for the next few hours, David and I would like to meet each of your Marvins. Peculiarities. Pluses. Minuses. Friends. Enemies. Whatever you can tell us about the man. Chris, we'll begin with you."

Chris sat facing Peter, his face frozen. "I can't tell you much, Peter. We just did things together. We talked about my job at the paper. He asked me tons of questions. About school. The foods I liked. If I ever smoked pot. We went to movies, out to dinner. He was always interested in what I was doing. The only times he talked about himself, it had to do with the agency."

"Did he ever talk about having a daughter? Your step-sister?" Peter asked.

"No. Until she called to tell me Dad was dead, I never heard anything about her. Heck, I don't know if she really is my step-sister."

"How often did she call you," David asked.

"Just three times. The first time was Tuesday. All she said was, "Hi, Bro." I said you must have the wrong number. She said, "No. You're my brother." Then she hung up before I could say anything. I thought it was a crank call. Then she called on Wednesday. She said, "Our wonderful father is dead. Your family's fault." And she hung up again. I knew he was supposed to go to Florida, so I called the agency to check. Ms. Birkey said he wasn't expected because they were shooting a spot in Florida. I figured if anything happened, she'd know.

"Then, my so-called stepsister called on Thursday. All she said was that we would be meeting soon."

Chris talked for about an hour. Arthur and Susanna listened to all of Peter and David's questions, still surprised at the relationship between Chris and Widdicomb. Finally, Peter suggested that Chris head upstairs to unpack and get ready for dinner. Before he left, he looked at Susanna and asked once again, "Mom, do I have a sister?"

Susanna shook her head, "I don't know, Chris. I really don't. But Peter and David will find that answer. I trust them."

After Chris left, the four of them continued.

"Whoever she is. She knew Marvin was dead before we did," David said quietly.

"That does not bode well," Peter added. "Now, Arthur, it's your turn, but before you begin, I must apologize. Mordecai gave me a Special Delivery letter that came for you."

Ryerson took the letter and tore it open. A simple drawing greeted him: Four arrows crudely drawn, each crossing at the other's fletching with one of the arrowheads dripping to represent blood. Four lines of text sat beside the arrows:

4 sharp arrows all in a line
One is finished, three are behind
When those three hear the arrow's call
    No one's left to get it all.

David reacted quickly with deadly dread. "Whoever killed Widdicomb isn't finished. This is a viable threat, Arthur. You, Susanna, and Chris are under attack. And this house, this location, this snowstorm is the ideal setting for murder."

"Why does it have to be us? Why not three people from the agency?" Susanna asked.

"Agency personnel are replaceable, Susanna," David answered. "Even dead, Marvin is still part of your family, as Chris' father."

"Besides," Peter added, "if something happens to Arthur, the agency is yours, Susanna, per your wedding gift contract. And if something happens to you, Chris is at the helm. And if Chris is gone, there is no agency—no one will be left to get it all."

"Arthur, I think it wise to contact guests in the morning and simply advise them that the Christmas celebration is being canceled."

"I think we need them, Peter," Arnstein interrupted. "A good group will help us keep tabs on the agency people. Widdicomb's killer has thrown down the gauntlet. We need eyes and ears."

"I see your point, David. I have misgivings…but I do agree."

"Arthur, who will be here from the agency?" David asked.

"Well, there's Hank Redfeather, Charlie Cabot and his wife,

Carol Nelson, and her assistant, Emma Patric, who happens to be her niece. You surely don't suspect any of them?"

David answered, "Arthur, everyone's a person of interest. Any others?"

"Let's see…two people from our Production Group. There's Jody Marks, one of our producers, and Phil Conroy, our editorial chief. I invited them both at the last minute."

"Any of your other guests, friends, or acquaintances of Widdicomb?"

"The Galas. They introduced Susanna and me to Marvin."

"Peter, you must be Arthur's shadow. I'll take Susanna, and when Leven gets here tomorrow, he'll be Chris's best new buddy. In fact, I think Mordecai should be with him as well."

Peter nodded his agreement and said, "Let us finish with Arthur and Susanna's recollections of Marvin. After dinner, you and I can build a true profile, and perhaps, we may be able to add substance to our enigmatic killer."

Arthur walked to the library entrance and pressed a buzzer at the corner of the door jamb. Within minutes Mordecai appeared to learn the evening's schedule and the plan for an early, light dinner.

Mordecai nodded and explained he would be taking the truck to pick up Detective Leven in Appleton at 6:00 AM, barring, of course, additional weather issues.

Ryerson thanked him and went back to join the others. "Shall we begin, Peter? David?"

For almost two hours, Arthur and Susanna searched the memories in their minds looking for expressions, incidents, comments, confrontations — anything that would resonate with a reason for Marvin's murder or the person who put the arrow in his chest.

When Alena knocked at the door to announce dinner, Arthur asked a single question before leaving the room. "This arrow drawing—it's not just some prank someone concocted to suggest a murder weekend like that Indian mystery by Christie…is it?"

"Trust me, Arthur, it is not a prank," Peter replied.

Chapter Thirty-One

Secrets Revealed

It was almost midnight when her tears stopped falling, and Susanna finally closed her eyes. She hadn't talked about Marvin in several years, and she certainly hadn't revealed so much about their marriage or life together to anyone. Not her father. Not Peter.

And now, even David knew her secrets: her embarrassments, her naivete, her misplaced trust, her blind attachment, her faulty reasoning.

She had buried memories of Marvin deep in her psyche, but Peter pulled each one of them from her mind as easily as pulling weeds and blossoms from an unattended garden.

> Marvin P. Widdicomb was a charming man. Good looking with dark curly hair, a contagious smile, and eyes...a color of blue that the sky envies.
>
> He was loving and generous with a wry sense of humor. A perfect lover, gentle yet passionate. Intense and demanding, yet ever so sensitive. And his power was such that you believed every word he whispered.
>
> He was everything Susanna dreamed.
>
> He would describe her beautiful after a driving rain plastered her hair into vine like tendrils and turned her eyelashes from dark to light, leaving rivulets of black across her cheeks. Beautiful, he would say. And she believed him...as many other women did.
>
> Women were charmed by his tenderness, his sincerity, his unbridled lovemaking, his caring, his promises of love forever.
>
> Susanna believed him, unaware of his effect on other women until an attractive brunette knocked on the door of her Kenilworth home and calmly announced

that Marvin P. Widdicomb was the father of her expected child — a child neither she nor Marvin wanted. A fetus to be aborted. An abortion to be paid for by Marvin P. Widdicomb.

Susanna stood there for several minutes, digesting the diatribe directed at her adoring husband. The brunette was cheeky. 'Will you give me a check, or shall I go to his office?' she asked, handing over a copy of a letter regarding the same abortion and familiarly signed: affectionately, your dearest Marvin.

As if a trance, Susanna told the brunette to wait as she walked to a kitchen desk, removed a checkbook, and endorsed a $4000.00 check to cash for her beloved husband.

Marvin P. Widdicomb was indeed a man loved, a man desired by every woman he met — blonde, brunette, redhead — as Susanna learned in the following weeks before she filed for divorce.

Of course, men were not exempt from the charms of Marvin P. Widdicomb, or were they? He was the end-all, be-all competitor — admired for his prowess with women, but unabashedly hated for his power to convince anyone he chose to agree with his assessments, his ideas, his recommendations.

A man who forges such love and hatred walks life on a wire. It really is no surprise that his life has led to his murder. Who did it? Many have been called, but one is chosen.

Saturday
December 23, 2006

Chapter Thirty-Two

Peter Sees Red...

It was 3 AM. Vivid dreams awakened Peter with a start. Dreams flashing images created in his subconscious.

Two paths meandered in his mind. One was yellow with vibrant blues and greens; the other, red and white. Two red clocks ticking loudly, red arrows falling from the sky, and red letters marching on a white path...an A, an R, an S, a C.

Peter shook free of the images, acknowledging the need to examine them thoroughly and redefine the messages hidden in their layers of meaning. Some are easy. Some require intense unraveling. But he needs them to rest and resonate with his thought waves so that every nuance can be revealed.

Wrapping a deep blue robe around his slender frame, he chose to seek solace in the kitchen with a cup of chamomile tea. The house was as still as a graveyard...moonlight and shadows turning tables and secretaries into gargoyles and creatures of the night.

This day before Christmas Eve promised to be bleak, with Alena preparing a holiday repast in one room while Peter devises a plan to prevent murder in another. He had been concerned about Susanna's safety once before when he and David worked together on the murders of eight Realtors. Susanna received the murderer's calling card shortly after her best friend became a victim. Leaving the real estate business had been on Susanna's mind; the murders just confirmed and hastened her decision.

Peter turned on the spotlights at the island, adjusting them to a soft glow, then started the electric kettle. The chamomile tea was in the second cabinet he opened, alongside a container of honey. Cups were on the cup caddy next to the kettle.

After preparing his tea with a modicum of honey, he added a splash of Jack Daniels, the bottle awaiting him on the tray next to the window beside the overstuffed grey suede chair. Nuzzling himself into the comfort of the down cushions, he retrieved a small notebook from the pocket of his robe and began to write between sips of his special tea toddy and closing his eyes to focus on his mind movies.

> *My subconscious stirrings are more than mental imagery. They are stories not yet written. Pictures not yet developed. Oftentimes, actions not yet defined or planned. And sometimes, actions recently committed.*
>
> *My task: strip away each layer, each color, each meaning to unravel the message.*
>
> *The yellow path. Is it the warm place introduced in the image of Arthur deplaning? Sun-filled, perhaps with colorful blossoms, or costumes mimicking Klee or Cezanne's paintings, or can the colors be a bird aglow with feathery hues? But if the color 'yellow' signifies the Sun, is it truly the Sun or the star at the center of the Universe. Or is it the star at the center of an ad agency or a family? And what if the 'yellow' signifies the Sun but is spelled with an "o".*
>
> *And what of the color "blue"? Is it a color or something the wind has done? Perhaps it's an anagram.*

Peter's clairvoyance reacts like a computer programmer erasing, coding, re-coding options until he is satisfied with his image interpretation and the picture is complete. As the clock strikes four, he writes something in his notebook.

Will murder strike next?

Chapter Thirty-Three

Leven, Leven Where Art Thou?

United Airlines Flight #925 from Florida circled Chicago's O'Hare airport for well over 20 minutes in a landing lineup of airborne jets. As the snowfall pauses, snow-eating bobcats scoop and shove record amounts of the fluffy white off the runways. And as quickly as the snow disappears, one jet after another plants tires on the ground, maneuvering to waiting gates manned by cheerful personnel ready to welcome anxiety-ridden passengers home or onto the next leg of their holiday trip.

Family and friends waiting for travelers watch with fascination the orchestration of jumbo jets sliding into place like toys on a board game.

Leven was happy to put his size 11s on solid ground. Shaking with cold, he made his way to a departure and arrival board to search for his connecting United Express flight to Appleton. His plane had arrived at Gate H22. He would be departing from B12 in one hour and ten minutes, thankful that for now, the weather was working in his favor. The snow had stopped, but another front out of Canada was coming, possibly within the next 24-hours. He would be well out of harm's way before it reached Wisconsin. Predictions pointed to a southeasterly route kissing the eastern shores of Illinois but hugging the state of Michigan. It might just miss Leven's Stockbridge destination.

After locating a Dunkin Donuts for his favorite cup of java, Leven headed to Gate B12. He made himself comfortable in a corner seat where he stretched out with his feet nestled atop his carry-on. It was over twenty years since Leven had a connection at O'Hare — not since leaving the city at fourteen with his mother and sister. He may have been born and bred a Chicago boy, but he was a Floridian now, loving the long hot days of summer, the ocean, the perennial blue skies, and the seafood. He absolutely, positively loved fresh seafood.

Thirty more minutes, and he would be on his way to ice and

snow and hot drinks and sweaters and boots and scarves. And, most likely, frozen seafood.

≈≈≈

It was 5:30 AM at the Ryerson lake house; David had joined Peter in the kitchen, grateful for Alena'a's waiting pot of coffee. Hot tea was not the key that unlocked his brain on an early, cold, and dreary morning. Mordecai was in the garage starting the truck and packing gear on the outside chance of a breakdown or a snow issue. Peter was still writing in his notebook.

"Do we know when everyone's arriving?" David asked the others in the room.

Alena replied. "Everyone should be here for dinner, so I would say sometime between four and five this afternoon. The snow is stopping, so the main roads will be in good shape."

"I just got a weather warning on my phone that another storm was heading our way from Canada," David said.

"We heard that also, but Mordecai checked with the Air Force base in Milwaukee an hour ago, and they said it looks like the storm would miss us. Michigan and east will get the brunt of it," Alena said.

Peter looked up, putting his notebook aside. "That is good news. Perhaps, David, you might convince Susanna to go cross-country skiing after our meeting. It would be a good release for her."

"Good idea, Peter. And as for our meeting, I've put together some suggestions. Why don't we meet in the library after breakfast?"

Peter agreed and told David about his dreams. "I only wish I could get to the scene of Marvin's murder. I know I would see so much more."

"I have an idea you'll be seeing more than you want after everyone arrives. I'm anxious to hear any updates from Leven."

Chapter Thirty-Four

Leven Lands in Appleton

WISCONSIN

It was close to 7 AM when Mordecai left the lake house under skies still dark and cloudy. Leven's flight was due at 7:15, but after Mordecai checked with United Express, it looked more likely to be 30 to 45 minutes late. O'Hare's outgoing flights were in a traffic jam.

The trip to the Outagamie County Regional Airport usually took about forty-five minutes, even on snowy days. The road was clear with occasional patches of black ice, but the mountains of white bordering WI-55 were not something one could ignore if the Canadian storm moved a few miles south of its current path. The road would be impassable.

Mordecai was traveling west on 114 to WI-10. Traffic was lighter than he expected, another 10-15 minutes, and he would arrive at the short-term parking area. For most people arriving at Outagamie Airport, the reaction to the 30,000 square-foot gate area was one of surprise. It may not have compared with Chicago's O'Hare, but it certainly was not a dinky airstrip in the middle of nowhere. Furthermore, it was the "airport that never closed" no matter how much snow fell.

At 7:55, United Express flight 1320 landed and began its taxi to Gate 4. Leven looked for some wood to knock on, grateful that both legs of his trip suffered only minor snow delays. One of the first passengers off the plane, he watched for signs to Door 2 for the short-term parking as he glanced at all the seating areas with natural light. Impressive, he thought. Looks nicer than Fort Lauderdale. When he saw the plaque inviting passengers to take off their shoes and rest — the floors are heated, he paused. "So, you've got hot floors," he said aloud. "We've got hot everything in Florida — nothin' cold, except the beer."

Grabbing his phone, he dialed the number Arnstein gave him. When his call was answered, Leven replied, "Mordecai, it's Detective Larry Leven. I'll be at the short-term parking in about ten minutes. I gotta hit the head."

"No problem, detective. I'm in a black Range Rover parked just to the right of Door 2."

≈≈≈

Leven waved when he exited the airport, walking quickly to the truck.

"Wow!" he exclaimed, jumping in the front seat after tossing his carry-on inside. "What's the bloody temperature. I'm as cold as a witch's tit in January."

"It's 22 degrees," Mordecai laughed. "We're due for a heat-wave tomorrow. A springy 28.."

The two men jawed weather, Wisconsin politics, and religion for some 30 minutes— agreeing, and agreeing to disagree, when Mordecai's phone rang.

It was Peter.

"Mordecai here," he answered, then listened intently. "Yes sir. He's with me. We're about 45 minutes away. I'll come straight to the hospital." He closed his flip phone, a strained look on his face.

"What's happened?" Leven asked.

"Ms. Susanna, Mr. Ryerson's daughter, has been shot…with an arrow."

Chapter Thirty-Five

Two More Arrows In A Line

CHILTON HOSPITAL

Arthur paced the length of the waiting room and back, again and again.

"Gramps, the doctor isn't going to give news any sooner if you wear a path in that carpet."

"I know, Chris. I'm just too nervous to sit."

"Mom'll be OK. I know it. I can feel it. I'm just glad I got there when I did. I couldn't find my gloves, so I told them to go ahead, and I'd meet 'em on the trail."

"It's a good thing you weren't there. You might have been a target as well."

While grandfather and grandson talked, Peter sat motionless in one of the blue, fabric-covered chairs, eyes closed, arms hanging loosely at his sides, palms down with fingers relaxed. Behind those eyelids, he examined a filmstrip of images racing across his mind, images that a voice directed him to review.

> How did you miss the white road with the red letter "S"? The simplicity of it deceived you. That's rare, Peter. The "S" wasn't marching; it was gliding along the path. Don't forget the ticking clock, Peter. Two of them. Need I say more? It is time to structure the story with all the recent images. Peter, you must organize them together, do not examine them singularly. Don't let emotion for a family distract your mind.

As Peter listened to his mind consort, his subconscious began its journey to discover and integrate ubiquitous images and their multiple meanings.

Moments later, Mordecai and Detective Leven entered the waiting room at the Chilton Memorial Hospital. They acknowledged

Arthur Ryerson but stayed in place as a doctor dressed in green scrubs walked toward Susanna's father.

"Mr. Ryerson?" he asked.

"Yes, yes. Is Susanna all right?"

"She's very lucky. If that arrow hadn't first met Mr. Arnstein's upper arm, your daughter most likely would not have survived. According to Mr. Arnstein, he noticed her ski was loose and put his arm towards her shoulder. That's when she turned to him and got hit. If he hadn't raised his arm and she hadn't turned, that arrow would have hit her back smack into a mass of major organs."

Chris, relieved to hear that David had saved his mother's life, walked to Mordecai and the two of them, fist-bumped.

"Thank God. What about Arnstein?" Ryerson asked.

"The arrow sliced his deltoid, but not seriously. There's considerable bruising as well, but he won't suffer any permanent damage. The impact on his shoulder was just enough to affect the arrow's trajectory as well as speed and angle."

"Your daughter's deltoid muscle took the brunt of the penetration. The arrowhead scraped the edge of the humerus. It caused the muscle to contract so forcibly the arrowhead tip was bent upwards around the bone. Luckily, no one tried to remove the arrow. Pulling on it would have caused severe arm damage."

Peter joined the doctor and Arthur. "Will Ms. Ryerson and Mr. Arnstein have to spend the night?"

"We'd prefer that did. I'm concerned about infection, and if one should develop, we can tackle it immediately."

Peter turned to Ryerson and said, "Arthur, I think we should alert security and let Mordecai stay with them."

"I think you're right, Peter. Doctor, can we see them?"

"Only a few minutes. I've ordered pain medication and something to help them sleep. Come with me right now."

Arthur and Peter, joined by Chris, walked into Susanna's room. She was already asleep: her face, as white as the sheet covering her while her frailness gave the heavy bandaging on her arm even more prominence. Her shallow breathing recounted the trauma she had faced.

Tears fell from Chris's eyes. He'd lost a father, one he liked but didn't know well enough to love genuinely. And he just came close to losing a mother he knew so well and loved with his heart and soul. A mother who was always there for him. A mother who loved him without restrictions or conditions.

Arthur's arm circled Chris's shoulder. Peter clutched Chris's hand. Susanna, Chris, and Arthur were family. That meant a great deal to Peter. It meant he had to make certain the arrows would never find this family of targets again.

The trio paid a short visit with David, advising him that Larry Leven was in the waiting room.

"I'd like to talk to him before what's in this IV does its work. Perhaps Mordecai can take him back to the lake house after we meet."

"David, we think Mordecai should stay here to keep an eye on you and Susanna," Peter advised.

"I'll stay," Chris interrupted. "and drive Mr. Leven back."

Arthur Ryerson put his arm around his grandson. "That's an excellent idea, Chris. I'll come back in the morning to bring everyone else home."

With a flurry of thanks, wishes for a quick recovery, and the promise to be back early in the morning, Peter and Arthur headed back to the lake house, while Chris hurried to bring Leven back to David's room.

Chapter Thirty-Six

The Party's Getting Started

Charlie Cabot and his wife were the first to arrive. Alena greeted them, explaining that the Ryerson family would be returning shortly to welcome the couple. Alena's friend, Flo, hired to help for the holiday weekend, took them upstairs to their assigned room.

The Galas' limo arrived shortly after — its back seat filled with luggage, suggesting a stay much longer than two days. Mordecai's cousin, Hezekiah, was quick to open the limo door to a rather large woman dressed to repel the clutches of Old Man Winter. On her feet, boots covered in coyote, somewhat of a cross between a moon boot and one designed for a broken foot. On her head sat an Ushanka, a traditional and stylish furry winter hat designed to combat frigid Russian winters. Unfortunately, Mrs. Gala's headgear was beaver with super-sized ear flaps and a visor that replicated the furry critter's face. It was scary. Completing her ensemble was a pup tent of mink wrapped around her generous body.

Mr. Gala was the very opposite of this wife, most likely 135 pounds dripping wet. To be sure, an odd couple, and yet, clients who evolved into two of Arthur Ryerson's closest friends.

~~~

Peter and Arthur arrived at the lake house while the Galas were in their room unpacking. It was almost 5 PM.

"Mr. Arthur, I am so happy that Susanna will be all right. What a thing to happen," Alena said, taking both of the men's coats.

"Thank you, Alena. I don't think I'll ever forget this Christmas."

"Yes, sir. But it will end well. I know that. Don't you think so, Mr. Peter?"

"I do, I do, Alena. I can see a blue sky and sunlight ahead," Peter answered aloud.

Secretly Peter's mind examined an image of two black

knights rushing and sliding through swirling snow.

Much will occur before light shines on these two knights.

"Has everyone arrived?" he asked.

"Five more are on their way," she replied. Turning to Ryerson, she said, "I told the Galas and Cabots that cocktails would be in the library after six and that dinner would follow at 8 PM."

"Thank you, Alena." Ryerson thought for a moment, then said, "Peter, why don't you head up and get dressed for dinner. I'll wait here until everyone from the agency arrives."

Peter nodded, then left for his room.

Once alone, he asked aloud, "Oh, Marvin P. Widdicomb, what have you done to wreak such havoc on this family? What caused you to change?"

≈≈≈

Carol Nelson arrived at 5 PM, and her niece/assistant, Emma Patric, arrived shortly after 5 followed some 15 minutes later. A round of hellos and a discussion of driving conditions were interrupted by the doorbell's ring announcing the last of the guests: Phil Conroy, the agency editorial chief who had driven up from the city; and agency producer, Jody Marks a few steps behind. As the pair entered, the last guest came up the drive.

The holiday mood was evident, despite the cloud of Widdicomb's death. Other than Ryerson and one of his Creative Directors, Charlie Cabot, no one from the agency knew about the bike commercial's re-edit. No one saw the 30-second spot scheduled for prime-time TV with the inserted scene of Widdicomb struck with an arrow.

Chapter Thirty-Seven

David Meets Larry Leven

When Leven walked into Arnstein's room with Chris, he saw an ashen face in the chaos of white sheets and blankets. A face so pale that the hypertrophic scar from the corner of Arnstein's eye to across his cheek was almost invisible.

Arnstein opened his eyes and shook his head. "Hey guy, you must be Larry Leven under all that down and Gore-Tex."

"And under all those blankets, you must be David Arnstein," Leven laughed, extending his arm toward Arnstein's right hand.

"I guess we're both out of our elements. But at least the killer's here with us."

"Ya think?"

"Yes, I do…"

"David, you really think the person who killed my dad is here?" Chris interrupted.

"Unfortunately, I do. What's more, I think the killer's at the lake house."

David proceeded to explain his and Peter's theory:

"We're both convinced that the agency is at the heart of Widdicomb's death and Susanna's arrow attack. Peter had a great idea…"

"Sorry, I don't know all the players, David. Who the hell is Peter?"

"Understood, Larry. Peter Dumas is a clairvoyant. Please, don't roll your eyes until I explain.

"Peter is a favorite with local police departments, the FBI, and high-profile clients who need help. He is one of the most exceptional people I've had the privilege of working with on an investigation. Call William Mac McHenry at the LAPD. He'll tell you about Peter's gifts.

"But I digress. Peter suggested that everyone in Marvin P.

Widdicomb's former family describe the Marvin they knew. It was eye-opening. Facts we would never have discovered in basic questioning helped us develop a blueprint of possible motives and persons of interest, or at least groups.

Widdicomb was a player. Women ate him up. Pregnancies occurred. Payback? Promises not kept? Monies not sent? Jealousy of former wife and son? There may be a slew of women, or possibly just one or two who know how to shoot arrows.

Widdicomb was destined to become a one-third owner of the agency based on a wedding gift, with restrictions — no divorce. Arthur Ryerson can speak with more authority on this. We think there might be a connection between agency ownership and a sudden call from a supposed daughter. A threatening call, actually, a couple of 'em to Chris. Could be Marvin does have a daughter who has it against the agency. She must know that RFB Advertising can't and won't give her the money or prestige she wants — whether she believes her mother was cheated or lied to by Widdicomb. Possibly, she isn't aware that Marvin had begun legal action based on his contribution to the agency."

"Very interesting. Some of what we've been honing in on may tie us to the killer if he or she is at the lake house or in the neighborhood," offered Leven.

"If the killer's at the lake house, won't they make another attempt on us?" asked Chris.

"We've made a plan to cover any in-house attempts, but we'll have to make accommodations for any outside activity," David answered.

"I think I've lost my interest in cross-country skiing for now, David, unless we catch him quick."

"What's at your end, Larry?" Arnstein asked.

"For one, I'm curious about Hank Redfeather. Is the fact that he's Native American a coincidence? Or is someone trying to frame him? What was his relationship with the Vic? Lots of questions, but whatever's going on, we should be able to nail him or rule him out pretty quick."

"How are you planning to do that?"

"DNA. The arrow was handmade by a real pro — Comanche style. Sinew is what locks the feathers and arrowhead in place."

Arnstein looked up and whispered, "So how does that get you DNA?"

"The arrow maker chews the sinew to soften it, then wraps it around the feather ends and the arrowhead on the shaft. Dries tighter than any glue."

"How did you know about the sinew?" Chris asked.

"A helluva art history professor at Florida State. Who'd a thought?"

"A very lucky break, Larry." Arnstein's eyes were fighting to stay awake. "Anything else?"

"Couple 'a things," Leven answered. "But look, you need recuperative shut-eye. We can talk tomorrow. Chris and I'll head to the lake house."

Before he could say goodbye, Arnstein was out for the count.

Stopping at Mordecai's post outside Susanna's room, the pair told him they were leaving and said to call if he needed anything. It was just past 5 PM when they walked out into the cold night under a black sky covered by a translucent cloud generously sprinkling gently, falling snow.

As they approached the truck, Leven opened the passenger door, saying, "So Chris, tell me about this so-called sister of yours."

Chapter Thirty-Eight

There's A Killer In The House

The Galas were getting friendly with the Cabots. Carol Nelson and her niece, Emma, were greeting agency colleagues, Phil Conroy and Jody Marks.

Then Peter entered the library. A peacock among penguins. A patchwork of Christmas colors and patterns sang brightly on trousers that gave black tie a new meaning. His jacket, emerald green velvet with a bright red silk handkerchief tucked casually in his breast pocket. On his feet, elegant ostrich boots in a matching shade of green. "Good evening everyone, Arthur will be down shortly. For those of you whom I have not met, I am Peter Dumas, a family friend. Hopefully, your trip to the Ryerson lake house was uneventful. I know that the weekend shall be bountiful with all the wonders of this magical holiday."

> *Suddenly Peter's mind flashed a series of colors dominated by a brilliant red and exploding from its epicenter, a gold earring.*

Henrietta Gala immediately rushed to Peter's side, thrusting her hand to grab his. "Peter, how very nice to see..." She didn't finish as her attention swept to a new arrival.

A tall tuxedoed man entered the room, raising his hand to say hello to Peter. He had a rugged face, not a handsome one, but undeniably attractive and framed by black curly hair pulled back in a reckless ponytail accented by a single gold earring hanging from his left ear.

"And who are you, mystery man? I am Henrietta Gala, like the apples."

Redfeather was not prepared for a woman like Henrietta Gala, who peppered him with a series of questions. Where are you from? Do you have family in the area? How do you know Arthur? Why do you only wear one earring? What is your line of business? Are you married? Have you always worn a ponytail?

Peter rescued him as Arthur came in to join the group.

Arthur hugged Henrietta and welcomed his friends and colleagues. "We've had a little turmoil here today, but everything is well, and I'm happy to be celebrating Christmas with all of you. The weather has been somewhat of an issue for a few other guests, so tonight, there will only be thirteen for dinner. I hope you are hungry and ready for some Christmas cheer."

He was interrupted by the doorbell.

A few moments later, Alena came to the library and whispered to Arthur Ryerson, who signaled Peter to join him.

Waiting in the foyer was a local policeman, his face, red with the cold, peeking out from the hood of a fur-lined parka. "Evening, sir," he said to Ryerson. "There's been a murder in Chilton, so we're warning all residents in a ten-mile radius that an armed and dangerous killer is on the loose."

"Who was the victim?" Peter asked.

"One of the tribal chiefs."

"Was the killer a tribe member?" Ryerson asked.

"We're pretty sure someone from the tribe did it. Funny thing, though, Chief Blackhawk was stabbed, but not with a knife. He was killed close-up with an arrow."

Peter looked at Ryerson, then asked, "What time did it happen?"

"Sometime between 2 and 5 PM this afternoon. If you see anyone suspicious, give us a call. They might be driving a heavy-duty white Ford pickup, pretty banged up."

"Thank you, officer. My daughter's in the Chilton hospital. She was almost killed by an arrow earlier today. And I don't think it's a coincidence. Tell the sheriff we'll be in to see him early tomorrow morning before we bring my daughter home. But before you leave, Alena will take you to the kitchen for some hot chocolate and her famous cookies. You need sustenance before heading out in that cold."

"Yes, sir. Thank you, Mr. Ryerson." The officer turned and followed Alena.

"Well, Peter. Do you think we should pack up the whole house and take 'em back to the city?

"No. In fact, this is a great subterfuge. We can blame Susanna's accident on a hunter or possibly a tribe killer, which will allow us to bring in some professional security. No one will be suspicious. Only the killer will know what we know. It could cause our killer to say something by accident, something that might identify him or her. Besides, he or she is already in the house."

The door opened suddenly, and Chris walked in with Larry Leven. Ryerson went to Chris and hugged him, asking about his mother and David.

"Everything's fine. Mordecai's outside Mom's room, David's asleep, and the police are making rounds. Gramps, Peter, you didn't get a chance to really meet this guy from Florida who can't stop shaking," he laughed. "Larry Leven, this is my grandfather, Arthur Ryerson. And this colorful character is the closest thing I have to an uncle, Peter Dumas."

Peter laughed and reached for Leven's hand. "It is nice to formally meet you, Larry. David has briefed us on your investigation."

"He's given me your resume, as well, Peter. We'll solve this together. Count on it."

"I wish we were meeting on more pleasant terms, Larry," Ryerson said, shaking Leven's hand.

"The feeling is mutual, sir."

"Arthur, why don't you return to the library. I will take Larry and Chris up to get ready for dinner. Tell them about the arrow murder in Chilton and our precautions."

"Arrow murder! Not another one?" Chris barked.

Chapter Thirty-Nine

Dinner Is Served

Conversation was bubbling when Arthur re-entered the library—the Galas playing an integral part keeping the group involved and in a jubilant mood, a task particularly ingrained in Henrietta's DNA. She was a born conversationalist regaling guests with humorous stories of trips she and her husband had taken worldwide. Her description of mounting a camel in Egypt, for example, would be manna for a stand-up comedian judging by the group's guffaws of laughter. Unfortunately, her demeanor and delivery would not be too easily copied by a comic.

"If you all think mounting a camel was a choice experience," Arthur interrupted, "ask Henrietta about her face-to-face with the tiger in Thailand. In fact, Hank, it just could be a humorous approach to the open of another bike shoot."

At that precise moment, the door opened to Peter in the lead, followed by Chris and Leven dressed in black tie per Arthur's instructions. Alena stood at the door, wearing her black uniform covered by a holiday apron resplendent with a sequined Santa and a few of his elves. "Dinner is served," she announced.

Peter and Leven drew Alena aside and asked that she perform a task for them at dinner. She listened to their directions as Arthur told the group to take their drinks with them.

The dining room was dressed to the nines. Garlands of green hung from the brilliant white combination of dentil and bead crown molding atop deep blue lacquered walls. Contemporary pewter sconces surrounded the room with soft candlelight. In place of the chandelier, the piece de resistance: a Christmas tree hung from the ceiling, upside down, covered in a blanket of the tiniest lights and dressed in clear crystal ornaments—birds, globes, flowers, toys, musical instruments, an assortment of very special things.

Carol Nelson paused at the head of the table. "Arthur, this

is the most stunning presentation of a Christmas tree that I've ever seen." A chorus of 'beautiful' and 'gorgeous' and 'spectacular' from the group underscored her comment. "How ever did you think of it?"

"I can't take credit, Carol. I'm equally in awe. The idea comes from a gift shop in a Dearborn Street brownstone just south of Superior. When I first saw it a few years back, I knew I had to replicate it, so I bought all the ornaments at the end of the season, and the owners gave us installation directions."

She smiled, saying, "It's a wonderful tradition, new and original, yet almost old-world."

"It is old world," he continued. "According to the shop owners, the source of the idea was the Prince Albert of Victoria and Albert. Victoria's mother spread the idea of holiday trees to London, but Albert brought it into the mainstream. And it's said that he hung the trees upside down at their first Christmas appearance in the palace."

"Well, here, here for Prince Albert," Carol chimed.

"I agree, Carol," said Charlie Cabot, and added. "I'm going to visit that shop. They know good ideas when they hear them."

"You should. Now, if each of you will hunt for the place setting with your name on a crystal ornament, we can re-introduce everyone and begin dinner."

Thirteen Sheraton chairs with seats covered in a deep blue and gunmetal grey stripe surrounded a pewter topped table sitting on triangular teak columns that appeared to sprout from the teak floors. Each place setting of white china rested on deep blue placemats with an arrangement of crystal and pewter goblets. A crystal ornament resting in a napkin folded like a rose completed each setting. From the center of the table, wintergreen reached end to end with touches of Bluestar.

After everyone found their seats, Hezekiah began to fill each pewter goblet with Arthur's favorite wine, the sounds of Christmas echoing softly from hidden speakers.

Arthur stood holding his wine goblet, saying, "I'd like to propose a toast to all of you here this weekend. This house is named after my late wife, Annie. Everyone who lives nearby knows it as Annie's Place. My Christmas wish is that you may discover the true meanings of the holiday—the meanings that Annie inspired in our home: gratitude and generosity, faithfulness and forgiveness, patience and peace, compassion and caring, and above all, unconditional love."

With eyes turned to Arthur, the group rose, voices ringing out, "To friends and colleagues." One paused to avoid being in unison with the others. Unseen by all but one man's eyes.

Conversation began in earnest, shortly interrupted by Arthur, who announced that a murder in Stockbridge had created the need to bring in additional security. "I didn't want you to question the appearance of strangers around the house and property. The killer is suspected to be a tribe member, so we really expect no issues. Also, several of you have asked about Susanna. Unfortunately, she was involved in an accident earlier today and stayed in the Chilton hospital for observation. She'll be here tomorrow."

Hank Redfeather turned to Peter and asked, "What happened to Susanna?"

"An arrow struck Susanna's arm. We think a deer hunter might have been startled by something while taking aim, thus losing control of the shot. Thankfully it is not serious."

"Did you find the deer-hunter?"

"No, the shot was definitely from a distance and we needed to get help. We have to assume that anyone shooting deer with bow and arrow is an experienced archer."

"Lucky for Susanna, he wasn't aiming at her."

Just then, Alena and Flo began serving the soup. "Thank you, Elena. One of my favorites. Gentlemen and ladies, you are about to savor a bit of heaven. Alena's cream of asparagus soup is extraordinary. I don't know if it's the whipping cream she adds or the fact that she sautés half the asparagus with butter and Worcestershire before blending it into the soup."

Emma Patric, sitting on Peter's left, agreed. "It's delicious. I'd love to get her recipe."

"Alena's cooking secrets are not something she ordinarily discloses. I often watch her cook and make assumptions. However, she rarely measures anything. I have attempted to convince her to write a cookbook. Alas, she continues to refuse, Miss Patric."

"Call me Emma, please. Mr. Dumas, may I ask you a question?"

"Ask away, Emma. And it is Peter."

"Peter, it is. Is it true you're a world-famous clairvoyant?"

"I would not deign to describe myself in such lofty terms.

Suffice it to say, I am an active clairvoyant, and my phone often rings with numbers, as well as country and area codes, I fail to recognize."

"Do you read minds, Peter?" Redfeather broke in.

"I read energy and images, and I listen to voices that speak to my mind, Hank. Fear not; the secrets of your mind are yours."

Redfeather smiled slightly, "My mind is an open book, Peter."

A sudden peel of laughter ignited mid-center of the table.

Henrietta could be heard saying, "So then I looked him in the eye."

"What had he done?

"Nothing particular. But …when a tiger begins to growl and raises his gloriously large head to open his mouth for the full impact of that growl — one is not prepared to see a tiger with no teeth. So, as I said, I looked him in the eye. I did not want to embarrass him and look at his mouth. He must have appreciated that, for he licked my cheek and casually walked away."

More laughter erupted as Jody Marks shook her head, saying to Henrietta. "You should be on the stage. I'm certain your delivery would make a reading of the dictionary hysterical."

Peter and Emma smiled then continued to chat, while Leven took the opportunity to engage Hank Redfeather in conversation,

"Arthur and Chris tell me you're part Native American."

"Yes. Comanche. Part Irish and German, as well."

"Does the Comanche part make you a pro with a bow and arrow?"

"Strictly for pleasure. Why so curious? Who are you?" Hank laughed.

"Sorry, I'm Larry Leven, Fort Lauderdale Police Department. I'm investigating Widdicomb's murder."

"No one's explained what happened. Can you?"

"An arrow did him in."

"So that's why you're interested in my bow and arrow skills. Well, you can forget me. I hated the guy, but I wouldn't waste a good arrow to shoot at him."

"Oh, he wasn't shot with an arrow; he was stabbed with one… about thirty feet from where you were shooting your TV commercial."

Redfeather looked at Leven under hooded eyes, then turned to the prime rib set before him.

Chapter Forty

Whose Ear Is Missing an Earring?

The snow was falling at a rate of one and one-half inches per hour, with predictions for an additional fourteen to sixteen inches by mid-morning. Peter and Leven were sitting in the kitchen, sorting the plastic bagged water goblets Alena collected and identified with each guest's initials.

"We can take them to the sheriff's office tomorrow so they can get them to the crime lab in Milwaukee," Peter suggested.

Leven laughed and said, "The snow and Christmas may have something to say about that."

"Larry, you must think positive. Besides, we now have two additional arrows to compare with the one used to murder Marvin. We advised the hospital to take precautions with the arrow that struck Susanna before giving it to the sheriff — he already has the one that killed Sam Blackhawk. The killer may not have been quite so careful with these two. Matching these arrows with the one in Florida can whittle the suspects to one of eight people, all but one, housed under this home's roof."

"Whose number eight?" Larry asked.

"Chris's supposed step-sister."

"Yeah. Yeah, I forgot. The weather's getting to me. All I see is white. I need a green Christmas with sun, grass, and flowers. Lots of flowers."

"I suggest you go to sleep, Larry. You have had a long day. Chris will be sharing the room with you. Hopefully, no one will attempt an attack tonight. The Galas are in the room to the right when you enter, and Phil Conroy is left. He is the editorial man from the agency. Neither room has a connecting door to yours. I had Chris lock the door after he entered, and this is the only other key."

"Thanks, Peter. You're right. I need some shut-eye. Are you coming up?"

"I need to clear my mind, Larry. I will be up shortly."

When Larry left the room, Peter poured himself a splash of Jack Daniels and walked to a chair next to the windows. The swirling snow beyond gave him the feeling of being within a snow globe, waiting for the flakes to settle, so he could see past the white curtain where images were beginning to develop.

I must organize the imagery from the beginning.

Marvin: translucency in a sea of color — yellows and pinks on a curtain of green. Rigid body, closed lips, hands across chest as in rest. Fading in and out.

Arthur: disembarking a plane, casual clothes, vacation?

Susanna: holding a red earring.

Arguing Male Shapes: one white cutout, the other black filled outline

Two Paths: Again, yellow with blues and greens on one path; the other, red and white. Two ticking red clocks. Red arrows falling from the sky. Red letters marching on a white path: A,R,S,C.

Two black knights riding black steeds through swirling snow.

Much will occur before light shines on them.

Another earring: brilliant red, and exploding from its epicenter, a gold earring.

With his images in appearance order, Peter was ready for his subconscious to begin sorting the puzzle pieces. He placed his glass on the sink and turned off the lights.

As he passed Larry and Chris' room, he decided to make a request. Knocking softly and barely above a whisper, he called Larry's name.

Larry opened the door and seeing Peter stepped into the hall. "What's up?"

"I have a request, Larry. I am certain that your forensic team has no doubt examined the crime scene with utmost care, but I believe they missed something."

"Impossible, Peter. These guys are real pros."

"Humor me. If I am wrong, you may chastise me publicly. If I am right, you may thank me."

"Okay, okay. What are we looking for?"

"A gold or red hooplike earring. Or a gold earring with blood on it. The size is difficult to assess, but I would venture a guess at three-quarters of an inch to an inch and one-quarter in diameter. I suggest looking under the bushes with pink flowers."

Leven, mouth agape, stared at Peter. "You gotta be kidding."

"I never kid, when it comes to murder, Larry. Thank you for following up." With that, Peter turned and headed to his room.

"Boy, Arnstein wasn't kidding about this guy. He's something else."

Chapter Forty-One

No Rest For The Weary

Shutting his eyes did not help him to go to sleep. And the sound of the snow permeating the room didn't help either. The windblown snowflakes striking the windows sounded like rocks pelted from an army of slingshots. Every fiber in Leven's hands was tingling, waiting for something to happen. Leven was like that; he could anticipate an important change about to transpire, something unusual — and not just something run of the mill unusual. Something big. No, Leven didn't have clairvoyant tendencies. But he did have heightened intuition. He couldn't say what was coming, yet somehow, he knew it was on its way.

He was impressed with Peter's gifts, but he personally didn't want to be blessed with them. A stomach that seemed to wrestle with some unknown force, fingertips that suddenly felt numb, and hearing that became acute — these were bad enough when his intuition was trying to tell him something. He couldn't begin to imagine the physical changes and feelings Peter had to endure.

He never explained his intuition to others he worked with, nor did he share it with his sister. He didn't want colleagues to give him some nickname, like the sergeant in the Miami office who saw a blue halo around suspects who turned out to be guilty. His name was Kurt Van Voorheis. His nickname, Voodoo Van.

No, Leven just sucked up his stomach pains, numbness, and hearing and just waited for it to happen., He rose from the bed too restless to lie there and walked to the windows across from where Chris was sound asleep.

The earlier snow had turned acres of white crystals into an icy white coverlet, the full moon adding patterns and shadows with stark highlights. Suddenly, a snowdrift seemed to shift. An animal? Leven thought, catching the movement from the corner of his eye. No. Something is moving toward the house. Something all in white.

Leven struggled with his pants, shirt, socks, and boots. He patted the bedside table for his gun and room key, then felt his way to the door. The hallway was low-lit by wall sconces with enough light to keep one from bumping into tables and hall chairs and helping to identify the first step of the staircase.

He heard the front door quietly open and close when he was midway to the main floor. He could see a pair of feet encased in white snow pants and white boots. "Identify yourself," he called out as he continued down the stairs, gun in hand

The figure hesitated, but as Leven looked down in the semi-darkness to check the number of stairs to the bottom, the door opened, and the figure rushed out into the snow.

Leven jumped the last four steps, falling hard on his ankle. When he reached the door, all he saw was a sea of white.

Christmas Eve
Sunday, December 24, 2006

Chapter Forty-Two

Arrows and Earrings...

Peter walked into a dark and empty kitchen. It was not yet 5 AM. He loved the solitude of the early morning darkness, almost as much as he loved the quiescent darkness of a late night. Soon the kitchen would be bustling, but now he is able to delve into his subconscious to study the images floating randomly.

> *The earring is the most invasive image to date, first appearing with Susanna. A circlet of red. A sign I inadvertently missed. I assumed it was Susanna's, or it represented an owner with red hair. Of course, the red color was blood. Blood of someone Susanna knew. It had to have been Widdicomb. But why the earring? I believe there is no question that an earring is hidden where Widdicomb died? Is the meaning a need to listen? Has Susanna overheard something? Should we pay attention to someone around her? Then, of course, the red explosion with the earring at its epicenter. That was the attack that wounded her and David. Or is there yet another meaning?*

A sudden flash of light interrupted his mind reading. Alena turned up the track lighting above the island as she entered the kitchen. As she walked toward it, Peter broke the silence. "Good Morning, Alena."

Startled, she paused and said, "Oh, Mr. Peter. You certainly gave me a start. I didn't expect anyone to be up so early."

"I should have gone back to sleep, but I believe this may be the only quiet time we shall experience today."

"Well, it certainly will be a busy day, that's for sure. What time are you and Mr. Arthur expecting to go see the sheriff?"

"Arthur left me a note and said we should get on the road by 9 o'clock. He wants to invite all the guests to take part in some activities while we are gone. I expect he will be down in a few hours with a list."

"Oh, you can rely on that. He had Mordecai gas up the snowmobiles and get the big dray ready to haul the Christmas tree to be cut down. Hezekiah brought all the decorations and lights in from the barn, too. It'll be a very traditional Christmas eve if Mr. Arthur has anything to say about it."

Just then, Larry Leven limped into the kitchen, dressed but wrapped in a blanket to ward off the cold. "Good Morning. Is it coffee yet?" he asked.

"Just a few minutes, Mr. Leven. I can make toast for both of you, but the fresh caramel rolls and everything else won't be ready for at least an hour and a half."

"Toast will be wonderful, Alena, as long as it comes with your raspberry jam. I dream about that jam."

"I'll make sure you get a few jars before you head home, Mr. Peter."

"Music to my ears, Alena."

She went to prepare the toast and coffee for the two men.

"Larry, you look as though you have not slept," Peter said, staring at the dark circles under Leven's eyes and his unshaven face. "And why are you limping?"

"I had a run-in with four steps and an intruder dressed in white."

> *Peter immediately fixated on the mind image he'd had of the two men fighting. One white cutout outlined in black. Certainly, a "good" characterization did not apply. One black figure whose intent was "protection" and should have been labeled "good".*
>
> *His mind consort was right. He was allowing his relationship and concern for the family to obfuscate his interpretations. He should have recognized danger for both Larry and David.*

Leven went on to explain. "For some reason, the snow cloud cleared for a short time, so the moon did some light magic, and I saw a snowdrift move. Then something white was heading toward the house. I don't think I ever dressed or moved so fast. I remembered my key and my gun, though.

"I ran down the stairs. I heard the door open and close. Saw his feet. Should'na taken my eyes off him. He took his chance in the dark, opened the door, and moved. I jumped the rest of the stairs and did a number on my ankle. By the time I reached the door, our visitor in white was smoke."

"Alena or Hezekiah would never leave the door unlocked, especially after the attack on Susanna or Chief Blackhawk's murder," Peter offered.

"Blackhawk? Any relationship to Redfeather," he asked with a laugh.

"Possibly. As to our conundrum, someone had a key, or someone inside left the door unlocked for their return or someone else's entry."

"I figured the same thing, but I wasn't about to wake up the house and do a room check after I locked the door. When is that extra security arriving?"

"Before we leave for Chilton."

Alena, carrying cups of hot coffee, interrupted the two men. Her next trip brought a plate of brown bread and whole-wheat toast and a bowl with a generous portion of homemade raspberry jam. Conversation ceased.

≈≈≈

While the two men savored the toast and jam, Alena began making her caramel buns. She was joined by Flo, the Native American woman from Chilton, who often helped with events at the lake house. As Flo started to prepare the potatoes for oven roasting, she secretly watched Peter and Leven.

Peter sensed and returned her hidden stare concentrating on the single earring on her right ear. She was a beautiful young woman with flawless pale skin and blue eyes –features that sent a silent alarm to Peter's mind.

Chapter Forty-Three

Susanna And David Get The Green Light

Susanna was awake when the doctor knocked at the door. "How's our patient this morning?"

"Should I be brave or honest?"

"Whatever floats your boat," he laughed. "Dr. Spensor here to check that wound."

"In that case, it hurts like bloody hell." She winced, touching her right arm. "I don't remember much. Just a sudden pain. What actually happened?"

"You were struck by an arrow, after it took a detour at Mr. Arnstein's upper arm. You were very lucky he was there. The outcome would have been touch and go."

"How is he?" she asked, concern in her voice, as thoughts ran through her mind. Was it Marvin's murderer? Is he here? Are dad and Chris safe?

"He's just fine. Just checked him over. Both of you will be sore for a bit, but unfortunately, Susanna, you'll have to keep wearing a sling. Use your arm as little as possible for a few days. You've had several layers of stitches, about twenty in total."

"Twenty!"

"The cut was deep. A few topical stitches weren't gonna do it. It was a clean slice, but as I said, deep. I want you to wear a sling and keep your arm relaxed. No lifting, and see how it feels to be a leftie, like me. Then it's physical therapy, lots of it. Now let me look."

He removed the gauze strips and examined the wound, nodding approvingly. "Looks fine. I've prescribed something for the pain in the event you absolutely need it. Just stop at the pharmacy before you leave. And no alcohol with those pills. Keep the wound area dry and come back the day after Christmas for a check and a bandage redo. The nurse will give you a list of do's and don'ts, along with some instructions. She'll be here in a few minutes to help you dress, and then you are free to go. Have a wonderful Christmas, Susanna."

"Ditto, Doctor Spensor."

Susanna's thoughts drifted back to the warning about the arrows. Are we safe at the house? Is the killer there? A light knock at the door interrupted her concerns. It was David Arnstein.

"How are you doing, Susanna?"

"Terrific, considering that I wouldn't be here to answer that question if it weren't for you."

"I guess I was in the right place at the right time. But Chris is the real hero. He got to us minutes after the arrow did its damage and got help."

"Well, to you and Chris, I will be eternally grateful." She turned to adjust the position of her arm.

David watched for a few moments — his eyes wide, a slight smile on his lips joined with a rash of feelings flooding his mind. He quickly shook free of any expression when she asked, "How is your arm?"

"Okay. Sore but manageable. Lifting a cup of coffee smarts a little. Which reminds me, I need another cup. I'm still groggy from what was in that IV to help us sleep. Let's meet in the cafeteria when you're ready. Arthur called and said he and the others would be here by 9:30 AM."

"A plan. But first, a question. The arrow? Was it a calling card from Marvin's killer?"

"Most likely. The police took it to the sheriff's office last night. And, Larry Leven is bringing photographs of Marvin's arrow, so we can at least make a basic comparison."

"I'm still having a difficult time believing Marvin did something so horrific to make us the target of someone's revenge. It's disconcerting to imagine someone wants to kill you. The hate must be eating them alive."

"It may not be hatred. It may be insatiable greed because of your dad's agency. Anyway, you better hurry; your dad will be here soon."

As he turned to leave, a nurse arrived. "Ready to get dressed, Ms. Ryerson?"

When David reached the hospital cafeteria, a group of well-wishers greeted him: Arthur, Peter, Chris, Larry, and Hezekiah.

"Good grief is anyone left at the lake house?" he asked laughingly.

"Definitely. They can't leave. Their cars are snowed in, and the plow's on the Ford pickup Grampa's driving," offered Chris.

"We didn't want to leave Chris alone, so it meant taking both vehicles. You, Peter and I are going to see the Sheriff. I get to drive the pickup. Arthur and Hezekiah will head back with Chris and Susanna in the Rover," Leven explained. "The main road's plowed, but that's about it. I have never, ever seen so much friggin' snow. Let's catch this creep so I can get back to sunshine and flowers."

Arthur laughed a deep throaty laugh, but his eyes weren't smiling. His daughter had nearly been killed. He was hard as nails in his business. Demanding yet negotiable. But his family was his heart, his world. If anyone hurt them, there was no question that he would cross the bridge from defender to deadly aggressor without a second thought.

Susanna walked in just as Arthur turned to say to the group. "I wonder where…"

"I'm here," she announced, reaching out to her father, her jacket rusted with the dried blood that survived the attack as she had.

"Your chariot awaits, pumpkin," he said as he hugged her, carefully avoiding her sling-encased arm.

After a round of good wishes and goodbyes and an introduction to Larry Leven, Susanna left with her father, Chris, and Hezekiah for the lake house. Peter and Leven stayed with David to bring him up to speed about the chief's murder, the intruder wearing white, and their possible link to Widdicomb's killer.

Chapter Forty-Four

The Sheriff. No Small Time Lawman Here.

The Sheriff's office was a few blocks from the hospital, but the streets were easier to maneuver than the snow-laden walkways, so Leven said, "We're taking wheels. I'm not walking in this mess."

Peter was in complete agreement. "You should not walk on that ankle any more than you must. And David, you need to take things slowly despite your need to get the adrenaline pumping."

Wheels it was.

"What's this business about an ankle, Larry."

"When I jumped down the last four stairs to catch that intruder, I landed hard. Twisted my ankle."

"Who do you think it was?"

"No idea. All I saw were feet. Could 'a been anyone in those boots. Man. Woman. Gorilla. Elk."

≈≈≈

When the three men walked into the Sheriff's office, all they could do was stare.

Sheriff George Tyler Bush was no relation to President George Walker Bush, but they might be kissing cousins. Sheriff Bush was a ringer for the President: Same white-sprinkled hair, same blue eyes, same height and build, same smile. And the Sheriff is as Republican as George W. The only difference? Sheriff Bush has a solid southern twang, having been born and raised in Louisiana. If he never opened his mouth to speak, he could pass for George W's twin.

"Don't just stand there with your mouths open. Tell me something new. I already know I look like the President."

"You certainly do," Peter agreed. "In fact, do you have a photograph I'd love to give it to George the next time I see him? He will be amazed."

"You know George?"

"Not intimately, but yes. We have close mutual friends."

"I'll get you that picture, but right now, how can I hep you boys?"

Watching Leven and Arnstein, it was difficult to decide whether they were more impressed at the President's look-a-like or Peter's acquaintance with the current President in office.

"Sheriff, I am Peter Dumas, a family friend of the Ryerson's, and these two gentlemen are David Arnstein, a detective with the Chicago Police, and Larry Leven, the Fort Lauderdale detective investigating the Florida murder of Arthur Ryerson's former son-in-law."

Sheriff Bush studied Peter with experienced eyes. He recognized that Peter Dumas was no pushover, despite his purple western boots. Something about Peter announced to those with a critical mind and eyes that there was something old, maybe even ancient about him. Something far older than his age. The feelings and recognition weren't new to Bush — he'd sensed that feeling before with the men and women who practiced voodoo in Louisiana. Their eyes spoke of lifetimes they've lived.

Bush listened carefully to Peter.

"We know you are investigating the murder of a tribal chief. We believe the death is connected to the murder of Mr. Ryerson's son-in-law, Marvin Widdicomb, as well as the attempted murder of Susanna Ryerson."

"Now, how do you deduce that?" Bush asked.

Leven, who had been standing behind Peter, took the stage. "First, Mr. Widdicomb was stabbed with a handmade Comanche arrow. Second, according to Arthur Ryerson, Susanna Ryerson was struck by an arrow that resembled this photograph of Widdicomb's arrow." He placed the photo on Bush's desk. "We need to see the Ryerson arrow that the hospital sent over, plus the one that killed the chief. If they appear to be identical and handmade, we need to have the sinew checked for DNA."

Bush eyed Leven with a smile in his eyes — the sheepskin-lined cap with ear-flaps still on his head, the scarf still wound around his neck, and the brand new, buttoned-up sheepskin jacket. "You must be from Florida, all buttoned up like that. I kin tell. It's that thin blood ya git down there. Bet you're wearing them Gore-Tex boots, too."

Al Leven could do was laugh. He could only imagine what he looked like without his Hawaii-styled shirts.

Looking at the photograph, Bush continued. "You definitely have a color and style match with the arrows we got. You do know, or maybe you don't, Chief Blackhawk was a well-known arrowsmith. If those arrows are from around here, he might' a made him. We should get his DNA as well."

"We need something else, George," Peter chimed in. "We believe the murderer is possibly staying at the Ryerson lake house. With that in mind, we collected water glasses from everyone at dinner for fingerprints. Just in case…"

"Gotcha. We'll pass 'em on to the forensic lab in Milwaukee. Being Christmas tomorra, we may need an extra day."

David, who showed signs of fatigue settling in his bones, asked another favor, "If the chief's crime scene is still taped off, could we take a run through later today or even tomorrow?"

"Tomarra'd be better. Early though. I live in town, so I can meet you there 'bout seven."

"Is that in the morning?" Leven asked hesitantly.

"You bet, son. My grandkids will be opening all their gifts at six. By seven, they should be in full playin' mode, so I'll have some time to spare. Let me write directions for you boys."

Peter watched the Sheriff, aware that his folksy manner hid a strong, bright mind. He was a man with depth who sized up an individual quickly and accurately. He was a man, who knew when someone was lying, who studied facial expressions, hand and eye movements, and tonality of voice.

Peter wondered where Bush had learned his craft and what specific crime had initiated his decision to become a sheriff in a small Wisconsin town.

When Bush finished drawing a simple map, he handed it to Arnstein, then shook the men's hands. "It's been a pleasure. Here's hoping we can hep each other. Now let's go to the evidence locker on your way out, and you can see those arrows for yourself. Then you boys get home and forget all about murder tonight and have a blessed Christmas Eve."

≈≈≈

Leven gave a big yawn after he got behind the wheel of the pickup. "Somebody's gotta pilot me back to the house. I can't tell one snowdrift from another," he said with one more yawn. "I'm gonna take a nap as soon as we get there."

David nodded. "Me, too."

"Since I will be providing directions, I suggest you make a few attempts to operate the plow, Larry. Some spots on my route back may be snowbound. Mordecai did give you instructions, didn't he?"

"Yeh, he did. I hope I got it straight."

"I am confident you did. I simply want to get back as quickly as possible. Hopefully, Alena left me something to nibble on in the kitchen. I did not eat much for breakfast," added Peter.

"Larry, if there's one thing you want to remember about Peter, it's that he never misses a meal or the potential for a snack," David said, closing his eyes.

Chapter Forty-Five

News from Florida

When the phone woke him from his nap, Leven looked at the clock on the bedside table. He'd been asleep for less than 30 minutes. "This better be important," he said aloud and answered, "Leven."

"Larry, it's Modulsky. How's the weather?"

"Don't you dare tell me it's in the low 80s there. The friggin snow here's about eighty inches deep. I had to use a plow to get down a section of road this morning. What's up?"

"Some news I thought you'd like. DNA on the arrow. Got it."

"Great, fax me details. I'll call back with a number."

"You were right about the hotel staff," Modulsky continued with excitement. "After we checked arrivals for anyone from the ad agency, we got a hit. When we checked at the hotel, we got a home run. Carol Nelson registered at the Aqualina on the 16th and left on the 19th, early. Used the name Carson. One of the car jockeys said a young woman paid him to keep tabs on Widdicomb's comings and goings. Number she gave him was for a burner."

"Description?"

"Pretty general. Dark hair, five-foot-three, early twenties. A looker. No tats, no scars, he could see. Expensive clothes, and oh, he never saw her with two earrings."

"Get him to work on a comp with an artist."

"It's scheduled. Morning after Christmas."

"Lots has happened here. Someone missed killing Ryerson's daughter with an arrow, and an Indian chief who happens to make arrows was stabbed with one. Both arrows look exactly like ours. The sheriff is sending them to the Wisconsin forensic lab—we may have something to match our DNA. I'll email a report tonight, with everything that's happened to date."

"How's Arnstein working out?"

"Nice guy. Smart, but we haven't had much conversation. He

was wounded by the same arrow that almost killed Susanna Ryerson."

"You're not kidding about lots happening."

"Arnstein has a friend I think you would like. Name's Peter Dumas, a clairvoyant, believe it or not."

"Wow. I've heard of him. Friend of mine in New York worked with him on a kid's abduction --the Governor's kid — his four-year-old daughter. Jack says this Dumas is the real deal. Man, you are rubbing shoulders with some heavy hitters and in tons of snow."

"Modulsky, one more snow crack, and you're on a plane to Wisconsin."

"Okay, okay. I just want to wish you a wonderful Bing Crosby Christmas. I'll talk to you Tuesday, Larry."

Before Leven could say anything, the call was disconnected, so he pulled the covers over his head and went back to sleep.

Chapter Forty-Six

Chit Chat...Fun, Fibs, And Deathly Facts

When Peter came down after his much-needed nap, not a soul was stirring. The guests had not yet returned from the morning's activities. The sound of muted voices sent him to the kitchen where Chris was playing Uno® with Alena and Mordecai. A security guard behind them hunkered down in a corner opposite the island.

"Who is winning?" Peter asked.

"I just called Uno," Alena answered. "But I think Chris has a trick up his sleeve."

" He's won three games," Mordecai announced. "The cards must be marked."

"I doubt they are," Peter offered. "He has beaten me more times than I care to remember."

Chris smiled. "I just play the cards I'm dealt."

"Sure," Peter laughed, just as David and Larry walked into the kitchen looking for food.

Alena smiled and said, "Lunch won't be ready for about an hour, but I can put some leftovers together for you."

"What would we ever do without Alena's kindness?"

"All I know is that I'm gonna miss this food when I'm gone, Peter. You noticed I said food, not place," Leven answered.

"Well, I just may have to send you a goody box when you get back to Florida, Mr. Larry."

"Alena, I will remember you in my will!"

"Come with me," Peter said, directing Arnstein and Leven to a pair of solid wood doors at the far end of the kitchen leading to a large octagonal room. "We will be in here, Alena."

When opened, the doors became one section of the octagon while each of the other seven was windowed with moving canvases of Mother Nature's art from ponds to pine trees, hills to valleys, clouds to blue-grey skies, falling snow to snowdrifts.

"I'm a city lover," Arnstein said, looking at the windows. "Hi-rises and brownstones turn me on imagining life inside the windows...but this view in this room makes me want to discover what life and all it has to offer is outside the windows."

"It is beautiful. Imagine fall and spring, a panoramic portrait in living, moving color," Peter sighed.

"I agree, guys, but it's time to turn our thoughts to murder," Leven cautioned and began to tell them Modulsky's news just as Alena and Mordecai entered with trays of food.

When Peter saw the basket of muffins, he asked, "Are those cranberry orange muffins, Alena?"

"Yes sir, Mr. Peter. Your favorite."

"Is there anything you make in the kitchen that isn't one of Peter's favorites?" Arnstein asked with a laugh.

Alena looked at him as she and Mordecai were leaving and nodded a gentle no, a big grin on her face.

Leven rolled his eyes, then continued to tell the men about the one-earringed, twenty-something who had been keeping an eye on Widdicomb and a sketch of her that would arrive the day after Christmas. "The word, according to Modulsky. And another gem he discovered was that Carol Nelson spent the weekend at the Aqualina."

"Wow, that is news," Arnstein said with surprise.

Although Peter was regaling his tongue with yet another muffin, it did not mean he was ignoring Leven's discourse on Widdicomb's stalker and visitor. He listened intently as his mind re-flashed both earring images and their realities. "Did your forensic team find the earring at the crime scene?" he asked Leven.

"No word yet," he answered.

"I know I've been out of it, but what earring at which crime scene?" Arnstein asked.

Peter gave him a recap of images that visited his subconscious and his request that Leven call for a search to find an earring that may have been overlooked.

"I think it's time we begin to question everyone from the agency as well as get their DNA," Arnstein said.

"Let's begin by asking Carol Nelson how she enjoyed her weekend at the Aqualina Hotel," suggested Leven.

Peter disagreed. "I think it best that we hold off on Carol. I would like to begin with Hank Redfeather. I want to know more about his earring."

≈≈≈

While the three men discussed the question line-up for the agency people, the Galas, Cabots, and Jody Marks returned from their cross-country skiing adventure.

Henrietta Gala sat down on the bench in the spacious coat room to remove her ski boots. "That was fun," she bellowed, "but now that I've explored the healthy side of life, I need a drink with a splash of Hot Toddy."

The rest of the party agreed. After depositing their gear, they strode to the library, where they joined the group who had been searching for the nonpareil evergreen with Hezekiah. Carol Nelson and Emma Patric, along with Redfeather and Phil Conroy, were already enjoying Alena's stuffed mushrooms and drinks prepared by Mordecai.

When Arthur Ryerson and his daughter joined the lively group in the library, a chorus of questions welcomed Susanna: "What happened?", "How are you feeling?", "Does it hurt much?", "How long must you wear the sling?"

Susanna gave a brief overview of her injury, ignoring any mention that it was an attempt on her life. As Peter and David suggested earlier, she circulated within the group, offering casual comments, but more importantly, listening for any hint that would help single out the source of the attack on her person.

Conversation soon settled on the tree-hunting experience with Phil Conroy sharing Hezekiah's lesson explaining the proper way to chop a tree base after removing several lower branches.

The group's prize was a gorgeous Blue Spruce, roughly ten feet tall and proportioned to an almost perfect pyramidal shape. Hezekiah had already groomed the branches and planted the tree in a stand next to a baby grand piano in the family room. Unlike the living room with its contemporary furnishings, hardwood floors, and avant-garde art, the Ryerson family room would be an escape into a warm and comfortable world at tree-trimming time. Its butter-soft sofas invite you to shed your aches and worries, classic wingback chairs challenge you to read the classics, and deeply piled floor coverings suggest snuggling toes sans shoes.

"Lunch should be ready shortly," Arthur announced and suggested that guests might care to nap, play bridge, read or chill after eating. "Tree trimming will commence at 5 PM. I expect everyone to attend, so you'll have plenty of time to dress for dinner. Dancing begins at 8:00, and we will share Christmas Eve dinner at 9."

After a series of oohs and ahhs, Ryerson made his way to Redfeather, motioning him aside. "Hank, I know this is awkward, but the detective who's investigating Marvin's death has asked to speak with everyone from the agency. I'd like you to take the first time slot after lunch. The meeting'll be in my office upstairs, third door from the staircase, on the right."

Redfeather watched him, his face expressing neither concern nor curiosity. "No problem,

Arthur. I can understand how upsetting Marvin's death has been for you and the agency. You know, I've never been a fan of Widdicomb, but I'll do anything I can to help."

"I appreciate that, Hank," Arthur replied just as Alena announced, "Lunch is served."

.

Chapter Forty-Seven

Redfeather In The Hot-Seat

After enjoying Alena's gourmet luncheon, most of the guests returned to the library to chat and savor goblets of wine from Arthur's wine cellar. Cabot acknowledged his preference for the '83 Merlot. "I love the boldness of the cherry, especially with that hint of chocolate. Outstanding, Arthur."

"I agree. We can thank Peter for his suggestion to add it to the wine list this weekend," he responded, taking advantage of Henrietta's tapping-the-sofa invitation to sit. "A sommelier, I am not. I couldn't tell if it was black cherry, plum, or black current, or if its taste said black pepper, chocolate, or baking spices. If I like the way a wine tastes and feels in my mouth, it's a winner." Charlie laughed as others joined their discussion.

Hank Redfeather began to move away from the group slowly. "I am not a wine connoisseur. I'm a Grey Goose man, specifically, La Poire. It has the taste and freshness of an Anjou pear, crisp and smooth on my tongue."

Redfeather was a contradiction in many ways—his dress, his demeanor, his taste in food and drink, as well as his solitary life existence. Real friendships were few and far between. He was always cordial- actually, borderline friendly. A great conversationalist, yet no one could really define his feelings. He rarely scratched more than the surface of any topic, never spoke his piece, thus always leaving the other party believing he was of their political or spiritual persuasion. An educated man. A thoughtful man. A loyal man to the few who more than scratched the surface of his mind. Several colleagues believed he was a close friend—little did they know.

He left the library to meet with the detective from Fort Lauderdale.

~~~

After a discussion, Peter, Larry, and David decided the questioning approach for the man about to enter the room. They chose to split the topics—David would cover the agency and his relationships, Peter, his personal side, and Larry, the Florida shoot.

≈≈≈

When Redfeather walked into Arthur's lake house office, his face did not indicate any surprise to find three inquisitors instead of one. But Peter's antenna sensed trap and rose to welcome the man and thank him for his cooperation. They shook hands—the 6'4" giant film director and the 5'6" clairvoyant. One dressed in black with his carelessly tied ponytail, the other in Ralph Lauren holiday colors, purple cowboy boots, and his carelessly tousled white mane of curls.

Peter directed Redfeather toward Leven. "I do not know if you have been formally introduced, but this gentleman is Detective Larry Leven."

Redfeather nodded and said, "We met informally at dinner." He shook Larry's hand.

Peter continued, "You remember David Arnstein, but I do not believe you are aware that David is a detective with the Chicago PD. Hank, we are on an investigative journey to discover not only Marvin Widdicomb's killer but also the individual who attempted to kill Susanna Ryerson."

"I thought that was a hunting accident."

"Unfortunately, it was not. As a result, you may find our questions impertinent and possibly invasive. We hope you will cooperate. You see, any activity, any new or sudden relationship may have been encouraged or initiated to gain information or personal knowledge of Widdicomb, Arthur's family, or the agency. Questioned here, in the privacy of Arthur's home, eliminates the need for subpoenas. However, if you choose to have an attorney, David can set up an interview time at the Chicago Police Department."

Redfeather heard the threat, despite Peter's gentle prodding. "No problem, Peter. Detectives. I'm fine here."

"Thank you, Hank. Now, David will begin with agency-related questions."

They sat in an informal grouping: two pairs of easy chairs separated by a large coffee table with silver coffee service and cups at one end, at the other, a pitcher of ice water with glasses on a silver tray. Redfeather helped himself to the ice water as Arnstein, seated across from him, opened the red leather notebook he always carried.

"Let's begin with your relationship with RF&B. How long have you worked at the agency?"

"Five years."

"What's your deal with Arthur?"

"Deal?"

"Are you an employee? Free-lancer? Do you have a contract?"

"I'm a freelance director on contract. I'm guaranteed a base salary plus a negotiated amount for any spots I direct for the agency."

"Does that mean you can work for anyone else?"

"As long as it doesn't conflict with my work at RFB."

"What was your relationship with Widdicomb?"

"Typical."

"What's typical for you?" Arnstein quickly asked, his eyes searching for any physical responses, any hint of disagreement between words and reactions.

Peter, too, watched every move Redfeather made; his eyes revealed nothing, his hands didn't stir, yet his long legs often shifted — first right ankle to left knee, then reverse, back and forth. A nervous twitch, discomfort at the questions, or merely a desire to leave, Peter wondered.

"He bitches. I listen. I ignore," Redfeather answered with no difference in vocal inflection.

"Is that the case with all account people, or just him?"

"Just him."

"His criticisms. Were they only directed at you?

"I don't know."

Changing direction, Arnstein probed Redfeather's other agency relationships. "How well do you know Charlie Cabot?"

"So, so. We've worked a few commercials together."

"What do you think of him?"

"Nice guy. Creative. Willing to take suggestions, provided they give the spot more impact."

"How did he and Widdicomb get along?"

"I don't know. I don't think Widdicomb worked on any of Charlie's accounts."

"When was the last day you were at the agency before leaving for the weekend?"

"I left Florida on Wednesday afternoon, so it had to be Thursday the 21st when I got the OK on the spot."

"Did you see the re-edit of the Cycle spot?"

"Didn't know there was a re-edit. We had the green light from Arthur and the client on Thursday."

"Someone cut a few extra frames in your Cycle spot — Widdicomb with an arrow in his chest?"

No shock. No reaction. No declaration of impossibility. Redfeather's response was simply a poker-faced question, "Did anyone catch it before the spot went into distribution?"

Leven's face expressed surprise at the absence of a reflective comeback.

Not missing a beat, Arnstein asked, "How well do you know Carol Nelson?"

Only Peter caught Redfeather's hand movement — the sudden extension of long fingers followed by the slow guarded return to its resting place on his knee.

"She's a colleague I respect and trust."

"Friends outside of the office?"

"A drink now and then."

"What about Jody Marks?"

"A great producer. On top of things. Good judgment. Always gets the job done."

"How long have you known her?"

"As long as I've been at the agency."

"What about Emma Patric, Carol Nelson's assistant?"

"Have no contact with her unless she's delivering something for Carol."

"What did you personally think of Widdicomb?"

"I hated the bastard."

"Any particular reason?"

"No," Redfeather said, his eyes cold and black, his voice sans emotion.

It was quick, but Peter caught Redfeather's hand as it gripped his knee — white-knuckled for barely a second.

Arnstein reached for a coffee refill and said, "That's it for me. For now. But Hank, we'll need a swab for DNA if you'll come with me. Everyone at the agency needs to comply."

"No problem," Redfeather answered, following Arnstein toward the door.

Peter stood and suggested the group take a break. "Why don't we resume in 20-minutes.

Chapter Forty-Eight

Susanna Takes A Break

When Chris walked up to Susanna, she was talking to Carol Nelson and Jody Marks. "Mom, could I talk to you for a minute?" he asked.

"Of course, pumpkin," she answered, excusing herself from the two women.

"Please don't call me pumpkin in public, Mom," he begged in a whisper.

"Anything for you, pumpkin," she said with a laugh. "What is it, Chris?"

"Alena sent me to get you out of the library. She thinks you need a nap. And I agree. You look like that gray color you had your bedroom painted."

"I do feel wiped. You both are probably right."

"Hezekiah and I will go up with you. I'll stay in the room and do some work. He'll be outside until one of the security guards gets off his break."

"Do you think all this is really necessary, Chris? I think your grandfather's getting paranoid."

"Mom, get serious. That drawing with the rhyme was not a joke. Dad was murdered, and someone tried to kill you. I don't know about you, but I wanna survive this weekend and help Larry, David, and Peter catch the bastard who killed my father."

"You're right. You're right. I guess I want this to be a dream. It's hard to accept that someone hated your father enough to kill him. Or that someone here in Gramps' house tried to kill me."

She followed Chris to the staircase where Hezekiah was waiting.

Susanna's bedroom was a suite complete with a sitting room where Chris comfortably settled himself on the chaise lounge, just to the right of his Grandmother Annie's Louis XV blue secretary. Even as a six-year-old, Chris loved to peek into the mini drawers behind the hinged top when his Gran opened the desk. And when he discovered the false bottom in one of the three front drawers at the ripe age of twelve, he decided this would someday be his desk—and no one would know its secrets, not even his mom. And Gran Annie agreed the desk would belong to Chris.

The room was wallpapered with a pale blue, white, and random gold striped covering that accented the gold trim on the desk. Chris closed the French doors separating the room from the bedroom to keep from disturbing his mother.

When he was sure she was finally asleep, Chris opened the desk's bottom front drawer and clicked a small back bar that popped open the false bottom allowing him to retrieve the envelope his father asked him to hide.

Chapter Forty-Nine

Redfeather In The Hot-seat — Part 2

When Redfeather rejoined the three men in Arthur's office, he appeared composed, looking somewhat bored. Peter's blue eyes gave no evidence of his deliberate examination despite watching every movement nuance made by Redfeather.

"I believe you are next to question me, Peter. Is that correct?" Redfeather asked, claiming the comfortable chair on the opposite side of the coffee table, directly across from his current inquisitor.

"Yes, yes. Thank you, Hank."

Both Arnstein and Leven acknowledged Redfeather then took their seats. Leven hadn't said anything to David or Peter when the meeting paused for a break, but from the look on his face, there were opinions formed and assessments made that were not at all positive.

"Hank, I am fascinated with your genealogy. Irish, German, Native American. Have you researched your history?"

"Somewhat."

"What are your tribal associations?"

"Mohican and Comanche."

"Those are distinctly different tribes from different parts of the United States."

Hank smiled. "Isn't diversity wonderful?

"How did that union come to be?"

"My great, great, great, grandmother was Anglo-American. Abigail Ann Packer. She was kidnapped as a child in the early 1800s and assimilated into one of the Comanche bands. Eventually, she married the band's chief and gave birth to a daughter and two sons. One of the sons who followed in his father's footsteps became chief, as well as a successful rancher."

A quizzical look on his face, Peter asked, "And the Mohican aspect of your family tree?"

"An army soldier from the Midwest kidnapped the 10-and-12-

year-old sister and brother. The boy killed their abductor and escaped with his sister. He and I wear the same name.

"The pair were discovered by a Munsee hunting group and taken to the tribal band leaders. They were embraced, for good reason. Their mother and father taught them well, made them learn the Comanche ways: horsemanship, hunting, and weaponry. The children became part of the Stockbridge-Munsee Band of Mohicans and part of my genealogy. Tribal merging often occurred when the government confiscated their lands, forcing bands to move and join other tribes."

"I noticed that you occasionally wear a gold loop earring. I recall reading somewhere that Comanche men usually have their ears pierced by a female relative, And wear hanging earrings made from shell pieces or loops of brass or silver wire? Is that accurate? Do you believe the boy followed the same Comanche tradition? "

"Yes, I do. And, you are correct. A female relative pierces a man's ear, but not just once. More often than not, she'd pierce the outer edge with six or eight holes."

"Are you or have you been married, Hank?"

"No."

"Do you have any family?

Redfeather hesitated, then said, "I have a niece."

"Are you close?"

"No, I haven't seen her since she was born."

"What is your niece's name?"

"I wasn't at the naming ceremony. I don't know her tribal name.."

"How about her mother and father? Have you seen them?"

"Her true father is dead. I have not seen my sister since she delivered Abigail."

"So, the child is named after your namesake's mother?"

"Her Anglo name, yes."

"Did you know the Mohican chief killed in Stockbridge?"

"Yes."

"Are you aware that he was an arrowsmith?"

"Yes. He was part Comanche."

"Was he related to you?"

"Very distantly. And yes, he made Comanche arrows."

"Are you aware that Widdicomb was stabbed with a Comanche arrow?"

"No one told me."

"Did the chief make arrows for your archery competitions?"

Redfeather stared at Peter with eyes as black as coal and a dark grey aura around him that seemed to grow as Peter watched. Both Leven and Arnstein held their breath.

"No. He taught me how to make traditional Comanche arrows."

Chapter Fifty

Party Hardy

Carol Nelson and Chris were gathering players for a friendly game of poker. Phil Conroy was in, and so were Mrs. Cabot and Arthur, who brought the chips and cards from the wall cabinet next to the game table.

Henrietta passed on poker. She preferred playing charades and instructed her husband to arrange chairs for two teams: Charlie Cabot, Susanna, and Mrs. Cabot, and Henrietta, Mr. Gala, and Emma Patric.

"Wonderful, wonderful," Henrietta exclaimed, suggesting a topic for the first round. "Let's do mystery books!"

The two groups separated and selected their book titles. Henrietta's group won the coin toss, so she was first up with her author and title: Agatha Christie's, 'And Then There Were None'.

Henrietta knew all the moves and started her group off on the right foot, being the inveterate game player she was.

"Seven words. First word. Three syllables." Using a small word symbol for the first letter and a very descriptive gagging sound for the second syllable, she was able to turn an A and GAG into Agatha with Emma Patric's help. Christie was a breeze once Henrietta's team guessed Agatha.

Despite her size, Henrietta floated before her teammates, turning hair into there and slipping on a sweater into wear. She then brought an oww of a hurt into a now, and a the into a then. It was apparent that Mr. Gala could decipher his wife's messages, even blindfolded.

Meanwhile, Phil Conroy was on a roll. It was his deal and he announced, "Five-card draw, Aces wild. Everyone ante-up."

Somewhat disappointed that his prowess with UNO did not filter down to poker, Chris failed to pick up his cards until Phil finished dealing.

The first card Chris picked up was an Ace.

The second, a King of Spades

The third, another Ace.

The fourth, a King of Hearts.

His hands were shaking a little, but his face showed no sign of what he no doubt was feeling. The first four cards were an unbelievable stroke of luck, but number five could take him to the moon. He slowly picked up the fifth card: another Ace!

After everyone checked their cards, Phil announced the start of the betting. Arthur opened with a 10-dollar chip, then Carol added hers and raised with two more chips. The pot grew as betting continued, with the others added their chips. When it was time to draw, only Arthur and Chris stood pat. Phil asked for three cards, Jody and Carol, two. And another round of betting ensued.

Arthur had an Ace and three Jacks. Jody had zip. Phil had two pair, fives and eights. Carol had three threes.

"I was convinced you were bluffing, Arthur. Now let's see what Chris has up his sleeve," Carol announced.

Ever so slowly, Chris revealed his cards. The Ace, the King of Spades, a second Ace, The King of Hearts, then a pause.

"Chris, you got the game with two pair. But do you have another King or another Ace?" asked Phil in awe of the cards on the table.

"He couldn't," Carol said in disbelief.

"Let's make a side bet," Chris offered. "Who bets I don't have either?" Everyone threw another 10-dollar chip in a second pot as Chris revealed his fifth card: the final Ace.

"It's a pity this isn't for real money," Chris sighed. "But a win is a win, and I'll take that anytime, whether it's luck or talent."

Carol Nelson looked at Chris. "The follies of youth. Winning is not everything unless it delivers a reward," she said icily. "Preferably a financial one."

Based on his reaction, Arthur was taken aback at the coldness of her comment.

Carol saw Arthur's look and quickly smiled to add a layer of humor to her words, just as Arthur approached.

"Carol, the detectives are questioning everyone from the

agency. They would like to talk to you after they finish with Redfeather. It'll eliminate the need for you to go to the police station."

"Whatever for?" she asked, her face tense.

"I'm assuming background on Widdicomb, and of course, to remove your name from the suspect list."

"That's preposterous! Perhaps I should call my attorney."

"That's your decision, Carol. Just tell David or Larry what you decide. They're in my office upstairs. Third door from the staircase."

She turned and left without another word.

"That's strange," he quietly said to himself. "Why the hell would she want an attorney. She was in Chicago".

Chapter Fifty-One

Redfeather In The Hot-seat — Part 3

Nodding to Larry and David, Peter rose to excuse himself. "I am going to set up our next appointment." Turning to Redfeather, he added, "Hank, we appreciate your time and your candor. Larry will take over now, but I will return shortly."

Redfeather gave a half-smile, crossed his arms over his chest, and watched as Leven took Peter's seat opposite him. It was a little like watching two gladiators, unequal in stature, entering an arena and eyeing an opponent, body tense, eyes wary, waiting for the first slash of sword.

Leven's first question pierced the air, "Are you a killer, Hank?"

"Yes, I am." Redfeather maneuvered skillfully. "Killed a few deer, an occasional rabbit even killed a rattler."

"Cut the crap, Redfeather. Did you kill Marvin Widdicomb? A simple yes or no will do."

"Doesn't matter what I say. If you have proof, then I'm guilty. If you don't, then I'm not."

Leven stared at him for what seemed several minutes. No sound, just two men pawing the air, eager to best the other.

"When did you arrive in Fort Lauderdale for the shoot?"

"I checked into the hotel on Thursday the 16th."

"Why so early? The shoot schedule began Monday, didn't it?

"There's a lot involved with shooting a commercial. I had a script go-over with the shooter and the animal trainer on Friday to discuss shooting the panther jumps on Saturday. On Sunday, I went over the shot list with the crew for the next morning, and later that night at dinner, we prepped the shot list for Tuesday."

"Did Widdicomb show up at your pre-production meetings?"

"No, he rarely did. His habit was showing up at the shoot and demanding a different version of a shot, racking up the costs."

"You hated him, didn't you?"

Redfeather hesitated for a moment, steeling his jaw and drilling his eyes into Leven's, then slowly he affirmed his question, pausing after each word, "I hated his friggin guts."

David Arnstein looked surprised at Redfeather's blunt admission. But then he really didn't understand Hank Redfeather—he only knew he was a man who said what he felt and made no excuses for it.

"Was Jody Marks at the meetings?"

"All of them."

"Was she staying at the Senesta?"

"She had her own car; I don't know where she stayed. She might of had friends in Fort Lauderdale."

"Did she know Widdicomb?"

"She worked with him."

"Were they more than friends?"

"How the hell should I know?"

"How about Carol Nelson? Did you see her in Fort Lauderdale?"

"No. Was she there?"

"Let's talk about the Tuesday shoot. What time did you get to the park?"

"The cab dropped me off before 8 o'clock."

"Inside or outside the park?"

"Outside."

"What did you do?"

"I went to see if any of the crew were at the shoot site. No one was there so I went back to the Starbucks outside the park for coffee. I sat awhile, going over some notes, then went back to the park. The crew arrived a couple of minutes after I got to the shoot area."

"Was it marked off?"

"Not really. But I recognized the potted hibiscus that the producers propped to bring more color into the shots."

"Did you see anyone go behind the bushes and hibiscus?"

"No."

"When did you start making your arrows?"

"A few years back."

"How did you meet the Chief Blackhawk?"

"I hired a genealogist to trace living relatives in my family. The chief's name came up and I sought him out."

"Where and how often do you make arrows. And where do you keep 'em?"

"I make arrows when I need them. I have a 40-acre ranch in Kenosha. Nothing fancy, but I'm able to keep a horse there."

"Did you make any arrows before leaving for Florida?"

"Do you really think I targeted Widdicomb? I don't like a lot of people, but they're still alive."

"When did you last see the chief?"

"About a month ago."

"Did you drive from Kenosha to the lake house or from Chicago?"

"Kenosha."

"What time did you leave?"

"About noon."

"Do you ever wear two or three earrings at once?"

"Sometimes. I have three piercings."

Leven's next question surprised Redfeather, "Hank, who do you think killed Widdicomb?"

He looked at Leven for close to a minute, then answered, "I'll have to think about that."

"Did your sister know Widdicomb?" Why Leven asked, he had no idea. Something in his mind triggered the question.

For the first time in the three interviews, Redfeather's face showed fear, unexpected but abruptly gone. "I don't know. I said I hadn't seen her since before her baby was born."

"You've had no contact with her?"

"No. She's dead. She died a while ago."

"Where's the baby?"

"I don't know," Redfeather said with a voice of ice.

"That's it for now. You're free to go," Leven announced as he stood up and stretched. "A helluva way to spend Christmas Eve."

Redfeather rose, nodded to David, then looked at Leven, "Better than trading places with Widdicomb." He smiled and left the room just as Peter was opening the door, accompanied by Carol Nelson.

Chapter Fifty-Two

Stranger Danger?

When Susanna awoke from her nap, the sitting room doors were open, and Chris was gone. She started to stretch, but her sling and bandaged arm, made it a painful attempt. The clock on her nightstand read 4 P.M. "Wow," she thought aloud, "that was some nap."

Shaking her head to wake, she called Alena on her mobile. When she heard, 'Hello, Miss Susanna…', she asked, "I know you're busy, Alena, but can you or one of the girls come up to help me take a shower and get dressed?"

"Flo is here from Chilton. She'll be able to help. I'll send her up."

≈≈≈

When Susanna opened the door to the security guard's knock, she was expecting Flo but surprised to see a Native American with eyes as blue as the sky and a complexion as fair as hers. "Thank you for coming to help me."

"No problem, Miss Susanna."

"I don't think we've ever met. I would have remembered your beautiful blue eyes. Only one other person I've known in my life had eyes as blue as the sky."

"My father is a white man. He had very blue eyes. These are a gift from him."

"Does he have something to do with the reservation?" Susanna asked as Flo helped her remove her sling.

Flo's answer was a direction, "Keep your arm still. I will first slide the arm of your sweater from your left arm, then I shall slide the sweater off your bandaged arm." She proceeded to do so, then pulled the sweater over Susanna's head.

After removing Susanna's bra, Flo wrapped the bandaged arm in plastic film brought from the kitchen. She was careful and quick. After turning the shower on and adjusting the temperature, she helped Susanna remove the rest of her clothes then held her arm as she stepped under the warm running water.

"I'll be okay now," Susanna said, turning the spigot to full force. "I'll call you when I'm ready to dress."

Flo smiled and left to enter the bedroom. There was something about her that gave Susanna pause. She was nothing like the other girls from the reservation who came to help at parties and special occasions. She had a distinct air about her that shouted, 'I am special'.

I wonder who her father is and if he's still around, Susanna thought to herself as she cautiously stretched, letting the hot, pressured water massage every tense muscle in her body. It would be a while before she stepped from the shower.

In the bedroom, Flo walked to the desk in the sitting room. She opened each drawer rifling through lace panties and bras, hosiery, and silken nightclothes. She seemed to measure the depth of each drawer until one of them met her expectations. Her hand felt the drawer side and back until she found a flat bar. A light press. A click. And the drawer bottom moved. Her hand examined the hidden space beneath it.

It was empty.

Disappointment colored her face, but Flo was a patient young woman. She had tremendous focus, most likely expressed in the meaning of her name: Flo, supposedly of Native American origin, meaning Arrow, and 'Kimi," her Mohican name meaning Secret.

She closed the drawers and opened a cloth bag she brought with her. She removed a baby blanket, designed with symbols in bright, beautiful colors: two opposite-facing arrows that meant War; a circle with a man, woman, girl and boy, standing for family; triple curled lines, indicating homecoming, the return of the warrior; a fire of concentric circles and curves, designating cleansing and renewal.

Flo unwrapped something nestled inside the blanket and placed it under the down coverlet on the bed.

Chapter Fifty-Three

Carol Spirals Out Of Control

"May I pour coffee for you, Carol?" Peter asked. Arnstein and Levin watched Carol Nelson as she responded to Peter.

"Before I get comfortable, I'd like to know why I need to answer questions?" she demanded.

"Purely informational," Peter answered. "We need to know as much as possible about agency relationships, particularly those involving Widdicomb."

"Do I need an attorney?" she asked firmly.

"Do you think you do?" David offered. She stared at Arnstein, then focused on Larry Leven, and finally, once again on Peter. "I've heard horror stories about statements being misconstrued and eventually used to indict innocent people."

"Carol, it is your decision," he said. "David can easily get a subpoena, and you may then be required to answer questions at police headquarters with an attorney present if you believe you are in jeopardy." Peter's vocal tone was flat, non-committal, while his mind watched an aura of red surround Carol Nelson. A blood-red aura that turned black, then red again. Over and over again.

> *She is hiding something, something she wants to keep behind closed doors. A secret? Personal? Yes. But is it her person? The auras are sharp, the changes sudden.*
> *She's protecting someone, and she is in danger. Why?*

"I'll be happy to cooperate, but only about relationships within the agency."

Leven rose. "That ain't gonna cut it, Ms. Nelson. You were in Fort Lauderdale on the 16th of December. You saw Widdicomb and lied about seeing him. You checked into his hotel. You left the city a few hours after his murder. Frankly, you're at the top of our suspect list."

Carol Nelson looked stunned, fear in her eyes. The confidence and aggressiveness she wore when entering the room shattered. "I didn't kill Marvin. I loved him. I'm not saying another word without an attorney," she stammered, desperately attempting to hold back the tears clinging to her lashes. She turned and ran from the room.

Tears slid down her cheeks, her breath escaping in short gasps. "Oh, Marvin, Marvin, why did I say anything about us. Why did you do it?" She stumbled forward, grabbing for the staircase railing. A pair of hands reached out to her. She felt them and missed the railing as she began to spiral down the stairs.

Chapter Fifty-Four

Carol Nelson Meets Her Fate

"You were pretty rough on her, Larry." David said, "Do you think she's responsible?"

"It's either her or Redfeather."

"There is another option," Peter confided, just as a scream sounded outside Arthur's office.

The three men rushed out to hear the tumbling sounds of Carol Nelson falling to the floor below. David was the first to reach her. Leven, still limping slightly, was next. Arthur came running from the Game Room. Peter called 911 from his perch at the top of the stairs. After speaking with the dispatcher, an inscrutable Peter Dumas stood and listened intently.

> He sensed another was here. He heard calm breathing alongside deep sobs. He closed his eyes to reconstruct the moment – someone in black. Perhaps still upstairs in one of the rooms? He moved slowly, sensing with his eyes and ears. The sound of faint footsteps rushing down the back staircase began to pummel his thoughts. He followed, but the first-floor hallway offered no clue to the figure in black – neither when it descended nor where it was bound.

Descending the back staircase, Peter found a few guests crowded at the front stairway landing. As he moved through the group, Arnstein looked up at him, nodding a gentle no.

The irony of it. Men and women garbed in holiday dress for an evening celebration, now gathering around a lifeless body, a dribble of blood at its mouth, a small pool of red at its head.

David and Larry doing their best to shield the body from searching eyes.

Arthur Ryerson standing immobile, his face blank in shock.

Emma Patric simply staring at Carol Nelson's body.

At the game room door, the sound of whispers.

Hank Redfeather: "It's Carol Nelson. She fell down the stairs."

Charlie Cabot, hand over his mouth, embracing his wife. Her lips pressed together with eyes wide in tears as she asks, "Will she be alright?"

Henrietta Gala: "Has anyone called for an ambulance?"

Jody Marks: "Will she need one? She doesn't look like she's moving."

Mr. Gala: "A life may go before the birth of the child on this blessed night."

Phil Conroy: "That sounds morbid, Mr. Gala. Perhaps she's just in shock."

Chris, arm in arm with Susanna at the kitchen door, whispers, "Is it an accident?"

Susanna whispers back, "I hope so, I sincerely hope so. And I pray she survives."

Behind them, Alena, Mordecai, and Hezekiah watch quietly, concern in each of their eyes. Flo stands a few feet back, her face calm, content.

Peter pauses, closing his eyes for a moment, then says to the group, "Ladies and gentlemen, please clear the hall and return to the library. An ambulance will be here shortly."

As they follow his directions, Peter moves toward Arthur's side. The piercing sound of a patrol car followed by the wail of an ambulance in the distance. "Thank God, the road was plowed again a few hours ago," Ryerson stated. "Is she in shock, Peter? Will she be okay? How did it happen?"

Peter placed his hand on Arthur's arm, making sure none of the guests were in earshot.

"I fear she is in critical condition, Arthur. She may not survive. Someone tried to kill her."

Ryerson bowed his head. A single tear escaped his eye falling down his cheek. "When will this end? I want to kill the son of a bitch."

Meanwhile, the guests confined to the library were soon joined by Mordecai and Alena, rolling a cart filled with ice, lemon and orange slices, and an assortment of nibbles. Mordecai opened the bar and offered to mix drinks for anyone who wished to imbibe.

Hank Redfeather was first to order a Grey Goose on the rocks. Charlie Cabot followed, asking for Scotch, straight up.

"Just pour me a double Jack Daniels, Mordecai, and leave the bottle open," Henrietta charged. "Is she stable?"

"Don't know, Mrs. Gala."

Gradually, everyone in the room approached the bar except Susanna. She sat near the window, legs protectively tucked under, watching the sky turn black above the snow-burdened trees.

The arrival of the sirens outside the house and their sudden stop startled the group to silence.

David waited at the door for the police officer, introduced himself and the situation.

"Her pulse is very weak. I don't know if she'll make it."

The officer checking Carol's body agreed with Arnstein's assessment and directed the EMTs, entering the house, to move as rapidly as possible. After a quick examination, the man started an IV, began a high oxygen concentration, and then stabilized her head before quickly moving her to the gurney. She was a small woman, just over five foot six and barely 125 pounds.

Once again, the sirens screamed as they raced to the hospital.

≈≈≈

Before heading to the library, Arthur, David, Larry, and Peter discussed Peter's sensory perception of Carol's .fall.

"Someone was there with her and left immediately," Peter stated, describing the time period as though he had been present, watching. "He or she has darker hair and is wearing something black. I can't see a face. I sense the figure was outside Arthur's office when Carol ran out. She was startled, forced to misstep. She reached for the handrail but was pushed away and fell. Then I heard footsteps retreating down the back staircase."

David interrupted, "What do we tell everyone? I don't think we should involve your clairvoyance."

"No. Definitely not," Peter confirmed

"You got it right," Larry agreed. "Let's say we think she misstepped and lost her balance. It was a tragic accident. Do not comment on her condition. Just say they're rushing her to the hospital. It'll appease the guests.'

"It might encourage the killer to attempt a move against Arthur and the family if Carol's survival puts him in jeopardy."

"I think you're right, Peter," David said.

Ryerson looked as though his age weighed upon his shoulders. "I don't know if I can do this," he sighed.

"Arthur, you can, and you will," Peter admonished. "Carol knew something and hid it. We must discover what it was. Our concern now is to keep you, Susanna, and Chris safe. You can express grief to your guests, but do it for an accident, not a murder attempt at this time. I am going to call Sheriff Bush and get him up to speed."

Chapter Fifty-Five

And Then There Were Seven

Peter, David, and Larry headed upstairs to dress as Arthur turned to enter the library.

All conversation abruptly ceased when he began to speak. "We should hear something about Carol in the next few hours. Her breathing was shallow, her pulse weak, but according to the EMTs, it all depends on the blow to her head and internal hemorrhaging. She hit the pewter post on the bottom-most stair."

"What a tragic accident," Henrietta proclaimed. "We must all think positive. Good thoughts can manifest miracles. I believe it with all my soul."

The rest of the group agreed in unison.

"It'll be difficult to be joyous while one of our colleagues fights to live, but Carol is that—a fighter. If anyone can survive this injury, Carol can. Now let's gain momentum in positivity as we begin to celebrate this most wondrous of seasons. Let's do it for Carol." Arthur almost gagged, preaching positive thinking knowing full well that Carol might never see another blessed Christmas, another birthday, another day.

Both Henrietta's words and Arthur's seemed to ignite the group. Whispered among them were phrases that reiterated Arthur's challenge to be joyous…for Carol. Like the Pied Piper, he led them to the family room where Hezekiah had positioned the 10-foot blue spruce, already festooned with miles of candle-shaped lights and their LED flames, seeming to flicker as though truly lit.

Alongside the tree sat a collection of baskets filled with ornaments: miniature frames with family photos, gloriously colored balls of glass sparkling with sprinkles of white, handcrafted Radco designs in a cavalcade of shapes and figures, handmade children's wishes crafted in clay, keepsakes, and engraved silver collections—a bounty of priceless memories spelling Christmas's past.

The glitter, the glass, and the silver sparkle drew curiosity from each guest, urging them to touch and place Ryerson memories on the tree. Indeed, it is a wondrous tradition.

Music underscored the activity. From the tenor notes of Bocelli to Bing, Presley to Parton, Manheim Steamroller to Mariah, each guest hummed, mouthed, or quietly karaoked the words of Christmas.

When Peter with his wounded warriors joined the guests, their faces spelled amazement seeing the effect holiday habits made on Arthur's family, friends, and colleagues — even on the one individual who most likely committed two murders and missed an opportunity for a third.

The music and the tree, dressed in memories, seemed to calm the group, nurturing the feelings they shared. Peter watched as his mind cataloged the list of possible killers:

> *Was it Redfeather? He had the opportunity. Is he the black figure in my mind image — his clothing, his hair work? Or is he the white figure with the black outline? The one who tried to steal quietly back into the house only to be foiled by Larry. And where was the white figure coming from? Redfeather knows how to make arrows — he was taught by the murdered Chief Blackhawk. Did Hank kill to silence him about the arrows? I do not believe he would destroy a kinsman. Why did he speak so hesitantly about his sister and his niece? Perhaps Widdicomb crossed paths with his sister. Could Hank's niece be Widdicomb's love child? I must concentrate on this connection. Is his niece the stepsister who called Chris?*
>
> *And then there is Carol. She was in love with Widdicomb. Did she have Widdicomb's child as well? He was a devious man who preyed upon women. He packaged his positive traits — his manner, his physical presence, his intelligence, yet he beautifully concealed his dishonesty, his ambivalence.*
>
> *Tonight, mind consort, I will need your help. I need to eliminate what is not relevant to each murder.*

And what of Carol's 'niece' Emma Patric? Who is she? Why does she not speak of her mother or father? What's more, did Carol even have siblings? I must ask David to do a search on Carol. Her death was delivered to keep a secret. Is it Emma Patric she was protecting?

And what of the girl from the reservation, Flo? Blue eyes, fair skin? Could she be Hank's niece? Perhaps we will learn something at the crime scene tomorrow with Sheriff Bush.

We can eliminate the Cabots and the Galas. Cabot didn't like Widdicomb, but surely not enough to kill him, or was it enough? But there is no Florida connection, no arrow availability. And of course, there is the dark horse, Jody Marks. Was she another woman Widdicomb bedded? It will be a long night.

Chapter Fifty-Six

Dancing To The Sound Of Music

As the hands on the clock neared 8 PM, Arthur announced that live music for dancing or simply listening would begin in the Octagon Room. "Follow the hallway toward the back of the house. Just before you reach the kitchen, you'll see two large double doors. That's the entrance."

The Cabots were the first to enter. Mrs. Cabot stood in awe. Mordecai and Hezekiah had repositioned the furnishings creating a large octagonal dance floor. A crystal chandelier crowned the center with a soft central light that turned the delicate contemporary pendants into four sparkling crystal fringe tiers. Outside the seven windows of the room were seven fir trees wearing miniature pinpoints of light against a sea of white under a black moonlit sky.

The dulcet tones of a cello began to fill the air with Strangers in the Night joined by a piano and guitar beautifully combined musically by a tuxedoed group of young musicians. The Cabots took to the dance floor, joined by a surprisingly foot-light Mr. and Mrs. Gala.

David Arnstein walked slowly to Susanna, offering his right hand. She looked into his eyes and smiled. Raising her left hand, she laughed for the first time in days. "We couldn't do this if we hadn't been shot in opposite arms."

"Oh, where there's a will, there's a way." He put his arm around her waist and led her to the dance floor. Peter watched them and smiled. Perhaps something good will come of all this trauma, he thought.

Hank Redfeather invited Jody Marks to dance. Phil Conroy chose Emma Patric. Even Alena and Mordecai, dressed for the holiday, took to the floor and moved to the music. The tunes played may not have been on the current hit list, but they managed to caress the dancers, creating gentle feelings and thoughts in their hearts: Time after Time, She's Like the Wind, One More Night, plus a little Cole

Porter magic.

Arthur, Chris, and even Peter did their duties as well, cutting in, changing partners, letting the music help soothe thoughts of Carol Nelson, and what tomorrow could bring.

***

At 9:15, Alena announced that dinner would be served in the dining room at 9:30. Several of the guests took to the floor for one more dance. David and Susanna were one of the couples. "I'm glad Dad didn't cancel everything," she said. "Normalcy helps bring calm, not panic, to our thinking."

"You're right. But perhaps in the killer's mind, panic will startle a new awareness, and that awareness will trigger observable actions upon which we can act. As long as the killer believes Carol is alive, she is the panic button, the obstruction to his plan."

"You mean killing off the Ryersons?"

"Yes, if that's the motive for the murders. But don't worry, no harm will come tonight, Susanna. I won't let anyone hurt you or Chris or your father." He tightened his arm around her as she nestled her head on his shoulder.

≈≈≈

The wall sconces all flickering softly in the dining room set the hanging tree's crystal ornaments on fire along with the light from tabletop candles. Even the pewter table seemed to glow as guests settled in their assigned seats. Peter and David had spoken briefly with Larry and agreed to keep possible suspect guests seated together. Hank Redfeather between Jody Marks and Emma Patric with Peter and Larry as bookends. Of course, any or all of them could be eliminated after their interview once there was a DNA confirmation.

Peter's main concern was Flo.

> *Is she a main character in our murder mystery, a walk-on, or merely a red herring? She could create a grand slam putting something into the food if her ulterior motive is revenge. But that wouldn't give her what she wants if she is who I think she is and if she wants what I think she wants. Alena and Mordecai will keep an eye on her. I must watch her reaction to Redfeather. And his to her.*

Dinner was more elaborate than the night before. The salad: Warm Baby Spinach, with sautéed mushrooms, roasted pecans, and blue cheese dressed in a balsamic vinaigrette; the entre, a choice of quail stuffed with Wild rice studded with cranberry chips, or smoked pork tenderloin medallions with Boursin cheese and cinnamon orange sauce; vegetables included roasted carrots with asparagus, Frenched beans peppered with bacon, and mashed potatoes baked with Gruyere and shaved Parmesan.

Ryerson waited with the toast as champagne bubbled while Mordecai filled each guest's crystal flute. A delicate chime echoed when Arthur finally tapped his water glass. "It's been an eventful time for our agency family this holiday. Marvin's death almost a week ago, and this weekend Susanna's arrow injury and Carol's staircase accident. Hopefully, Carol will survive as my daughter has. Let us raise our glasses to her health and welfare…in the hope that the blessings of this Christmas include her survival.

Voices rang out with "To Carol." A hush then settled over the room.

Eventually, a few of the guest whispers grew into glowing accolades after each bite of Alena's Christmas fare. Other guests discussed interviews about murder.

≈≈≈

"Have either of you been through the third degree with Peter and the detectives?" Redfeather quietly asked Jody and Emma.

"Not me," Emma whispered back. "Why would they interview me? I had nothing to do with Mr. Widdicomb."

"It's probably cuz we worked in the same agency," Jody offered. "And as for me, I was lucky enough to set up the scene where he was killed."

"That's right, you did. All those hibiscus plants. Did you see him at all while you were in Fort Lauderdale?" Redfeather asked.

"No, I didn't see him," she replied defensively. "Why would I see him? I didn't even know where he was staying."

"You know he was killed with an arrow, don't you?"

"An arrow! I took archery in college," Emma gulped.

"So, neither of you are off the hook," Redfeather chuckled.

Chapter Fifty-Seven

Magic And Murder At Christmas

After dinner, most everyone chose to end the evening with a nightcap in the family room and another look at the tree, perfect with the collection of Ryerson family memories.

Peter, standing before the Blue Spruce, fondled his glass of Jack Daniels, then suddenly announced, "Is it not strange that a pagan ritual would come to be one of the most worldwide symbols of Christmas?"

"Didn't the custom begin with the Germans?" asked Charlie Cabot.

"History suggests they were the first to bring the evergreen into their home in the early 16th century and decorate it with sweets and ribbons and paper flowers. But before Christianity began its trek through the planet, homes in the Northern Hemisphere celebrated the Winter Solstice as the return of the sun god from the cold of winter, and they used evergreen plants for decoration — a reminder that God would glow when summer returned."

A group gathered around Peter as he continued, "Many ancient peoples used evergreens to decorate in honor of their gods and beliefs: The Celts decorated druid temples to signify everlasting life. The Vikings honored Balder, their god, for light and peace.

"The ancient Romans feasted in honor of Saturn, their god of agriculture. But...in the early days of Christianity, Christian Romans set that last day of the Solstice celebration as Christ's birth date — no doubt a contrived move to turn the bawdy Roman party into a celebration of the birth of Jesus."

"Fascinating," Henrietta exclaimed. "Especially the part about purposely setting Christ's birth date."

"This is what history suggests," Peter replied. "We believe what we choose to believe."

"Well, regardless of Celts and Romans, I believe that Queen

Victoria gave worldwide status to Christmas trees because she loved Albert," Mrs. Cabot acknowledged. "The real tradition began when she gave her thumbs up for his decorated evergreens in the castle. And I'm thrilled she did. It's such a beautiful and inspiring sight."

"I think I read somewhere that Martin Luther was the father of a lighted candle on the tree," Arthur added. "And look at what's evolved. Miniature lights surrounded by memories, forever green hopes and wishes, sprinkled with love and joy. Thank you, Peter, for helping to end this night on a lovely tradition."

One by one, the guests left, heading to their respective rooms. Peter, David, and Larry stayed behind as Arthur checked the night schedule for the security people—rarely seen, yet always present and watchful.

When Flo came to help Susanna, Gary reminded her to double lock the door after entering. When she did, he left for a short break, so he never witnessed Carol Nelson enter or leave Arthur's office. Or get pushed down the stairs.

≈≈≈

"It's been a helluva day," Larry sighed. "

"You can say that again," David agreed.

"Perhaps it would be beneficial if we did a recap and laid out the facts along with our reactions," Peter suggested.

Just then, Arthur joined them with Chris in tow. "Chris has something he would like to show us," he said.

Before Chris could identify the contents of the envelope he held in his hand, Peter interrupted. "What you want to show us is extremely important, Chris, but I fear it might color our thinking and possibly send us on the wrong path. Let us assemble what we know and what we need to learn. Your revelation then can be looked at with respect to discovered facts, our interpretations, and our intuition."

"Your call, Peter."

"I have been concentrating on the imagery in my mind, and the observations of reality I have made. There are missing pieces that we must discover and assign to the killer's profile. But at the same time, it is imperative to identify the most likely suspects and determine who has the most genuine motive, Native American knowledge, archery experience, and, most important, proximity to all the crime scenes, at least as far as we can ascertain. Furthermore, what has forensics discovered at each of those scenes that contribute to our killer profile? And, in turn, to our suspects.

"Larry, you seem to focus on Redfeather. How does he measure up, and what in his persona doesn't fit?"

"Well, so far, no motive. And until we get the sinew DNA from the Wisconsin arrows, we got squat. But he was in the park within the time and kill zone for Widdicomb's murder. His farm/ranch is in Kenosha, so he coulda made Susanna's attack in the morning. He knew Sam Blackhawk, so there's that connection. He's part Native American, and he's a competitive archer, even makes his own arrows. And he hated Widdicomb, but as to why he'd kill him, or the chief, or attack Susanna, I haven't got a clue. And I'm stumped when it comes to Nelson."

Peter looked at Larry for a few moments, then quietly said. "Redfeather's sister and her child may be behind his intense dislike of Widdicomb."

Arthur looked shocked. "His sister? She died a while back."

"Yes, but the child is alive."

"Peter, do you think the kid is Widdicomb's?" Larry asked.

"There is a strong likelihood."

The door to the room suddenly slammed open. Susanna stood there holding an arrow, a security guard hovering behind her. "It was in my bed!" she screamed, shaking the arrow.

Arthur grabbed his daughter into his arms as Leven forced the arrow from her grip.

"It's like the others," he called to Peter and David.

Chapter Fifty-Eight

Who Done It? And Why?

Once Susanna calmed down, Peter asked her several questions: Who was in your room earlier in the day? Did you lock the door when you left? Who made the bed? How long were you gone from the room?

After hearing her responses, Peter explained that the arrow was left as a warning. "It was not from the killer," he assured her. Assuaging her fears, her father and her dear friend convinced her to return to her room and get some sleep.

"You will lock the door; Gary will be right outside," Arthur whispered, motioning toward the security guard. Somewhat mollified, Susanna walked hesitantly back to her room, her father and Gary on either side of her.

"Peter, how can you be so certain the killer didn't leave the arrow?" David asked.

"If the killer entered that room with the arrow, she would be dead."

"She said she didn't lock the room when she left it before dinner. Anyone could have walked in, so we're no closer to narrowing this mess down," Leven said, shaking his head in disbelief.

"No, we are much closer," Peter advised. "Let us not jump to conclusions. We must complete our suspect list."

"Well, you gave Redfeather a motive for murder, if his niece is Widdicomb's bastard. Now we have to come up with the why Chief Blackhawk was eliminated and why Susanna almost was. Then we got our killer."

"Larry, Larry. We have a possible motive for one murder, and it is not yet verified."

"Peter, I can get verification on the birth. Perhaps his name is even listed as a parent," David offered.

"You are right, David, but there are a few other individuals for which we need background and birth checks, so let us wait until we all decide which ones they may be.

"Now, let us continue. Until Carol Nelson met her killer at the top of the stairs, she too matched some of the criteria we set forth. She was in Fort Lauderdale during the period Larry describes as the time and kill zone. She admitted to having feelings for Widdicomb, as well as being engaged in an affair with him. A possible motive could have been discovering he did not have marriage on his mind but simply a roving eye. Also, there is a strong likelihood of Carol having had a lovechild with Widdicomb. He seems to be a man who thrives in planting his seed with his fans. And if there is a lovechild, which I am inclined to believe there may be, could she or he not only kill Widdicomb for financial revenge, as well as the mother for not securing authenticity and financial security? And what if Widdicomb tried to add the child to the notches on his imaginary bedpost."

"Wow, you make excellent points. And that lovechild could be here in the house. Emma Patric? Jody Marks?" David responded.

"Worth checking. Either one could be the one-earringed chick checking out Widdicomb at the Aqualina. Don't forget Modulsky's got an artist set-up with one of the car valets for a sketch, morning after Christmas. We should also have DNA on the bed coverings from Widddicomb's suite."

"If we all agree, we need the full histories of Jody Marks, Emma Patric, Carol Nelson, and the blue-eyed woman from the reservation, along with her mother," Peter offered.

David looked askance at Peter, "Blue-eyed woman from the reservation?"

"Flo," he responded in a quiet voice. "The woman who served you dinner tonight. Have you ever seen a Native American with fair, fair skin and eyes the blue of a summer sky, and wisps of chestnut hair escaping from under a wig, or perhaps missed by a deep blue-black dye? The same blue Widdicomb eyes that captivated female after female. The Americanized Flo, meaning arrow. Hank Redfeather's niece.'

"He said her name was Abigail, and he never singled her out," Leven said questioningly.

"He said he hadn't seen her since birth, and he hasn't. But she knows him. Her eyes followed him at dinner. Recognition was in her, but not in him."

"I never caught that," admitted David.

"Is she the step-sister who called me?" asked Chris, who had been listening intently to every word; Chris, who had watched immobile, helpless, in shock when his mother appeared holding the arrow.

Peter embraced the young man whose life in a matter of days learned revelations, actions, and secrets that would forever impact the footprint of his future.

"No, Chris. I don't believe so. But once we verify her ancestry, you may find a sister you will treasure. Now, why don't you share the contents of the envelope."

"My dad gave this to me about three months ago and told me to keep it safe. I did. I put it in Gran-Annie's old desk."

Peter smiled. "Do you mean Annie's blue desk, the Louis XV secretary?"

"I guess. Well, when I was six, Gran said I could have it, and she showed me a secret hiding place in the desk. Even mom doesn't know where it is. That's where I told dad I'd put his envelope. He told me if anything happened to him, I should give it to Gramps. It's a letter and a copy of his will. Gramps read it after dinner and said I do have a step-sister—I'll read the letter to you."

> Dear Chris,
>
> *I must be gone – if you are reading this. Choose one: disowned, fired, murdered.*
>
> *I have made a wreck of my life. Don't ask yourself why I have done the deeds I've done. Know only that you are one of my saving graces. I cannot say my only grace for reasons to follow. Know that I love you and have loved you despite my walking away. I did it to cope.*
>
> *Your mother had every right to banish me from our home. Ah, but she didn't banish me from you. That was my doing. I couldn't bear to see you only one weekend each month. I thought I'd wait till you were an age that allowed freedom of choice, time, and location. And when you reached it, I was too ashamed to contact you.*

But love made me overcome shame, and the times we met were some of the most wonderful hours I've ever spent. Seeing you, a man, not a boy, gave me pause. If you could forgive me, perhaps I could be forgiven by your mother and someone else I loved.

A man is fortunate when he finds that one woman sets his heart on fire and his mind ablaze. And many men believe she is his for life, despite any dastardly thing he does. False. There are boundaries, my boy. Boundaries.

I made every effort to change, but a pretty face, a well-turned ankle, an ample bosom, a tight derriere, and blonde locks always sang to me, 'just one more time.'

But then I met someone at the lake house after your mother and I formally split. She was from the reservation. As I said, a man is fortunate when one woman fires his heart, soul, and mind, but he is blessed when it happens a second time.

You have a stepsister from that union. Her name is Flo, a name supposedly of Native American origin, meaning Arrow. Her Christian name is Abigail. Her namesake was a white ancestor who married and assimilated into the Comanche tribe generations ago. Her Mohican name is Kimi, and it means secret. My secret arrow stole my heart when she was born, much as you did.

Some women have claimed I am the progenitor of their child, but a check and an attorney-provided release dismissed any future claims. Oh, there are other children, but they are not mine legally. That is a distinction only given you and my secret arrow. Her mother died after Flo was born. Not being a man with proper traits to raise an infant, I left her with Sam Blackhawk, whom she would believe was her father. I saw her often when visiting Sam. And she blossomed as you have with a nurturing parent and friends.

And so, to you and your stepsister, I have left in trust all my worldly possessions. Having been a somewhat successful man, those possessions are extensive. Share them equally with your stepsister. She's a precious young woman. She's smart like you. She's kind; she's caring. Perhaps my initial traits were proper and somehow mantled you both. Welcome her to the Ryerson family. Guide her. Help her with her education. Protect her. Love her.

I regret the actions that took your mother from me, yet I cannot explain why I did what I did. Nothing is chance. Our actions deliver destiny — be it on our self-chosen path or the path we are divinely directed to follow. Perhaps in my next life, I'll stay on my divine path to satisfy karma.

Never doubt Christopher that I loved you, and your mother, with all my heart and soul.

With boundless love, your imperfect father

Chapter Fifty-Nine

Hide And Seek

After Arthur left, Susanna said 'good night' to Gary stationed outside her suite; then she double-locked the doors.

I hope Peter is right. I'm too young to die. I need to be happy once more, she said to herself.

Thinking back again, she remembered that Flo was alone in the room when she was in the shower. It couldn't have been her. She's so sweet.

"Susanna," she said aloud. "Don't be ridiculous; Lizzie Borden was sweet, too. And look what she did."

Susanna's mind began recreating her steps before dinner. Emma Patric was going to her room two doors down when she and Gary walked to the stairs. Jody Mark's door, next to Emma's, was opening when she and Gary began descending. Did I see Jody? She asked herself. No, no. Just the door starting to open. Did I hear a man's voice? No, it was probably from downstairs.

She walked slowly to her bed. Someone had been in the room to turn down the bed covers. She stared, afraid to pull them further. What if there's another arrow or something worse?

She was about to call Gary but hesitated. Are you going to let an arrow take over your life? She asked herself.

She ripped the covers free.

No arrow.

Nothing but a hot water bottle. She smiled; *Alena's been here.* Relieved, Susanna let out the breath she'd been holding.

For the next ten minutes, she tore through the room, opening closets, drawers—any place someone could hide an arrow for a possible second visit. She finally climbed into bed, eyes-wide-open, waiting for an unknown visitor who wanted to kill her...until her eyelids finally closed.

Chapter Sixty

Words From The Dead

No one spoke when Chris finished reading his father's letter. There were tears in his eyes, and blinking rapidly, he fought to keep them from sliding down his cheeks. Peter embraced the young man, his face filled with sadness.

"I'm happy I was getting to know him, even for that short time," Chris sputtered. "Maybe, if someone didn't kill him, we all would have forgiven him...been friends."

"I am certain of it," Peter whispered. "He cared, he loved, he was a friend— in body and now in spirit. In his book The Prophet, Kahlil Gibran offers that absence is only a clarifying and fortifying force for the bond.

He wrote: *When you part from your friend, you grieve not; For that which you love most in him may be clearer in his absence, as the mountain to the climber is clearer from the plain.*

"I think Alena is still in the kitchen. Let us get you some of her orange tea and maybe that cookie you love. I know I could do with something hot to drink." Motioning to David and Larry, Peter ushered a solemn Christopher from the room.

"Wow. That was explosive," Larry exclaimed.

"Peter always finds the right words. As for Widdicomb's letter, it certainly puts a new wrinkle in the motive category. Legitimacy rises above money," David said thoughtfully. "And of course, legitimacy can get money."

"You know, this Widdicomb sounds like a decent guy, with a big hang-up."

"A huge hang-up," David said thoughtfully. Laying his head back against the sofa cushion, he ran his fingers through his hair. Then shaking his head, he surmised, "Nelson knew. I bet she had it out with him in Florida. She must have found out about his marriage and child.

"And since there's a possibility that she had a child with him, she could be his killer. Maybe Patric is her daughter."

"Or wait a minute…we keep thinking the kid is older; he or she could be a baby, a toddler."

"I remember Cabot talking about his family. I think he said he had a six-month-old son. But would Cabot kill Widdicomb because of a baby?" David questioned.

"Yeah, if his wife was involved with Widdicomb."

"I don't know, Larry. That's a big if."

Larry began to pace from one window to the next. "God, I hate this. We need DNA verification. I love Christmas, but it sure is fooling with the time clock."

Peter walked in just then, "Well, Mordecai took Chris up. He will stay with him until you head to the room, Larry. Any thoughts on the letter? Larry? David?"

David explained their thinking about legitimacy and money and Patric and Marks while Larry gave a pitch for a younger age of the lovechild.

"Interesting. I will not divulge my thoughts on the matter. I am still defining images. So, let us call an end to this most eventful day, and as Poirot always advises, rest the grey cells. We must leave early to meet Sheriff Bush."

The three men ascended the stairs.

:

Christmas Day
Monday, December 25, 2006

Chapter Sixty-One

The Scene Of Chief Blackhawk's Murder

The temperature dipped to ten above zero, so Larry Leven layered up. The roughly 170-pound man now resembled Bibendum, commonly referred to in English as the Michelin Man*.

David had to stuff him into the back seat of the pick-up.

"Larry, this truck does have a heater. Are you wearing everything that was in your suitcase?" David asked, laughing.

"You won't be laughing if this truck breaks down, and every repair garage is closed for Christmas, and you freeze to death. How come you guys are warm, and you don't look like you're wearing anything under those jackets?"

"Larry, the secret is light layering that wicks away moisture," Peter said, trying desperately not to laugh out loud at the elephantine figure in the back seat. "You will soon feel as though you are in a sauna and that moisture will have nowhere to go. I fear you may become ill."

"Great, so I'll be in 80-degree temperatures when I get home, and I'll have pneumonia."

"I'd unzip if I were you," David suggested, struggling not to laugh as tears began to roll down his cheeks.

The ride to Stockbridge took about twenty minutes, filled with the sound of tires crunching on the snow-covered back road and the sound of zippers unleashing layers of clothing in the back seat of the truck.

~~~

When they arrived at the tribe's old Community Center, Sheriff Bush was waiting. "Merry Christmas, boys," he shouted, walking to the truck. Looking at Leven, he said, "Are you warm enough in those jeans and that jacket, boy?"

"Larry has been doing a striptease in the back seat," Peter announced. "He, unfortunately, equated warmth with wool...layers of it.

We convinced him to pare down."

"I git it. It's that Florida thang, fear of the cold. Now let's get crackin'. My grandkids should be through playin' with the new stuff in about an hour and a half. Then it's my turn to tire 'em out."

They walked to the Center entrance as Bush explained that the Center had been closed for the weekend Sam was murdered. "But Sam Blackhawk was putting some data into his computer." Bush unlocked the door and continued. "He was in the back office. Musta heard someone come in and got up. Whoever stabbed him knew where to aim. Got him straight in the heart. He fell back, hit the chair he'd been sittin' in, and fell over, hands around that arrow."

"Who found him?" Peter asked.

"Flo, his daughter. He didn't come home for dinner, so she came here to git him."

Peter's eyes closed momentarily. "Does she have family?" he asked.

"No one real close."

As they spoke, Arnstein and Leven began poking through papers, opening drawers, and examining books on the shelf behind the desk. Arnstein skimmed the titles and looked surprised to see the variety of books: novels, instructional books for computer programming, college textbooks, autobiographies, Native American histories, and more.

One book, in particular, caught his eye. It was not very large, but the almost shabby cloth cover announced its place in the reader's pecking order. He reached for it and began skimming through the pages. It was a book of poetry: Walt Whitman, Edgar Allen Poe, Emily Dickenson, Robert Frost, Maya Angelou, E.E. Cummings. Pages curled from constant turning, worn down by thumbs. On the title page, an inscription: To my secret arrow, Love M

David's eyes misted. He handed the book to Peter.

Meanwhile, Leven began examining the Chief's computer. Considered a geek to some, many Fort Lauderdale detectives would often slip into his office with a program glitch, a crash, a how-to, or how-do-I-get-rid-of-this for Larry to solve. Leven always clicked a few keys and let the magic happen.

He motioned for the group to see what his clicking had discovered.

> *Dear M,*
>
> *Flo is doing well. She is working at the lake house over Christmas weekend. She asks when her Uncle M will come to visit. Will you be there? If so, can we arrange a visit for you to see your secret arrow at our home?*
>
> *Also, I have had several calls from a woman asking about you. Why you visit? Who you see? She says she is a friend of yours and anxious to meet when she comes to the Midwest. She refuses to say her name. She says it is a surprise. I give her no specific answers. When I ask where she lives, she says far away. I don't understand. I have her number on my mobile, but I left it at home.*
>
> *I am leaving the office shortly. Kimi is preparing dinner. I will finish this tomorrow and send it to your private email.*

"Verification," Peter observed. "We have one of Chris' stepsisters. A true and legal one. She must be protected."

"How do we know she isn't the killer?" asked Leven.

"She is innocent. There is too much love here. Consider Sam's letter to Widdicomb, the warmth and protectiveness the Chief offers with his words, as well as Flo's interest in Uncle M's visit. She is a bright and accomplished young woman, according to Marvin. I am certain she is the one who delivered the arrow warning to Susanna. I've watched her. She is quiet but extremely observant; nothing gets past her. She may know more than she realizes. And if the killer does not know it, he or she will come to realize it…very soon. We must protect her."

Satisfied, they discovered all they could; the men prepared to leave. As Sheriff Bush began to lock up, Leven asked if they retrieved the Chief's phone from his home.

"I don't recall seeing it listed with the evidence, but I'll stop at the station and double-check on my way home. I'll call you if we've got it. If not, we'll have to ask Flo to git it for us."

"If need be, we'll bring her back to search for it, Sheriff."

They said their goodbyes and, with firm and warm handshakes, wished each other a very Merry Christmas.

≈≈≈

They followed deserted roads back to the lake house. The few places the pick-up passed were bright with colored lights from Christmas trees sending greetings through giant picture windows. Inside, families were tearing through ribbons and wrappings while some of the children gazed at the snow outside as it began to fall in earnest. It would be a sledder's paradise.

"It looks like we may be stuck at the lake house til the spring thaw," Leven moaned.

"Larry, look at the bright side. It is a beautiful white Christmas Day. And, you will soon be savoring Alena's holiday breakfast-brunch."

"Peter, I've come to realize what you and I hold most dear. We may grow old and fat together."

"I don't think Peter's ever going to be fat," David offered. "All that food just fuels those grey cells of his. Right, Peter?"

"I cannot compete with Monsieur Poirot, but food somehow quenches a need to rest and supplants it with an insatiable desire for mental stimulation. My mind needs exercise, so I must use it, which brings me to today's schedule, my friends. Breakfast-brunch is an ongoing event at the lake house, at least until dinnertime, so I suggest we start our interviews with Flo and then the Cabots. We can eliminate them as suspects, and I believe they may know more than they think they know."

Chapter Sixty-Two

Arthur And Chris Get Some News

Most of the guests were still in their rooms when the three men arrived back at the lake house. Arthur was in the library watching the news. It was shortly after 8 AM.

"Too bad this isn't New Year's Day. I'd sure like to watch all the bowl games on that baby. I'd be right in their face," Leven remarked, looking at the drop-down projection TV screen that had to be six feet across.

Arthur laughed. "I hear you, Larry. That's why whenever I'm able, I'm up here for the first week or so in January. Where are David and Peter?"

"Peter headed for food. And David's getting Chris. We learned a lot at the Blackhawk scene."

"Good or bad?" Arthur asked.

"I'd say informative and interesting."

Before Leven could elaborate, David walked in with Chris, followed by Peter carrying a platter of orange cranberry muffins.

"Are two of those for me?" Leven asked as he hurried to Peter's side.

"Of course, my friend. Just a little to tide us over until we have an appropriate meal after Arthur and Chris get our report."

Leven mumbled a yes, as much as anyone could mumble with a mouth full of orange cranberry muffin. He opted to comment on the taste as well. "Ohn, Ohm, gud."

Ignoring the mumbles, Arthur repeated Larry's description of what the Blackhawk scene revealed.

David responded. "Interesting? Definitely. Informative? Without a doubt for Chris."

"What ja learn, David?"

"Your stepsister's here in the house, Chris. She served you dinner last night; her name's Flo, like your dad wrote you in his letter.

And the man she believed to be her father was Sam Blackhawk, the chief who was stabbed with an arrow not long after someone tried to kill your mom."

"Is she the one who called me?"

"I don't think so, Chris. But then, I don't know what Flo knows."

"She knows what Widdicomb told her," Peter offered. "We must question her immediately. I am afraid she is in as much danger as you and your mother."

"Wow. And she's here in Gramps' house."

Another revelation, Peter thought. At least this one is a positive one for him.

Content with the mind-altering goodness of Alena's orange-cranberry muffins, Leven added, "We learned about a female who was anxious to meet with Widdicomb, as well. There was an unfinished email on Blackhawk's computer."

"So, is our killer really one of the guests?" Ryerson asked.

"Unfortunately, Arthur, I believe we have broken bread with the killer at several meals. But I'm certain the eventual reveal will be an unexpected one," Peter answered. "Chris, we will seek out your stepsister. Give us a little time, then join us in your Grandfather's office."

Chris nodded, looking a little dazed. He had reason. In one week, the father he lost as a boy and reunited with as a young man was murdered. He discovered his father was not the man he thought he was. He learned that his father's killer threatened to kill his family. His mother barely escaped being a victim. And now, he was going to meet a stepsister. Not just any stepsister, but one who is part Comanche and Mohican.

Nothing in Chris's experience prepared him for the last seven days: his job, his friends, his girlfriends, his hopes, his goals…his entire life. "I think it's time I took a hard look at myself," he said quietly.

Chapter Sixty-Three

Flo-Kimi-Abigail Speaks Up

Peter chose to speak with Flo before sitting down for brunch. His uneasiness about her safety telegraphed the need to surround her with security. Should I make Redfeather aware of his niece? He asked himself. Or will his acceptance of Flo's existence confirm the killer's assumptions and thereby endanger her?

He closed his eyes, inviting his mind consort to help direct his actions. A minute meditation was a common phenomenon that Peter employed when he was at a crossroads in his interpretation of imagery, thoughts, or questions. A bare sixty seconds, and it was as if he rebooted his mind, clearing the cache of insignificant clutter. He looked up when he heard the light knock at the door.

Leven jumped to open it. Flo stood there in her black uniform with its crisp white apron and bib. Her eyes, wide and ever so blue. Her hair, entirely hidden under a blue-black wig. Peter walked to her, his smile declaring welcome and his arm directing her to one of the chairs around the coffee table.

She looked neither frightened nor questioning but solely at peace. Leven watched her, most likely wishing he could display such a warm and friendly poker face instead of his this-is-what-I'm-thinking face.

David offered Flo, "Coffee or water?"

"I would like some water, please," she said with a quiet smile.

Peter, shuffling some papers, looked up and said, "My condolences on the death of your father."

"Sam Blackhawk was not my real father. My uncle Marvin is my birth father."

"Did Sam tell you that?"

"No, Mr. Peter. I searched for my birth records and saw his name recorded as being my father."

"Was that upsetting?" he asked.

"No. He did the practical thing. His life did not accommodate a baby. My interim father provided a stable home and a tribal family for my development. I loved Sam before I knew he was not my father. I love him still. And I loved my father before I knew he was my father. I love him even more now."

"Did you not question your fair skin, hair, and eyes."

"No. Sam explained that I look like my grandmother six generations ago. She was a young girl, fair with light hair and blue eyes, kidnapped by the Comanche tribe. She fell in love, and her love was returned. I love her story. I am honored to bear her name and to look as she appeared.

"Why do you wear a wig?"

"Sam and my father thought it best that I drew no attention to myself. Blue eyes are a rarity in our tribe, but not absent. But hair as fair as mine is not common among us. My father and Sam wanted to protect me."

"Do they tell you from what you needed protection?"

"Sam said jealousy could become weaponized. I didn't understand, but it was my duty to obey."

"How did Marvin Widdicomb come to be your Uncle?"

"Sam explained that he was related through the Algonquin tribe, something similar to the story of my grandmother. I liked my Uncle. He brought me books, and he read them to me. He took me all over the world with his stories. I've been to Paris, to the Louvre, and I've been to Rome. I've been to so many places that I someday want to see. He said he would leave something for me after he passed into the afterworld. I was to look into the drawer of a blue desk in Miss Susanna's room. I did. But nothing was there. He may have died before hiding it."

"We have it, Flo. Your stepbrother will show it to you."

"Is his name Christopher? My father said I would like him."

"Yes, I believe you will," Peter acknowledged. "Christopher is Marvin's child with his first wife, Miss Susanna."

"She was almost killed like my father."

"Did you leave the arrow in her room?"

"Yes, it was a warning to be careful."

"Why did you leave a warning?"

"Sam made arrows for other people. He made six of them

that were sent out one week before my father died. When Alena told me my father was stabbed with an arrow, I thought it might not be a coincidence--Sam murdered with an arrow and someone trying to kill Susanna with an arrow. They may try again. They have three more."

"Where did Sam send the arrows?"

"I don't remember. But the address should be on the invoice."

"Flo, we need your help to discover who ordered those arrows. But first, I must ask a question. Are you aware that Hank Redfeather is your mother's brother?"

"Sam told me just before I left to get here. He said I would see a man who does not know I am his sister's daughter. Sam said Redfeather is a good man. I would like to meet him and learn about my mother."

"You will, Flo, or do you prefer to be called Kimi or Abigail. I apologize for not asking sooner."

"I like Kimi, but I love Abigail."

"Then, Abigail, it shall be."

Throughout Peter's questioning, David and Larry watched the endearing seventeen-year-old — her poise, intelligence, and extraordinary beauty. The way she answered questions— thoughtfully, respectfully. There was emotion showing in her eyes, but it was privately held in her heart and mind, not in her facial expressions. Hands folded lightly in her lap, her back straight as an arrow, she was a proud, young woman and deservedly so.

"David Arnstein and Larry Levin are detectives, Abigail," Peter announced. "Along with Chris, they will take you to the office to retrieve the address for the arrow shipment. You must also take them to your home and find Sam's mobile phone. We need the number of someone who was searching for Marvin Widdicomb. Sam referred to it in an email he was writing, one he planned to send to your father."

The door to Arthur's office opened suddenly. Chris entered, his eyes targeting his newfound stepsister. Abigail stared back, smiling.

≈≈≈

Before leaving for Chilton, the group assembled in the kitchen for an awaited taste of Alena's spectacular ham and gruyere souffle. Peter opted to remain at the lake house to question the Cabots, so he resisted the urge to splurge on the souffle.

Charlie Cabot was first to meet with Peter in Arthur's office, but not before a second helping of the souffle, fruit, and orange cranberry muffins. He managed to squeeze two sausages onto the plate as well.

"Would you prefer to finish before heading upstairs?" Peter asked.

"Nope, I'm fine, unless you'd rather I did," Charlie answered. "I don't want to be impolite, especially since I didn't see you have anything to eat."

"I am not very hungry, Charlie," he said indifferently, hoping his stomach would not sound the alarm for lack of food.

Peter reached for the silver service and poured coffee for himself and Arthur's Creative Director. "I would like you to describe your discovery of the re-edited version of the bicycle commercial. Please do not spare any details, no matter how insignificant you believe they are."

"Sure, Peter. Let me think a minute," he said, stuffing sausage and souffle into his mouth. "The office building was locked when I arrived. The security guard let me in after I showed him my I.D. He told me no one else was in the building, but Carol and her niece were there for about an hour earlier in the morning — probably around 8 AM. That's when the security guards change shifts.

"I went directly to my office..."

"What time was that about?" Peter asked.

"...hmmm 'bout 9:30. Stayed about 20-25 minutes, checking all the presentation folders for the client meeting in January. I wanted everything in shape, so I wouldn't have to be concerned the first day back from our bonus vacation.

"I took a cassette of the mock spots for our client, Anderson Financial, and headed to the studio in the lower level. Wanted to take another look. The studio was deserted. Dark except for some low-wattage ceiling lights in the corners. I popped the cassette in the slot and watched the commercials. After I ejected it, I reached for the cassette case, but it wasn't empty. It was another case next to mine labeled Cycle, Inc.

"Hadn't seen the new spot, so I thought I'd give it a peek. Carol said it was dynamite.

"I was mainly watching for the dissolve between the bike and the panther. It was dynamite. But something else caught my eye. It looked like a man. I replayed it and watched for the man instead of the panther. And there he was — Marvin, with his hands on an arrow in his chest.

"I called Arthur right away."

"How difficult is it to edit in a piece of footage?"

"Digital footage is easy to edit."

"Could it be done in this studio?"

"Sure, we do edits here for rough cuts, all the time. You need the digital footage, though. You can edit a video copy, but it would look like hell, and it would be noticeable immediately when aired. You'd be looking at several generations down."

"How long would it take?"

"With the original footage, a competent editor, and the equipment in this room — well under an hour. And that includes making a cassette copy."

Chapter Sixty-Four

The Second Trip To Chilton

While Abigail was reading the letter from the secret drawer in the blue Louis XV secretary, Leven answered a phone call from Modulsky. He turned on the speaker so David could hear the call firsthand. "Merry Christmas, Modulsky. I hope you've got some news. The good kind."

"Merry Christmas back. I got lots to tell you. Me and the boys have been busy. First, we were able to get the artist's rendering this morning instead of tomorrow. I'm faxing you a composite of the chick checking out Widdicomb at the Aqualina. I'll text it to you, too. I hope it matches someone in Snow Town, USA."

"Modulsky, if it does, you're on your way to this winter wonderland to make the arrest. Besides, you keep telling me a change of scenery works wonders on everyone."

"But Larry, you deserve all the credit; you should make the arrest. And I got even more good stuff to tell you that'll make it happen. Number 2, you asked forensics to find an earring. We got it, man. They found it in one of those hibiscus pots. It musta bounced off the edge onto the dirt inside. That's why they missed it the first time. I faxed pictures and measurements. There are markings on it, some kind of design, so you might be able to match it. Don't forget we have that earring we found in Widdicomb's room. We should have DNA on it and the coverlet tomorrow. We can check the design on it to see if it matches."

Larry fist-bumped David, then said, "I'll have another job for you to check. Six arrows were shipped from Wisconsin. We're driving to get the ship to address now, so I'll text it to you with any other details we discover. It looks like this murdered chief made the arrows for someone, so soon as we get DNA confirmation that agrees with the sinew report you sent, we strike out big time on the killer making those Comanche babies. Gotta go. We're almost at the chief's office.

All kidding aside, Modulsky, you and the guys deserve kudos for all the work, especially on a holiday. I hope you have a great Christmas dinner tonight, guy."

"You too, Larry. I'll watch for the text."

"What's your gut say about the sinew?" David asked when Larry put his phone into his jacket pocket.

"I think it'll match the chief's DNA."

"I agree."

Abigail, who had been talking to Chris about the letter, managed to catch a part of Modulsky's call. "Pardon me, Mr. David, but I forgot to mention something earlier. My father once came to see Sam with a woman. They didn't see me, but I saw them. I was coming home early from school."

Arnstein was quick to respond. "What did she look like?"

"She was not very tall. Pretty. And she had beautiful red hair. I couldn't see her face very well."

"Did Sam mention her name? Or say why they came to visit."

"No. But the woman and my father looked as though they were very close friends."

Larry pulled out his phone and checked if the drawing Modulsky sent was in his message. Folder. It was. "Hey Abigail, did the woman look anything like this drawing."

She took his phone and studied the face on the screen. "It could be, the eyes seem familiar, but the hair is too light. And the woman was older."

Arnstein pulled up to the scene of Sam Blackhawk's murder as Leven retrieved his phone from Abigail. He had a questioning look on his face as he recalled something his instinct said was important, but unfortunately, out of his memory's reach.

Abigail unlocked the door, and the group followed her into the office, where she immediately headed to an old 4-drawer vertical file. She opened the second drawer and rifled through the invoices, but the one she was looking for was gone.

"It's not here," she said. "I know I filed it."

"Do you remember anything about the name or the address?" Leven asked.

"I'm not sure, but the name of the company was Mr. Cycle Ink, and it was going to some hotel. I remember the invoice said to stamp the shipping label Hold for Pick-up. But I don't remember the hotel name or the street. Sam packed and labeled everything. I just took it to the post office."

"No problem, Abigail," Leven responded. "I think I know the hotel."

They locked up and headed to Sam and Abigail's home, a short walking distance from the office. It was small, a happy-looking house. One floor. The towering trees around it gave it the look of a dollhouse covered in snow inside a snow globe. A twisting path led to a shiny red door on a home built of wood with red-framed windows.

When they approached, the door was ajar.

Abigail ran quickly inside to find a sea of chaos. Chairs overturned, drawers left open, contents spilling from cabinets, clothes ripped from closets. Tears began to fall from her eyes. Her happy home was cold, corrupted by an evil spirit.

"Wow," Chris uttered. "Someone was looking for something."

"Sam's mobile!" David cried.

"Where did he keep it?" Leven asked.

"Sam always put it in one of his boots," offered Abigail.

Both Leven and Arnstein bee-lined for the boots in the hall closet. There were several pairs all in a line. Half of them erect. They overturned and shook each pair until a small clamshell phone tumbled from a fur-lined boot. "Got it," yelled Arnstein. "It's dead. We need the charger."

Abigail rushed to one of the bedrooms, equally in disorder. The charger was on the floor, partly covered by a patchwork coverlet with Comanche and Mohican symbols embroidered on each square.

While the phone charged, the men helped Abigail attempt to make order out of chaos. Leven motioned Arnstein aside. "That figure dressed in white sneaking into the house…10 bucks says it did the deed."

"Most likely," David agreed. "But whoever it was, had to use one of the cars or one of the snowmobiles to get here."

"I didn't hear any engine noise, car or snowmobile."

"We have to check the area where you first saw the figure. Maybe they ditched the snowmobile and hiked a mile or so back. Let's get to the lake house and see how Peter made out, and then we can use one of Arthur's snowmobiles to search."

In the 15-minutes before they left, the phone charged enough for them to search the incoming calls. Within the past ten days, one repeated number stood out: The Ryerson Agency phone number.

"Every other number is local. Another dead end," Leven said, slamming his hand against the door.

Chapter Sixty-Five

Preparations For Sam Blackhawk's Funeral

Chris opted to stay at the house with Abigail and help her ready it for Sam's deathwatch. As soon as his body is released, Sam would be dressed for tribal members to pay their respects. A fire would burn outside for three days and nights with friends and family staying round the clock.

Abigail chose a traditional, blue-patterned ribbon shirt for Sam to wear. Blue was his favorite color. Her choice had two deep blue and maroon ribbons stitched horizontally, decorated with six vertical ones in light blue — three on the right, three on the left anchored at one end to the horizontal ribbons. Plain buckskin britches completed Sam's death clothes.

He would be placed in a simple wooden box. And Abigail would burn soy candles—White Birch along with Wild Raspberry Sage, Sam's favorites.

Although close to tribal members at the official reservation site in Wisconsin's Shawano County, Sam had always planned to be buried in Stockbridge. He was one of several tribal members who chose not to move when the tribe, once again, had been relocated. He was tired of government treaty moves, acquisitions, tribe re-establishment, forced relocations. His people had traveled on a trail of tears—uprooted from their homes, their lands, to start over and over again. Sam said, "No more. Stockbridge is my home in life and in death."

He would be buried in a cemetery near the shores of Lake Winnebago. He believed it was right and just, in keeping with the meaning of the Mohicans: The people of the waters that are never still.

Native Americans have a strong belief in the circle of life. What dies allows new life to be born. Sam Blackhawk was a Christian with a deep love for his culture. He practiced rules and rituals of both believing and knowing that they can and do co-exist.

It was difficult preparing for the funeral, difficult for Abigail to accept Sam's death. He had given her so much. He had been her stand-in father. The man who taught her to believe in a higher spirit, to trust that the spirit would be the guide to her true path. The man who encouraged her. The man who was there when she was ill. The man who held her hand walking to school. The man who helped braid her hair. The man who kept her mother's memory alive.

Chris helped Abigail bring order to the chaos the killer had delivered to her home. She was organized and worked with a sense of calm that deeply impressed him. He felt almost as though she was the elder and him, her kid brother. It awakened something in him that would impact his life. He could feel it.

Chapter Sixty-Six

Back At The Ranch

Peter was drinking a hot cup of coffee when Christine Cabot walked into the kitchen, looking for him. "Arthur said you needed to speak with me. Is this a good time?"

"It is perfect. Come with me to the Octagon Room, where we may drink in the beauties of nature as we talk."

Mrs. Cabot followed Peter into the room. The Christmas Eve dance floor was hidden once again under cool grey alpaca rugs. The contemporary sofas and armchairs were back in their respective places. Mordecai and Hezekiah had risen early to restore the room to its nature-viewing ambiance.

Snow was gently falling outside, adding even more to miniature white throws resting atop branches sprinkled with pinpoints of holiday lights on each of the seven trees at the windows. "I love this room," Mrs. Cabot announced. "The window walls make me feel as though I were in a glass cocoon set in the forest. All alone, relaxed, and filled with a rare calm one doesn't encounter too often."

"I, too, enjoy this room," Peter responded. "It is a perfect place to talk of both good and bad. The peacefulness helps to soften bitter and angry feelings of regret. Nothing said here will escape to others, unless of course, confessions open a door that should not or cannot be closed.

"Mrs. Cabot, did you have an affair with Marvin Widdicomb?"

She stared at Peter, eyes wide in shock, her mouth agape. Her body slumped like a balloon pricked, releasing the air inside. A minute passed as she tried to speak. "How did you know? Carol told you, didn't she," she asked breathlessly.

"I understand your need to know, but no one has told me — especially not Carol. I did not think anyone knew. My only reason for asking was to clarify your relationship with Marvin and determine if your child is his or Charlie's."

Her hand covered her mouth to hide her words, feigning shame at what she had done and fearful that speaking the words would be a proclamation to the world. "I don't know. I'm afraid to find out. I don't want to hurt Charlie." The words tumbled from her lips, then washed over them like a waterfall, splashing, thundering. "It was stupid. I wanted to be special, different — a femme fatale instead of a frumpy suburban housewife. I wanted someone to know I am a woman, not just a mother, wife, caretaker, cook, or carpool lady. Marvin made it easy to be me. He took pleasure in me being me. He put me into another world that asked nothing of me, no Give me. Help me. Drive me. Get me.

"Being with him was like being a concert. A crescendo of feelings: Quiet. Deafening. Romantic. Thrilling. He played me like an orchestra. From Mozart to Billy Joel. From Sade to Beethoven. A night with him was a year of Charlie."

Peter watched as she wrestled with her thoughts and words. Thoughts that preferred secrets preserved and words that demanded expression. Words were the winners.

"Oh, I love Charlie, don't get me wrong. He's thoughtful, kind, and loving. But there is no adventure with Charlie. No edginess, no risk-taking. He is life on a calm sea. No waves. No excitement. Not ever."

"I see. Sometimes one needs sudden bursts of emotion to appreciate the calm," Peter offered.

"Yes, yes. And Marvin delivered bursts of romantic chaos. Love in the afternoon. In an office. And not just physical love. We'd touch intimately in a back booth of a restaurant. Or we'd make love with words. Words that caressed on the phone, in a text. Words that drew pictures.

"I didn't love him. I adored him."

Peter sat back, somewhat surprised at this very attractive yet frumpy, suburban housewife's explosion of personal need and the untapped joy Widdicomb gave her.

> *No, she did not love him. Nor did she adore him.*
> *She adores the sexual blessings he bestowed. She is a woman who wants love on finite levels and willing to gamble on losing the foundation of her life and family to bring temporary excitement to her experiences.*

*What will come of her now that Widdicomb is gone?
No doubt, he would have left for a new lust when he
tired of her. Was she aware of that? Will she search
for a new partner? Will her desires grow unrestrained
and seek out new levels of risk. She has much to learn;
I feel sorry for her.*

"When did you last see Marvin?"

"A few days before he left for Florida. I went to the agency to meet Charlie for lunch and stopped at Marvin's office." She smiled a coquettish smile, "We did the nasty on the sofa in his office." She took a deep breath, and abruptly, her demeanor changed. A look of pride beamed on her face, her head erect, her shoulders straight, uncompromising.

"He asked me to meet him in Florida on Saturday."

"Did you go?'"

"Unfortunately, Charlie had to work, and I couldn't find a babysitter. I'll only have the memory of our last exciting time together in his office."

"Did you see anyone when you left his office?" Peter asked.

"Just Carol Nelson. I looked up, and she was at the end of the hall. I don't think she noticed me."

Peter was satisfied that Christine Cabot had no part in Widdicomb's murder. He knew, too, that Charlie Cabot was equally innocent. But Peter could not claim innocence for Charlie's ignorance of his wife's manifestation of self-indulgence

*Christine Cabot is the most self-serving excuse for a
woman I have ever encountered in all my experiences.
She's hollow, utterly devoid of humanness: her lack
of accountability, her audacity saying she loved her
husband and did not want to hurt him, her absence
of genuine grief for Marvin's death. And what of her
children? No loving words, just remorse at the lack of
a babysitter so she could meet her paramour. No concern to determine the father of her child, be it Charlie
or Marvin.*

Our suspect list grows shorter, or does it?

A few minutes after Christine Cabot left, there was a knock at the door. "Enter," Peter called out.

"It's just me," Arthur responded as he opened the door. "Alena said earlier that you and Mrs. Cabot were meeting. Didn't want to disturb."

"She has gone. Thank goodness. I have never met a female I disliked more. Poor Charlie."

"That sounds ominous. And I'd like to hear your reasons, but I just heard from the hospital. Carol survived the night but took a turn for the worse at about 7 AM. She never awakened. Death was called at 8:35 this morning."

"I believe Marvin's executioner has been punished."

"Peter, are you saying that Carol Nelson killed Widdicomb?"

"Indeed, I am."

Chapter Sixty-Seven

Checking The Details

On the way back to the lake house, Larry's stomach was doing a number on him. His hands were tingling. His legs felt numb. And the ever-falling snow was hitting the windshield like a rash of pebbles. The noise was deafening. Larry's intuition was in overdrive, most likely recalling something important he'd forgotten.

While David concentrated on the road's slip and slide condition, Larry pulled his phone from his jacket pocket and called Modulsky. After several rings, he listened to the detective's gravelly voice spitting out his no-nonsense message: "You got somethin' to say. Say it."

"I sure as hell hope you're doing a number on a turkey, a ham, and a slab of beef, big guy. Hate to call on Christmas, but you know me, murder comes first. With everything else you're getting ready to send me tomorrow, I need a few more things. I'll put them in a text. By the way, I had a dream last night. You were riding shotgun on a snowmobile. It was a glorious sight. I really think you should fly out here and play in the snow." He clicked off laughing, then turned to David and said, "If you thought I looked like the Michelin Man, you'd be shaking in your boots if you caught Modulsky in a down snowmobile suit. He'd look like King Kong."

"A big guy, huh."

"Six foot seven. Three hundred and thirty pounds. And he moves like Baryshnikov."

"Did I hear that right? Baryshnikov?"

"So, you don't think I enjoy the finer things in life? My mother made me take ballet from ten to when I turned thirteen. That's how I learned to fight."

"How did ballet teach you how to fight."

"I became Mohammed Ali in a make-believe ring. The better I danced and flitted around anyone who made fun of my lessons, the easier it became to land a surprise punch. I'm sure a few kids asked to take dancing lessons after I beat 'em up."

"Larry, you are one-of-a-kind," David said. His expression, genuine. His voice, filled with awe for his new, innovative, and unconventional friend.

They joked and repeated stories of things they both did as kids, forgetting how and why they met for a few moments.

After Larry texted the list to Modulsky, he shared with Arnstein the evidence his acute intuition forced him to remember: a red hair on Widdicomb's body and no camera check before 7 AM.

"We've got three redheads, Larry. Marks, Patric, and Nelson. Of course, Patric's hair is dark. It's more auburn."

"Yeah, but the DNA doesn't care if it's auburn or fire-engine red."

"By the way, we should have stopped at the hospital to get the news on Nelson. Although I doubt she'll ever wake up."

"I feel the same, David. It's a pity she didn't tell us anything."

"Perhaps Peter has connected some dots that will tell us what she knew."

Chapter Sixty-Eight

The Widdicomb Murder Is Solved.
Will Justice Be Served?

While most of the guests opted to stay comfortable in robes and slippers, Peter chose to dress for the occasion. A pair of red patchwork trousers set the mood topped with a crisp white shirt and a pop of emerald green from a patterned silk cravat at his neck. An elegant red velvet jacket finished the ensemble. But the piece de resistance? The western boots made of ostrich and dyed blood red. His finery was indeed competition for the holiday's jolly fat man in his red suit.

Peter and Arthur decided not to visit the group with news of Carol's demise. Peter planned to discuss his solution to Widdicomb's death with Leven and Arnstein upon their Chilton return. So, when Peter descended the stairs, he headed straight for the dining room to indulge in the mastery of Alena's prowess in the kitchen.

The ham and Gruyere souffle became his primary focus. He'd watched her on Christmas Eve cutting the ends of many loaves of bread, sandwiching buttered slices with Gruyere and thin slivers of a roasted ham glazed in brandy, brown sugar, and butter. He watched as she cracked dozens of eggs, mixing them with cream, butter, brandy, and cinnamon for a liquidy custard that she poured over the triangled sandwiches, standing erect in large rectangular pans which she placed in the refrigerator.

This morning she began baking those petite triangles drenched in that liquid custard, and Peter was looking at the most recent pan from the oven. He filled his plate, adding fruit and his favorite cranberry orange muffins. He headed for the library, where Mordecai waited with a glass of champagne. Peter was in heaven. Not even murder could interrupt.

If Peter were a smoker, he would be lighting up a Cuban cigar after his meal, but he didn't smoke, so he accepted another flute of champagne from Mordecai, who offered to bring him more muffins.

Peter smiled and nodded, yes, just as Larry and David entered the library. "Where is everyone?" Larry asked.

"In the Octagon Room, enjoying nature, exquisite food, and superb champagne." Peter sighed and took a deep breath. Unfortunately, it was time to talk murder. "Marvin's killer is dead," he said, his face free of emotion.

"What?" Leven and Arnstein asked in unison.

"Carol Nelson did not regain consciousness. She was pronounced dead shortly after you left," Peter answered. "My mind convinces me — it is her. Your evidence will prove me correct. Check the cameras at the park at least one hour before Widdicomb arrived. I see her on the tape, but she appears to keep her face from being recognized. Light rain has stopped. She wears casual clothing, tan shirt, and slacks, and she carries a black umbrella. A black baseball cap hides her hair, but a tendril of red looks caught on a gold circle earring she wears. Perhaps the ME found hairs on Marvin's clothing."

Larry stared at Peter. "He found a red hair. I called Modulsky this morning to get the DNA. And the tech guys found the earring you told me to look for. It was in the hibiscus planter. We also have a gold earring we found in Widdicomb's room. We'll have the DNA tomorrow."

"What tied all the images together for you to focus on Nelson," David asked, "especially since she was a murder victim?"

"Ahh, an accidental occurrence related to me by Christine Cabot."

"So, she did know something," David said, nodding.

"She did know some things but was unaware of the havoc an accidental occurrence would wreak. Carol's rendezvous in Fort Lauderdale was to be with the man she loved. It is evident by her failure to mention the trip, and her DNA presence, as you will soon discover. Christine Cabot was involved physically with that same man, and the week before, as she so poetically described did the nasty on Marvin's office sofa. According to Mrs. Cabot, Carol may have seen her departure. Aware of Widdicomb's penchant for bedding anyone in a skirt, it no doubt made an impression upon Ms. Nelson. As the English playwright and poet William Congreve wrote in the late 1600s:

Heav'n has no Rage, like Love to Hatred turn'd,
Nor Hell a Fury, like a woman scorn'd.

"What about the arrows shipped to Florida?" Leven asked.

"Did Abigail find the address?" Peter responded.

"No, but she said it went to a hotel."

"I would contact the Drake in the city. It would have been convenient for Carol."

"Did she even know anything about arrows? And why would she order six?" asked David.

"A gift for her friend, Redfeather. He reacted when you asked about her. They were friends. Close friends. I spoke with Redfeather this morning. I asked if he exchanged gifts with anyone at the office. He named Carol and Jody Marks. I also questioned if either of them knew of his archery competitions. He said Carol did, and Jody may have. I taught Jody how to shoot; she was a natural. He offered that he and Carol discussed his Native American background and proclivity to using authentic Comanche arrows."

"Did Carol have a baby with Widdicomb?" Leven asked.

"I do not know for certain, but she may have, and by tomorrow, we will know for a fact when all the information David requested will be at our fingertips. She is our killer. She met with Widdicomb at the hotel, slept with him. Most likely asked him about Cabot's wife, and he probably bragged to his paramour that Christine was begging for his attention. Carol was an intelligent woman and no doubt knew he was cheating, yet once again. She'd been with him off and on for years — the proof of her child's birth may verify that there were other men in her life. But his dalliance with Cabot's wife, most likely, was the final straw.

"She knew the location of the shoot. She was with him the night before. She knew when he was scheduled to leave in the morning. She overlooked the possibility that you would check if any other agency personnel made the trip to Fort Lauderdale. If she had used someone else's identification, she might have been scot-free. She also overlooked the earrings, though — a huge mistake.

"There are many exits at the park, allowing her to walk away after plunging that arrow into Marvin. Get your evidence together, Larry. I know that Marvin's killer is dead. The question is, should Christine's affair be made known? Her family, destroyed? Should Chris and Abigail learn the true why their father was killed? Should Arthur's agency suffer because of the loss and scandal?

"I see no reason to create even more misery. Can we create a story that tells the truth but limits the back story? I pray so. I've told Arthur my belief in her guilt, but nothing more. You have no evidence of Christine's affair. I sincerely doubt she will ever admit to it. Or that Carol saw her leaving Marvin's office. Carol cannot confirm it.

And you may get a child's birth record, but I doubt it will identify Marvin as the father.

You may have physical evidence, red hair on the body, and DNA on earrings, and a coverlet in Marvin's room, but a good attorney can turn that into something circumstantial in a heartbeat to protect her good name.

The arrows? They were a gift. Anyone could have removed them from her office and re-wrapped them. The re-edited spot? There is no proof that she did it?

And the original footage of Marvin after the arrow entered his chest? Most likely burned, and no way to tie it to Carol, that is, if Carol actually shot it. And frankly, I doubt that. The tape at the park? She hides her face. And finally, you have a clairvoyant's mind movie which cannot, I repeat, cannot be used in evidence."

"My mind movie is over for Marvin's murder. I am producing a new one for Sam's and Carol's death, as well as the attempt on Susanna." He stood and looked at them, "Who knew about the arrows and had the opportunity to get them from Carol. Who discovered that Marvin had a legitimate child? Who prepared to murder for money and legitimacy?

"I am spent. I must speak no more of murder today. It is a blessed day, and I want only to think of good for its remaining hours."

"Collecting and reporting the evidence of Widdicomb's murder is your task," Peter said, his voice quiet, his head bowed. "There is another murderer in this house who has killed, first an innocent man, then Widdicomb's murderer, and finally the attempt kill a third. We have tomorrow to identify her before she ravages this family. Her rage intensifies."

He left the room to join the killer, who was quietly enjoying the spirit of the holiday celebrating with the others.

David fell onto the sofa, "He's right, dammit. He's right."

Leven walked to the cart and grabbed the half-filled bottle of champagne and two flutes. He handed one to Arnstein, filled it, then filled his glass. Sitting across from David, he rested the bottle between his knees and chug-a-lugged the bubbly liquid.

"I can't figure him out. He directs us to clues, offers motives, uses that brain of his like he's playing Mozart on the violin. Then he gives us reasons why we shouldn't; no, can't report the back story connecting the dots to Nelson's motive for killing Widdicomb."

"Maybe it's simply redefining her motive. First anger. Then rage. And finally, acceptance of who and what he was."

"You mean she was fed up," Leven said, raising his voice to continue, "and not going to take it anymore. Like that guy said in that network movie."

"Peter Finch. Sort of. Except Finch didn't die, he just won an Oscar for that performance. Maybe Nelson gave Widdicomb a chance to let every woman who knew him know it was truly his last performance."

"So, she edited the spot?"

"The edit room is in the building's lower level. She could have gone there anytime while her team put all the campaign materials to bed. No one else had a reason to go down there. And no one else was in that building after hours until she arrived the next morning."

"What about Patric? Or Marks? "

"I don't think Patric has actual production experience, but we can check it out. And I think she arrived a little later than Nelson. Marks is a producer. She could have done it. But who shot the footage?"

"That video may be the final nail in someone's coffin."

Chapter Sixty-Nine

Jody Bares Her Soul

When Jody Marks saw Peter enter the family room, she was ready to corner him. Excusing herself from Phil Conroy and the Cabots, she headed to the pair of chairs facing the window where Peter had settled himself. Before joining him, Jody grabbed a flute filled with fortification. Her hands were slightly shaking.

"Mr. Dumas, may I join you," she asked as she held onto the back of the chair next to him.

"Of course, Jody, but only if you promise to call me Peter." He smiled, and calm seemed to cover her. Even her hands ceased their shaking.

Peter had that effect on most everyone. One could turn to him and admit they committed murder, and Peter, most likely, would smile and say, 'Oh, that is a pity, but do not worry. Everything will be right again. Now tell me what you did, the entire week before the murder.' Of course, that didn't happen too often, but occasionally, it did.

He had this look on his face. It said he was eager to hear a story. It invited soul cleansing, and for the most part, honesty. His blue eyes seemed to become blue-black when he believed they were lying and yet no word spoken garnered a judgmental look.

He looked at Jody and sensed her need to release something buried deep in her breast.

"I have to tell you something." The sudden gush of words spilled from her lips as she took her seat.

She looked directly into Peter's eyes. "Carol Nelson is my mother."

"I did not see that coming," Peter said, images floating, cataloging, regrouping in his mind. But…nothing gave credence to her story — no imagery and, more importantly, no sensory perception on his part.

"She took a big sip of her champagne and continued. "She gave me up for adoption when I was born. She was 19-years-old, a sophomore at a city College. She met a man at a party in Lincoln Park, and she slept with him. I was the result—an inconvenient pregnancy. But it worked out."

"You will have to excuse me. I am unfamiliar with adoption procedures, Jody. How did you discover your birth mother?"

"I pretty much have always known. Carol knew there was no way to support a baby; her parents died in a car accident four months before I was born. Their deaths left her with enough money to finish college, so she chose an adoption agency that embraced open adoptions. I had the best of both worlds: a loving mother and father and a loving birth mother. Eventually, Carol and I did meet, and we became close. She mentored me. Helped me become a producer. She even celebrated some holidays with my parents and me. It was a good relationship, not a mother-daughter one; she was more like an aunt who I could talk to about the advertising business."

"Did anyone at the Ryerson Agency know?"

"No. As far as anyone knew, Carol was my mentor, and we were friends."

"You want to know if she will be all right."

"Yes. And I want to know if it was an accident or deliberate, Peter."

"I will be honest with you. Carol died this morning, shortly after 8 o'clock. She never regained consciousness."

"Hah aaa," she cried, holding her fist over her mouth, a cascade of tears flooding her eyes.

He reached over and held her hand. It was a terrible way to learn about a birth parent's death. It would have been easier if she had not known Carol or appreciated her as a relative and a colleague. It was not a gift one chooses to give or receive on a Christmas Day.

She wiped her eyes, stood, and forced a smile to her lips. "Yes, or no, as to accident," she asked quietly. Peter turned his head slowly right, then left.

Scrunching her face and squinting to stop the tears, Jody took his hand, holding it tightly for but a moment, then turning, head down, she left the room.

Peter bowed his head, moving his lips quietly in prayer,

sprinkled with phrases his mother had taught him. May God bless this child. Shield her from the negativity of those who will judge. Exorcise her mind of the harsh words and memories to come from misguided tellers of tales. Commit her thoughts to remember only the good deeds of a mother — a mother thoroughly flawed by the hurt of unpredictable love.

Chapter Seventy

Whose Blind?

Leven was stretched out on one of the library sofas when Susanna walked into the room. "Oh, I thought David might be here."

"Nope. Thought I'd grab forty winks while David made a few calls."

"Where is he?"

"I think he went upstairs. He should be down soon," Larry answered, his eyelids at half-mast.

"Dad told me about Carol. It wasn't an accident, was it?"

"We don't think so, but there's no real proof that it was or wasn't, Susanna."

"I think Carol had a thing with Marvin. If not, she had to be the only woman at the agency who wasn't."

"Why do you say that?"

"There was always this tension when she met me with Marvin. They could be laughing or joking, but a wall went up when I walked into the room, I asked Marvin about it, but he said I had too vivid an imagination. I don't think so. And after the divorce, I received so many notes telling me about his one-night stands in his office and congratulating me for leaving him. No one said anything positive about him in any of those notes. Yet, he and Carol were always close. She either was in love with him, or blind."

"In love," whispered a voice behind her.

She suddenly turned as David moved toward her. Unblinking eyes staring at her tousled pale-colored hair, her green eyes. She stared back. A minute passed until the spell was broken by Leven's question asking if David had any news from the Chicago PD.

"Well, a package arrived at the Drake for Mr. Cycle Inc about a week before Widdicomb's murder. According to the clerk, he remembered the woman having red hair, same color as his wife's. The woman left a card when she signed for the package. The name on it was Jody Marks."

"Jody!" Susanna said, sitting suddenly, a look of surprise on her face.

"Doesn't mean it was her, Susanna. It's easy to get someone's card and used it for an ID." Arnstein turned to Leven, "No chance for prints. They tossed the card."

"Well, Nelson has… had red hair."

"So do Marks and Patric. We need something concrete to tie on one of them. We need to search for the place where the killer aimed that arrow at Susanna. Have you ever hunted animals, Larry?"

"Nah, I'm strictly a killer hunter. Why?"

"I've got a hunch. Let's you and I go for a snowmobile ride."

"David, you can't manage a snowmobile with your arm. Ask Hezekiah or Mordecai to help," Susanna suggested.

"You're probably right."

"I can drive," volunteered Leven.

Susanna chuckled, "Larry, you can land both of you into a hospital. You've never driven a snowmobile."

"What's to learn? You start the engine and step on the gas."

"I'll go and get Hezekiah," she laughed.

"She's right, Larry. You can flip one of those babies in a heartbeat if you don't know what you're doing."

"OK, OK. What are we looking for?"

"A blind."

"A blind? What, a venetian blind? You're kidding me, aren't you?"

"No, I'm not kidding you. We're looking for a deer blind."

"Oh, well. That tells me a lot. What the hell is a deer blind?"

"It's where hunters hide while they wait to kill a deer. Our archer didn't just walk out and happen to see Susanna. Our killer hid while she waited to kill Susanna. If we find that blind, we may find something she left there."

"Gotcha."

The door opened, and Susanna walked in with Mordecai. David explained what they needed to find.

"There are several blinds built in trees not far from the house. Birdwatchers use them sometimes," Mordecai started. "Since Mr. Ryerson bought more acreage and added fences, hunters go elsewhere. I think we should not take the snowmobiles. The paths are too narrow for them, and the snow is far too deep off the paths. Best, we dress warm and cross-country ski. I'll pack some supplies."

"You expect me to ski someplace? I wouldn't ask you to swim in the Everglades if we were hunting for an alligator blind!"

"Come on, Larry. Cross country skiing is just like walking, but the skis help you walk faster."

"I suppose I gotta wear big jackets and pants?"

"Mordecai will get you outfitted to keep warm, and you'll be warm. Oh, Mordecai, I forgot. Hezekiah must go to Chilton to bring Chris and Flo back to the house," David reminded him.

"Yes, Mr. Ryerson is planning to go with him. They will soon be leaving."

"David, what is Chris doing with Flo in Chilton?" Susanna asked.

"I'd rather Chris tell you, Susanna. It's a long, complicated story."

"Does my father know?"

"Yes, he does."

"Then I'll ask him." She turned and left the room, slamming the door shut.

Chapter Seventy-One

The Transgressor's Words Strike The Heart

Susanna found her dad just as he was leaving with Hezekiah. "Dad, I'd like to come with you to get Chris."

"We won't be long, pumpkin. You should be resting that arm."

"I want to know what Chris has to do with Flo. And I want you to tell me."

Arthur Ryerson drew his lips together, pondering what he should do, then looked at his daughter and said, "OK. Let me get some papers, and I'll meet you at the truck."

Susanna grabbed a coat, boots, and gloves from the hall closet, then hurried to the pickup, idling in the driveway. She climbed in the back as her father exited the house and jumped into the truck. He handed her an envelope with folded pages. "It's a letter from Marvin to Christopher. It should explain everything."

She began to read as Hezekiah headed to Chilton.

Arthur turned to watch Susanna. At first, she looked thoughtful, then suddenly, her eyes closed, most likely recalling the sadness and anger learning of her husband's infidelities. *How could I have loved this man? He was deceit in hyperdrive. Was he devoid of conscience?*

She continued to read her face taking on a questioning look— brow creased, lips closed. *He admits that he walked away from Chris! Why didn't he tell me how he felt about visitation?*

Then suddenly, her lips turned upward in a slow smile, her eyes mellowed. *He loved twice. I'm glad. My goodness, a daughter. So, Chris has a stepsister. Marvin, despite the anger, the angst, and the heartbreak, I forgive you. Your demons may have possessed you, but they didn't destroy the real love you had in your heart. I will share your daughter with Chris. I'll help her, too.*

Tears. Happy tears slid down her cheeks. She smiled at her father as her tears released years of anger, mistrust, and sadness.

In another five minutes, they pulled up to Sam Blackhawk's

home. The happy house with the red windows and doors welcomed them inside. Chris introduced his mother to Abigail, who reached out for Susanna's hand, but instead, Susanna wrapped her arms around Marvin's daughter.

Chris explained that Flo preferred to be called Abigail.

"Well then, Abigail, why don't I help you pack a few things to take to the lake house? You're part of our family now. You're Chris' sister, and I will be...let's see...how about an Aunt?"

Abigail glowed.

Chapter Seventy-Two

Daddy's Girls

While Larry was getting outfitted by Mordecai, David answered a call from a detective at the Chicago PD. "Hey Arnstein, got some answers for that info you wanted from the Chief."

"Hey Jerry, what are you doing there on Christmas Day?"

"Not much. It's as quiet as a morgue here, so I can't complain. My kids are celebrating today with my wife and her in-laws. Yesterday was our time with my family. Worked out great. How bout you? Chief said you were in Wisconsin for a long weekend. Nice."

"Not so nice. One murder and one attempt. And there's a detective here from Fort Lauderdale who's investigating the death of one of my host's employees. So, any of that info you have for me might give us a break. I want to enjoy some of this long weekend."

"Hear ya, buddy. First up, Carol Nelson. Family: One married sister, Natalie Patric, and her adopted daughter Emma. Occupation: Creative Director at Ryerson, Foot, and Burner, twelve + years. Started as a copywriter. Active in Linked In, 1500+ connections, minor activity on Facebook and Twitter. Member of six professional groups. Recipient of several creative awards for both print and radio-TV advertising.

"Owns a Gold Coast co-op on the corner of Elm and Lake Shore Drive — pricey building. Does not own a car. On the board of her co-op association. Fairly private woman. Actively dating two men, according to her doorman. One, a big guy, Marvin Widdicomb, who often spends the night. The other, a hair younger than she is–tall guy, dark hair, always wears a ponytail. Never stays the night, according to the doorman. Only have the first name: Hank.

"No lawsuits, no issues, well-liked by colleagues. Never been married. Age: 44-48. Both public and private papers document birth date changes. Somebody changed her birth records in the State capital. Accounts pre-1965 indicate one birth date, while accounts post-65 register the same month and day but with a different year of birth. In either period, there is no record of a marriage. However, she gave birth to a baby girl a few months after her parents died in a car accident near their home in Appleton, Wisconsin. The baby was put up for an open adoption that gave her communication opportunities and possible future contact with the kid. The birth records identify the father as Unknown. Friends claim that the father was a Marvin Widdicomb, the girl's steady boyfriend.

"The kid's name was identified as Baby Nelson. The adoptive parents christened the baby Jody Marks. They reside in Appleton."

"Great. That'll help. What about the Patric kid?"

"Not much. Her birth mother was a debutante who got heavy into drugs. She was a year ahead of Nelson at Northwestern. A sorority chick from a high-brow family who got pregnant. The folks talked her into signing adoption papers and rushed the baby away to an Evanston Adoption Agency, which seems to have been the go-to for Northwestern girls who got into trouble. No open adoption with this one. Grampa and Gramma didn't want their daughter to have any connection or memories of the kid. They didn't know that their daughter's friend, Carol Nelson, had an older, married sister who registered with the agency—all cleared and all approved. Natalie Nelson Patric couldn't have a kid of her own.

Eventually, the teenage mom wanted that baby back and somehow got wind that the Patrics were the adoptive parents. She began harassing them. They got a restraining order, and when her parents refused to help, drugs became her crutch. She died of an overdose. Never saw the baby."

"Any indication of who the father was?"

"It said Unknown on the birth certificate, but I talked to the parents—they're still living in Winnetka. According to them, their daughter Gemma always hooked up with Nelson and her boyfriend. He's their best guess—real personable, good-looking Lady Killer. The name is Marvin Widdicomb.

"Emma Patric worked her way to graduation at NYU and went to work at ABC-Television in New York. Her stepmom got cancer last year, and Patric left her job to come and help her. Natalie Nelson Patric died about three months ago. The birth grandparents won't have anything to do with their granddaughter."

"Wow. You did an incredible job, Jerry."

"I can't take all the credit. We got a couple of new, and I mean really new detectives on board. No caseload. And these guys are so tech-savvy, they could probably find Jerry Hoffa with all their apps and Apple phones, watches, and tablets. I think they can make all of our work a helluva lot easier if we can keep 'em in front of those computer screens."

"Detection of the future. Except…someone has to talk the bad guys into confessing, and a computer screen isn't going to do it. Jerry, I owe you…big time. Hope it stays quiet for the rest of the day. Merry Christmas and give my best to Marie and the kids."

"Merry Christmas back on you, Arnstein. Get the bastard to confess. If anyone can do it, you can."

Arnstein put his phone in his jacket pocket, closed the red notebook he always carried, and went to look for Larry and Mordecai. When he walked into the kitchen, Peter was standing at the window. "Peter, have you seen Leven?"

Peter turned, smiling as he nodded to two figures in the snow, "I believe he is the one who keeps slipping on those skis."

"Oh, no. Mordecai's giving him lessons," David said, laughing. "We're off to check out some deer blinds. Maybe our mystery guest in white used one to wait for Susanna before letting that arrow fly."

"Good idea, David."

"And I just heard from one of the detectives at the station." He briefed Peter on Jerry's information.

"Ahh, a new wrinkle for a motive," Peter said thoughtfully. "And your news confirms the story Jody Marks offered me."

"Her birth may be authentic, but that doesn't release her from the suspect list."

"No, and I believe she may be concerned about legitimacy and money, David."

"Perhaps not, but knowing and not being accepted is a difficult pill to swallow. Regardless, I think we're in the home stretch, but we've got to find something concrete. I'm beginning to worry about DNA with suspects who may have the same father. I'm going to ask the security guards to keep an eye on both of the women. Do you think you can manage checking out their rooms? I'd sure like to get my hands on the rest of those arrows."

"I doubt they will be in either of their rooms. But I will do my best to discover the hiding place. Good luck at the deer blind."

Chapter Seventy-Three

Peter Makes a Breakthrough

Peter was conflicted. He never experienced so many mixed messages. Interviews that contradicted his mind images, confessions he could believe and yet not believe, evidence pointing in one direction yet suggesting another, and motives still evolving. Did I err? Am I losing my gift? He asked himself.

Reality was interfering with images from his mind consort:

Clear your mind of contradictions, Peter. Only then will the truth be revealed. Focus, Peter. Focus. Why do you listen to what people want you to hear? I've given you images, and you ignored them, misinterpreted them. This is not like you, Peter.

Doubt is not in your DNA.

Carol Nelson loved Widdicomb. But she loved him for his mind. Would she really kill him? A woman scorned, yes. But she was scorned continuously by him, and yet his lust was never strong enough to make him or her walk. They were intellectual lovers! Friends, colleagues, comrades. They could discuss anything. That was their true love. He was the first man who acknowledged her entity – a woman with a mind he admired and respected. Their physical relationship was a necessary evil, not an expression of love. His true expressions of love were given only to the women he wed.

Think back to the revelations directed your way. The true path to the killer is in your mind.

Peter closed his eyes and focused on the earliest images his mind consort had sent and began once again to reassemble the puzzle pieces eliminating words he'd listened to, expressions he'd evaluated.

But his start at the beginning was interrupted by the later image of the two black knights sliding and rushing through the swirling snow, followed by a brilliant red explosion with an earring at its epicenter. And the white path. He stopped suddenly, knowing what was about to occur.

He ran to the kitchen, gave Alena instructions for the security guard, grabbed his jacket, and ran to the barn, following the white stone path he's seen a thousand times in his mind and dismissed. It was right there before him

He reached for his phone and called Arthur, but there was no answer. Then, he called David.

≈≈≈

Alena found the guard outside on the snow-covered patio, smoking a cigarette. "Hasn't anyone told you those are bad for you?" she asked, shaking her finger at him.

"Yes, ma'am," he answered, a sheepish look on his face as he crushed the cigarette in the snow.

Shaking her head, side to side, Alena gave him Peter's instructions

"Do you know where she is?" he asked.

"She's in the Octagon Room," Alena answered. "Red hair."

≈≈≈

There was one woman with red hair sitting there. He checked out the room, then took a chair from the kitchen and placed it outside in the hallway.

Chapter Seventy-Four

Blind No More

Leven was beginning almost to enjoy skimming across the snowy path. "This cross-country skiing is really cool. I couldn't walk this fast. And I'm not even breaking a sweat."

David called back to him, "Next, we get you to snow ski down a run."

"I'm for flat ground, Arnstein. If God wanted me on a mountain, he would have made me a goat."

Mordecai, roughly twenty yards ahead, shouted, "Blind's ahead on the right."

Arnstein caught the trees but couldn't spot any blinds. It reminded him of some movie he'd seen: The White Birch facing the enemy like the first-line-of-defense foot soldiers preparing to attack; behind them, a cedar copse hiding the archers with flaming arrows aimed at a target unaware of its destiny.

When the two men joined Mordecai, he pointed to a large Cedar tree. "Hunters love the Cedar trees for blinds," he said. "They appear dense, but removing a branch or two can create enough room to maneuver a bow. The needles stay green all year, great camouflage. And when you break a few twigs on a branch, the cedar oil can help to mask your scent. Perfect for hunting deer."

Mordecai led them to one of the trees with small boards hammered to create a ladder. Slipping off his skis, Arnstein started to climb. He was about forty feet up when he saw a flat boarded area. "Hell, you can live up here," he said as his flashlight began to scour the space. "Someone's been eating granola bars." He carefully lifted the wrappers and placed them in a plastic bag from his pocket. His phone rang as he sealed the bag. It was Peter.

"Yes, we found the blind. I should say Mordecai found it. We would have walked right past it." David paused while Peter talked.

"Are you sure?"

"As sure as my name is Peter Dumas."

"Keep trying to call Arthur. We'll head toward the road for Chilton. Who do you think it is?" He listened, then said, "Okay. Got it. Let me ask Larry." He turned and called down, "Hey Larry, are you carrying?"

"Do birds sing? Of course, I'm carrying."

"Leaven's got his gun," David said to Peter. "See if you can find one at the house. Why don't you get Redfeather to drive you both to Chilton? Watch for us along the road."

He scrambled down the makeshift ladder and told Mordecai and Leven what Peter believed.

"Mr. Peter does not fail in his predictions. We must hurry," Mordecai said, strapping on his skis.

"Okay. If you guys believe it, I'm with you."

"Larry, it's time to break a sweat. Let's move."

Chapter Seventy-Five

On The Road From Chilton: Big Meets Bang

Susanna helped Abigail finish packing while her father, Chris, and Hezekiah completed moving upturned furniture back in place.

"Whoever broke in for the Chief's phone did a number on this place, Mr. Arthur."

"Just to get a telephone number. Incredible, isn't it?"

Hezekiah nodded, then asked Chris if Larry or David found the phone.

"They sure did."

"Where was it, Chris?" Ryerson asked.

"In the hall closet, inside of a pair of his boots. Guess he didn't want to hear it ring when he was home. And Gramps, whoever was looking for my dad, called the Chief from the main number at your office."

"Maybe your dad was calling."

"Not according to Larry."

"Hopefully, everything will reach a climax when all this DNA comes in tomorrow, Chris. Now, let's get Susanna and Abigail and head back to the house. It's Christmas. I'd like us to try and bury all the misery, murder, and malice that's followed us to the lake house; let's share what's important — our family and friendships."

As Arthur spoke, Susanna walked into the room. "You are so right, Dad. We're ready."

Abigail turned the lights off, locked the door, and followed the Ryersons to the truck where Hezekiah waited.

"I don't know about you guys, but I could eat a horse and chase the driver," Chris admitted.

Arthur laughed. "Alena's roasting a turkey and a standing rib roast. You will be feasting soon, Christopher."

While buckling his seat belt, something on the rubber mat caught his eye. "There's my phone. I thought I left it at the house."

Ryerson picked it up and saw three messages from Peter. "Something's happened. Peter's called three times."

His call back was answered on the first ring.

"Arthur, where are you?"

"On the road back to the lake house. What's happened?"

"There's going to be an attack, an explosion."

"An explosion? Involving us?"

"Yes, tell Hezekiah to be particularly careful at the two bends. I see an arrow and the truck centered in the bull's eye of a target."

"Peter, an arrow isn't going to hurt this truck or the steel-belted tires it rides on — it's like an army tank."

Just then, Arthur felt a sudden and severe jolt. The driver's side front tire blew out. Hezekiah tried frantically to control the truck as it began to slide and skid across the narrow road toward a grove of tall trees: majestic Red Oaks, 60-70 feet tall with their distinctive deeply ridged black bark, and 75 to 80 feet tall Bur Oaks with massive branches matching the wingspan of a Boeing 737.

Protecting the trees' base was a slight incline created by a natural limestone ridge roughly two to three feet high. The passenger-side tires hit it like a bowling ball, but the rock and the trees it protected did not fall over. The impact forced the truck to rebound, falling hard on the driver's side and rolling over to a sudden stop with gasoline seeping into the snow.

Ryerson, head bleeding, was not moving; his slumped body was held in place by a safety belt and a deflated airbag. Hezekiah shook his head slowly, attempting to clear his mind, his left arm hanging loose at his side. Pain painted his face. In the back, Chris, with eyes wide open, assessed their situation. Acknowledging his mom's and Gramps' lack of motion, he began to maneuver around the deflated side airbag to push the door open. His stepsister, in full flight mode, started working at his side. "We've got to get out of here, Chris. Can you smell the gas?"

"Yeah, it could explode. Let's get this open." After several body and arm slams, the door opened, allowing the pair to get out. "You try to open my mom's or Hezekiah's door. I'll get my grandfather's."

While Chris broke away the rest of the window on the passenger door, Abigail started to pull on the driver's side door. Now fully coherent, Hezekiah released his safety belt and turned his body to push with his right arm. He bit his lips in response to the pain of his dislocated left shoulder. With Abigail pulling and him pushing, they were able to open the door. Hezekiah struggled to get out of the truck. Holding onto the door for leverage, he once again bit his trembling lips and forced his body off the running board, now above his head, as he rolled onto the ground. With the smell of gas assaulting his nose and mouth, he nodded to Abigail to help him get Susanna free.

Chris, pulling with all his weight, tears rolling down his face, finally opened the passenger door. He reached in to release his grandfather from the safety belt and yanked hard under his arms to pull him free without striking his head.

Arthur Ryerson was unconscious, oblivious to his danger and his grandson's resolute actions. Chris did not stop pulling, despite the snow forcing him to his knees at times. His determination to get his grandfather to safety was his sole goal.

Meanwhile, Hezekiah and Abigail were able to free Susanna. They pulled her across the road over another limestone bluff. "Hezekiah, you stay here with Susanna. I have two arms to help Chris. Keep warm until we get help."

Abigail met Chris at the back of the truck, and both of them dragged Arthur Ryerson to safety behind the bluff. Everyone was covered with a thin film of white dust from the airbags, their chemical odor competing with the gasoline fumes.

In less than a minute, the engine exploded.

"That should not happen," Hezekiah said in surprise. The fuel pump relay keeps the electric fuel pump from functioning once there's been a collision. The chance of a fire is almost nil. Someone tried to kill us."

"You can say that again," Chris said, pointing to the driver-side truck tires. The front one was blown away, but the back tire deflated from the arrow embedded in the tread.

Chris searched for his phone to dial 911 as he walked toward his mother.

Chapter Seventy-Six

A Family In Crisis

They were ten minutes beyond the deer blind when they heard the explosion. It wasn't very loud, but the black smoke rising gave them an extra incentive to push even harder. When they got to the county road, David saw the Range Rover barreling toward them.

Arnstein removed his skis and jumped into the car when Redfeather pulled over.

"We will follow on skis," Mordecai announced. "You will need space for the injured."

"Mordecai and I can check the scene for anything that'll give us a clue," Leven added.

David nodded, and Redfeather stepped on the gas. They were less than a mile from the accident, and as they approached, they saw Chris and Abigail waving. The red and yellow of their jackets glared in the late morning light, a contrasting beacon to a truck across the road blackened by the red and yellow flames.

Chris and Abigail were kneeling next to Susanna. She was in shock, confused— her pupils dilated, her pulse weak, drifting in and out of consciousness yet holding on to Chris's hand, alternately squeezing tightly, then lessening til limp.

David ran to Susanna's side, taking her hand from her son and holding it tightly in his. Chris thanked him, then went to his grandfather. Arthur was still unconscious. Peter barely felt a pulse. He took the blanket he carried from the car and wrapped it tightly around Arthur's motionless body. Hezekiah had removed his jacket earlier and placed Arthur on top of it. Now he was shaking with cold. Peter called Redfeather to help him get Hezekiah into the Rover and gave instructions to wrap him in the blankets they brought from the house.

Arthur's head injury concerned Peter greatly.

Chris saw concern in Peter's face. "Peter, we had to drag him from the truck. I tried to be careful of his head, but it wasn't easy.

Abigail slipped two small flat tree branches wrapped in her sweater under his jacket collar to keep his head from rolling back. Is he going to be okay?" Chris asked as tears once again sprang from his eyes.

"We will know better once we get him to the hospital, Christopher."

"I called 911 as soon as we got him away from the truck. They said it wouldn't be long."

"If they are not here in the next five minutes, we will have to take him and your mother in the Rover. So, find anything you can we can use to keep his head immobile."

"I'll go with Chris to find something to support him," Abigail said, but Peter asked that she stay at Arthur's side until he saw to Susanna.

David's face was in turmoil as he described Susanna's reactions to Peter. "I wrapped her in one of the blankets. Glad you thought to bring them."

Peter nodded, then checked Susanna's eyes and pulse. "I think the blood at her hairline is the result of a cut. She may have a concussion, but I am more convinced that it is shock. She's had her share of trauma this weekend. I think, however, Arthur took the brunt of the accident."

The wail of an ambulance pierced the silent agony of the family's friends. Behind it, the familiar cry of a fire engine.

≈≈≈

The EMTs worked quickly, stabilizing Arthur Ryerson and then Susanna. One of them went to the Rover to check on Hezekiah. After a quick appraisal, he said, "Your shoulder's dislocated, and there may be damage to the rotator cuff. We'll have to put you out to get that shoulder back and take x-rays. I'll make you as comfortable as possible until we get you to the hospital."

Hezekiah nodded quietly, his face a map of pain.

The EMT turned to Peter, "I'm going to give him something for the pain, and then let's get these middle seats down and wrap him to avoid as much movement as possible." He looked at Redfeather, who was sitting behind the wheel, "Give me a few minutes, then stay in the middle of the road and avoid any of the side drifts. The road was clear from the hospital, so you should be fine. Just follow the ambulance."

They worked quickly. The EMT staying with Hezekiah as

Redfeather and Peter drove up to Chris, David, and Abigail. "I'll be back to get you as soon as we get Hezekiah to the hospital," Redfeather said.

The ambulance ahead wailed its cry as the Range Rover followed.

Chapter Seventy-Seven

The Scene Of The Crash

Chris and Abigail followed David to the smoldering truck across the road. The fire was contained thanks to the firemen's quick work, but the air still pulsed with waves of heat. David walked to the crew and flashed his badge and I.D.

"Nasty fire. Good thing, everyone got out. Here's what's left from the cause of the blowout." The captain held the remains of an arrow in his glove: a barbed arrowhead and a charred part of the shaft studded with bits of blue and red coloring. David reached for it but was stopped by the captain's warning, "Still hot."

"Is this enough to cause the explosion and fire?" David asked.

"Nope. Front tire blowouts cause some of the worst accidents, but it had to be a combination of things. These tires are steel-belted, but there's no steel in the sidewall, so it's vulnerable. Looks like this arrow, most likely, started the chain reaction. The size and barbs on this arrowhead had to hit that sidewall like a bomb. The pressure on the inside blew out the tire, causes it to shred and release the arrow with help from the moving rim. The rim probably cut the arrow shaft as well."

"Wouldn't an experienced driver be able to correct the truck's direction?"

"With this kind of damage, and no doubt the suddenness of the vehicle's erratic response, one in a thousand drivers might not overreact. That brings me to number two: overreaction and snow mean sliding, skidding. Number three, the slight incline had to adjust the impact on the limestone wall. The truck slid up to it, probably smashed it with the force of the tire bottoms, and because the truck was on an angle, it rotated and flipped back onto the driver's side. The speed, momentum, and incline forced it to continue rotating onto the roof.

"Now, I'm just guessin', but I think I'm pretty close."

"Sounds more than close, but what about the actual fire?" David probed.

The captain was about to speak when Chris stepped up. "Hezekiah said the chance of a fire was practically impossible. He said the fuel pump relay keeps the electric fuel pump from functioning in a collision, so it protects the inside of the truck."

"He's right, young man. But first off, fumes from the fuel are more flammable than the gasoline itself. For example, the rubber hose that feeds the free rail could have been punctured during the collision releasing small amounts of gas and trapping vapors under the engine cover. When the vehicle settled after crashing into that limestone bluff, an arc could have occurred in the electrical wiring harness.

"That electrical arc is what ignites the vapors creating a chain reaction that then reaches into the fuel lines. And bam, you've got a fire and an explosion. We need to do a forensic exam. The arrow in the tire is enough to get one started."

"There were two arrows," Chris added. "I saw one at the beginning of the tread on the back tire of the driver's side as we were dragging my grandfather away from the truck. The tire was flat but in one piece."

"That tire didn't burn, so we'll probably find the arrowhead embedded in the tread." David added, "I'll call Sheriff Bush. Nothing will happen until tomorrow, but I know he'll get on it as soon as possible."

"Can we get you all to Chilton?" the captain asked.

"No, our ride should be here shortly. One of the injured is en route to the hospital in the Range Rover, and the driver's coming to get us. Thanks to you and your crew Captain. And thanks for finding that arrow."

Leven and Mordecai arrived just as the firetruck began heading back toward the hospital.

"Wow! I expected it to be totaled, but it's like looking at butter that's been melting. Well, I don't have to ask if you found anything, but I'm asking anyway. Did you?" Leven asked.

"We didn't; the firemen did." Arnstein showed them the deadly leftovers of an arrow weaponized to inflict severe damage. "Whoever shot this knew exactly what they were doing. And they were very good at it."

Mordecai walked closer to the Ford Ranger, stopping a moment to pick up a long branch; he used it to poke at the nest of hoses, circuitry boxes, and wires curling around the exposed engine like a den of snakes. A rail cross-over hose was split and cracked from the fire. His immediate reaction was that it might have been helped.

The sound of a horn turned Mordecai's attention to the road and the approaching Range Rover. David and Chris ran toward the driver, who pulled to a stop.

"What's the news, Hank?"

Redfeather signaled a thumbs up. "The IV in the ambulance did the trick. Susanna was coherent in the ER. Her blood pressure was down, but the doctor got it back up before I left. She was lucky. She hit her left side on the door after the airbag depleted, so no additional damage to her right arm."

"How about the cut on her forehead. She was bleeding pretty badly."

"Three stitches. Nothing serious. Arthur, on the other hand, was still out when I left. Peter said he would get back to us as soon as the doctor had some news. As for Hezekiah, he dislocated his shoulder and busted his left arm—two breaks. They put him out and set the arm. He's pretty bruised as well. I can only imagine how painful it must have been to get that door open."

David agreed. "Hezekiah is an incredible man, the kind of guy you want with you when you're in a jam. Does Peter want us back at the hospital?"

"No. He wants everyone back at the house as soon as everything is finished here. Chris should stand in for his grandfather. And he wants a security guard with him and Abigail—around the clock. Peter wants you and Larry to come back before dinner. And he wants you to take it easy. He's worried about your arm."

"I'm fine, Hank. Alena wrapped me up like a mummy. I'm a little sore from sliding on those skis, but a good soak, and I'll be okay."

Larry looked at David with a slight smile on his face. "A Hezekiah match," he laughed. "Me? I'd go back to bed if my arm met an unfriendly arrow."

"Not the Larry I know."

"I wouldn't bet on that, Arnstein. But before we head back to the house, I'd like to walk around a few minutes, take some shots with my phone."

"Good idea. We'll wait in the Rover."

Chapter Seventy-Eight

Life Continues

Chilton Hospital

The minute Arthur Ryerson entered the emergency room, the doctors ordered a CT scan—the first test performed when a traumatic brain injury is suspect. The scan helps doctors assess a situation quickly, using a series of X-rays to get a brain's detailed view. If Arthur had a fracture, any bleeding in his brain, a clot, or any swelling or bruising of his brain tissue, the scan would discover it or rule out a traumatic brain injury resulting from the collision.

Peter waited patiently while Arthur and Susanna were in X-ray. At least Susanna's regained consciousness, he thought, and Hezekiah is over the worst and resting.

The doctors anesthetized Hezekiah to set his broken ulna and pop his dislocated shoulder into place. Peter watched the gentle, loyal, and resourceful man asleep in his assigned room. His face, appearing masked by some translucent film, the color of the sheets and blankets that swaddled him.

The room's silence seemed to beg for a sign that Hezekiah would speak, that he would confirm all is well. But he lay there, silent, lips pressed together, eyes closed.

One listened when Hezekiah spoke, for he rarely used empty words to fill the air with sound. He was a cautious man. An honest man. A man who gave much consideration to the words he spoke and fiercely loyal to the Ryersons and Alena and his cousin, Mordecai.

Arthur Ryerson believed and trusted him, same as he did Mordecai, who had been with him for over thirty years. For Hezekiah, it was only the last five years that he discovered the generosity and trust Arthur and his family shared with him. He had been released from prison after fourteen years for assaulting a man who assaulted his wife. Hezekiah almost beat him to death. The judge sentenced him to thirty years, but good behavior and a lawyer hired by Ryerson saw him set free. It was a happy day but shrouded in black. Hezekiah missed his wife that glorious, bright, sunny morning; she had waited for him, but life left her one month before his release.

Peter continued to watch him, waiting for his eyes to flutter, his lips to part and ask, most likely, 'How is Mr. Arthur and Miss Susanna?' Peter realized it would be several hours before Hezekiah's medications would wear off, and he wanted to be there to assure him that everyone would be okay. He wanted him to see a face he knew, a face he could trust to be honest with him.

A nurse entered the room, interrupting Peter's contemplation, "Ms. Ryerson is asking for you, Mr. Dumas."

"Oh, thank you. May I ask you to find me as soon as Hezekiah wakes?"

"Of course, but that shouldn't be for several hours."

He smiled and said, "I will be here."

***

Susanna was sitting in a chair next to the bed where she had been lying. She was wearing an oversized hospital gown and robe sprinkled with butterflies frozen in flight; her clothes carefully folded on a bench across the room. Her down jacket minus a goodly amount of goose down from the left arm, the result of a tear from the shoulder to just above the wrist. Her grey ski pants spattered with dried blood and jagged tears. A white ski sweater awash with bloody streaks as if painted to resemble a narrow burst of color from neck to mid-chest. Her leftovers from a terrifying collision with a limestone wall, accomplished by the expeditious flight of an arrow.

Peter sat in the chair next to hers. As her hands grasped him, Susanna's eyes exploded in tears, crying, "Why?"

Chapter Seventy-Nine

Eeny, Meeny, Miny, Moe
Will The Killer Stay or Go?

Ryerson House

As soon as Redfeather pulled into the driveway, Arnstein and Leven jumped from the Rover to look for the security guards assigned to Patric and Marks.

Patric's guard stationed outside the Octagon Room was comfortably seated in one of the kitchen's tall back chairs.

Arnstein rushed to him, "Where is she?"

"Still in the Octagon Room."

Arnstein looked into the room. No Patric. No anyone.

"No one's there!"

"She couldna left without passing me."

"Who else was in the room?"

"Just the Cabot couple, but he left when I brought the chair out here. His wife came out about ten minutes later."

"Did she say anything to you?"

"She asked me if I could help her carry a tray to the kitchen. I did. It took about two minutes."

Jody Marks' guard was stationed on the second floor a few feet from his quarry's room. Leven knocked on the door. He could hear a Christmas carol playing softly. He knocked a second time. No answer. David searched for a key on the ring Alena had given him. Finding the right one, he opened the door. The room was empty.

"I was behind her, no more than five or ten seconds. I heard the door slam," the guard explained.

"Get the guard downstairs and search for both of them," David said, his fist silently rapping the door frame.

A few minutes later, the security guards appeared with news. One of them reported the women's location. "Mrs. Gala said they told her they were going cross country skiing together. She saw them heading east on the trails. They didn't wanna watch the parades on TV."

"Let us know as soon as they return," Leven instructed.

"I feel like someone's leading me around by my nose."

Leven slowly nodded, "I know the feeling, David. But we are so close."

≈≈≈

Most guests enjoyed helpings from Alena's cornucopia of delicacies to tide themselves over until dinner, scheduled for 7 PM.

"I feel like I'm on a cruise ship. The food just keeps coming," Phil Conroy announced, tapping his stomach affectionately.

"It's always like that at the Ryerson lake house. Alena's mantra must be Food is next to godliness. Before I met Arthur, I was a trim 170 pounds," gushed Henrietta Gala, smiling as she thrust her generous belly outward, proving perhaps that food might be closer to her lips than to godliness.

While Phil and Henrietta raided the miniature quiche tray, others watched Mickey Mouse tower over Iowa's St. Ignatius High School Band as they marched in step playing his theme song. Still others read or snoozed under the glow of the memory-dressed tree in the family room.

Leven was a snoozer. David was a reader whose eyelids occasionally drooped — on one of those occasions, a security guard tapped his shoulder.

Chapter Eighty

Show Me The Way To My Home

The hospital

"Susanna, we've got to stop meeting like this," Dr. Spensor's comment drew a smile to Susanna's lips—the first since dancing with David on Christmas Eve. "Everything looks fine. If you promise to rest at home, there's no need to stay overnight. Stitches look good. And the arm's healing beautifully. The crash banged it a bit, but all in all, you were lucky."

"I sincerely hope that luck stays with me," she said, tightly grasping Peter's hand. "How is my dad?"

"No traumatic brain injury. He should be fine but needs to take it easy— nothing strenuous or excitable. Quiet conversations, and I mean quiet. No television, nothing that will trigger symptoms. No reading, no games, no computers. No mental stimulation. Just rest. He refuses to stay, so I've given him a list of precautions. Here's a copy for you." He handed the paper to Susanna. "He may suffer headaches, and it's okay for him to take acetaminophen like Tylenol. Avoid ibuprofen like Motrin IB, Advil, or aspirin—they could increase the risk for bleeding. Someone should be with him for the next 24 hours. If any of the symptoms I've listed reappear, call my number immediately. If I don't hear from you, expect me at the house mid-morning."

"Why was he unconscious for almost 15-minutes?"

"Everyone reacts differently. I've had patients who were unconscious for 24 hours, others not at all. Don't worry. The imaging we did showed absolutely nothing of concern. So, I have one prescription for you and your father—rest, rest, and rest. And with that, I rest. Again, Merry Christmas to both of you."

"Merry Christmas," Peter and Susanna said in unison.

"Well, that is good news," Peter sighed. "David and Larry will be coming here in a bit, so I suggest you take one dose of the Doctor's prescription and rest. I will be in the waiting room."

Susanna nodded agreement and climbed back onto the bed.

Relieved to know her father did not suffer a severe injury, she closed her eyes.

Peter watched her drift to sleep then left to seek a quiet place in the waiting room. It was time to get serious. His first action was to call David.

When David answered, Peter briefed him on everyone's condition, followed by questions about Emma Patric and Jody Marks.

Peter listened to David's narrative, convinced that now he was on the right path. "Did you and Larry find anything at the deer blind or the collision site?"

"A couple of granola wrappers where someone waited at the blind. And the fire crew found the arrow that hit the front driver's side tire. It's the same as the others. The back tire was also hit, but in the tread, not the sidewall, so it just lost air, unlike the front tire that blew apart. Larry took photos of the pickup and the surrounding area.

"I left a message for Sheriff Bush. Told him what we found and that I'd drop off the granola wrappers for prints and DNA along with the arrowhead."

"When can you leave? Perhaps Larry should remain at the house to keep an eye on things."

"Larry should stay. I'll be there within the hour."

"I will check on Hezekiah again, but I do not think he should leave with us."

They said their goodbyes, and Peter headed to Hezekiah's room.

Peter found him just waking when he opened the door. "Good, you are awake, but I am certain you are still fuzzy in memory."

"You can say that again, Mr. Peter," he responded with eyes at half-mast, blinking rapidly.

"Hezekiah, it has been a challenging day for you. I am going to recommend you stay the night. You will be in much pain, and the doctor and nurses will be far more able to regulate your pain medication. I will be taking Miss Susanna and her father back to the house where someone can stay with each of them through the night. Thankfully they require no medication other than Tylenol if necessary."

"Are you sure, Mr. Peter?"

"Yes. The doctor will check you tonight and tomorrow morning. After a night's sleep, undisturbed, your healing cells will be restored, and you will be more able to cope with the pain of your injuries. What's more, the doctor will be coming to the house mid-morning, so I'm asking him to bring you home where we will take on the rest of your care."

Hezekiah nodded with eyes struggling to stay open but losing the battle. Peter smiled and quietly closed the door as he left.

≈≈≈

In the waiting room, Peter closed his eyes and ran images forward and backward in his mind. He knew who killed Widdicomb. And why. And who was responsible for Chief Blackhawk, Susanna, and the collision.

> *I was misdirected by my interpretation of the earring, the explosion of red. They defined several actions, not just one. I made assumptions I should not have made. The letters on the path, B, S, C, A, R – Susanna, Chris, and Arthur Ryerson, and the 'B'? For Blackhawk.? Or does the R signify Redfeather, and the 'C and B', Chief Blackhawk? Or Carol and Blackhawk? And the 'A', Abigail? Or is it Arrow? It must relate. But there is no question in my mind now as to the solution. Twice arrows fell from the sky. Two attempts to kill. Two ticking clocks. Two black knights. What do they bring? Who is next?*

Chapter Eighty-One

The Skiers Return

Ryerson House

It was almost 3 PM when Emma Patric walked into the Octagon Room, her cheeks rosy from the cold.

"You look like you could use a drink to warm you up," Leven said as he walked to the bar. "What can I get you?"

"I'll have a glass of whatever wine is open."

"How was your skiing?" he asked.

"Great. I love cross-country skiing."

"I thought you went out with Jody?"

"We started together, but I took the trail toward Chilton. I saw you getting lessons from Mordecai. How did you fare?"

"David's arm was bothering him, so we headed back. I was just getting the hang of it. Did you hear a kinda muffled explosion? Sounded like it was close to Chilton."

"Now that you mention it, I did hear a low-level blast—but it sounded pretty far away. I wonder what it was."

Leven gave her a wine glass filled with a Cabernet Sauvignon, which she cheerfully accepted just as Jody Marks walked in and said to Leven, "I'll have one of those if you're pouring."

"Sure thing."

"Hey Jody," Emma called, "did you hear a small explosion where you were skiing?"

"I was wearing my earbuds. All I heard was Kelly Clarkson's Breakaway Album. She blows my mind. What a voice."

Leven watched the two of them. The look on his face didn't offer any clue to what he was thinking. Maybe we are being led by our nose, he thought.

~~~

Arnstein was standing at the Octagon Room's kitchen entrance, waiting to get Leven's attention. When Larry turned and saw him, he excused himself and followed David into the hallway.

"I'm heading to the hospital, Larry. Peter wants you to stay here and keep tabs on those two. We'll bring Arthur and Susanna back, but Hezekiah will stay overnight."

"You think I should let everyone know about the accident?"

"I think you better, but don't mention the arrow. Give credit to the pickup hitting a limestone wall because of an icy stretch and a tire blowout."

"If they're coming home, that means everything's okay, right?"

"According to Peter, Arthur's got to take it real easy. I doubt he'll be social tonight. Susanna's distraught but physically OK. I'll drop off the arrowhead and the wrappers at the sheriff's office."

"Drive safe, buddy. We don't need another mishap."

Chapter Eighty-Two

The Epiphanies

The Hospital

The roads were clear, but only David's car was moving east to Chilton. Most travelers had reached their destination—homes with grandchildren, homes with in-laws, homes with friends or colleagues. All of them with welcoming scents of roasting turkeys and hams, gaily wrapped gifts, and good cheer.

Others are alone or celebrating their holiday volunteering at soup kitchens, shelters, or children's wards where they'll share smiles and conversation, food, and winter-warm gifts. The givers and receivers will both be happy to experience the true meaning of the holiday, joining together as strangers and leaving with bits and pieces of each other's heartfelt feelings.

David hadn't had a Christmas destination since his wife and child died. As the years passed, the three-dimensional, full-color album frozen in his mind had become veiled, translucent. It was getting more and more difficult to bring up the faces that never aged. David Jr. was a few months old that fateful day. He would be eighteen years old now, but Arnstein would never know how he would look. Like his mother? He would ask himself. Or would he look like me?

As he neared the spot where the Ford Ranger was totaled, he was relieved to see it had been towed. Susanna and her father needed no reminder of what someone had destined for them. It was 4:30 and getting dark. He opted to stop at the sheriff's office before meeting Peter.

When he pulled up to the station, a skeleton crew greeted him, offering cookies, chocolates, and an assortment of cheese and crackers along with a generous cup of cocoa. Arnstein passed on the munchies but accepted the cocoa, then chatted for a few minutes wishing all a wonderful Christmas.

The desk sergeant directed him to the Evidence Locker, where Arnstein signed in the arrowhead and granola wrappers he had earlier placed in separate plastic bags identified with location, date, and time.

"We need prints and DNA ASAP," he told the duty clerk.

"Sheriff Bush called and said he would be here around 7 AM. We'll get 'em right out."

Arnstein gave a wave as he left the station and drove to the hospital where Peter waited.

~~~

When David walked in, Peter was asleep on a chair in the deserted waiting area, so he took the bag Alena packed with fresh clothes for Susanna and went to the registration desk to get her room's location. She was down the hall, a few doors away, a police officer stationed at the room's entrance.

David walked in to find her, and like Peter, asleep as well. He watched her slow and steady breathing, her blonde hair cascading across the pillow. They met a little more than a year ago, and he looked for any excuse to see her, talk with her, his feelings growing, month after month.

They met when Arnstein was lead detective on a rash of Realtor murders. One of the women killed was her close friend. She was murdered, showing one of Susanna's listings at a Lake Shore Drive hi-rise. Arnstein gave her the news, but he never told her how her friend Terry died. And he never would.

Susanna had introduced Arnstein to Peter Dumas. And, when she received the killer's calling card, a gift of Boucheron perfume, Peter and his clairvoyance became an integral part of the investigation. Cut from the same cloth, Peter and David became instant friends, and Susanna became an integral part of David's life. But his feelings were kept secret, though he wrestled with revealing them. This family weekend was to be the disclosure of his confession. But murder has a way of interrupting life.

Susanna stirred and woke suddenly, looking up to see David. She smiled. He melted.

"I....I..ah, Alena packed some clothes for you. I'm glad you're okay. Peter should be getting Arthur, so soon as you're ready, meet us in the waiting room. I guess the doctor signed the releases."

"Is Hezekiah coming?" she asked.

"No, he's staying over, and the doctor will bring him to the house tomorrow when he comes to check you and your dad. I'll get the nurse to help you." He smiled awkwardly, put the duffel bag on the chair, and left.

Susanna had never seen Arnstein appear so uncomfortable. He looked like a blushing schoolboy. And yet, his confidence almost intimidated her the first time they met. But she soon learned beneath the confident manner were subtleties that endeared him to her. He wasn't just kind; he was thoughtfully kind— heeding and understanding the layers of need. He seemed to aim his kindness at one's source of anger, one's degree of sadness, one's measure of self-guilt. Those nuances of knowing what to say precisely and how to say it brought sudden relief to those recipients of his kindness. He was a warm and caring man with principles that crowned his confidence.

Susanna believed that one felt safe, cared for, protected, even loved with David in your corner. She considered him her friend, but recently her feelings for him had evolved. She was falling in love with David Arnstein. She loved being with him, talking with him, listening to the way his mind worked, and she wanted their friendship to move to another level. *Did he feel the same,* she would ask herself. *Is that why he looked so uncomfortable? Why, oh why, did murder have to interrupt this weekend with him?*

≈≈≈

Before Susanna and Arthur joined them, Peter cautioned David to not speak of the accident, the arrow, or anything about the murders. He explained that Arthur was to have no excitement, no mental stimulation.

David understood but was shocked when he saw Arthur in the wheelchair. Physically, he appeared to have aged some ten to fifteen years since early this morning. Even Susanna recognized the change that had occurred within a matter of a few hours. Her father looked tired, fragile; his skin was pale, almost translucent allowing his veins' blue to roadmap his neck and hands. His incredible mass of white curly hair lost its fullness; it was flat, dark with lackluster curls.

Susanna blinked back, tears forming at her eyes. Whosoever intends to destroy us is making inroads. But I will not stand by and watch them succeed. A sudden firmness at her jaw, darkening of her eyes, and an uplifting of her shoulders, straight and strong, added dimension to her determination.

Ordinarily, Susanna chose to compromise in disagreements and overlook negative comments. Still, in a world where one can destroy a reputation with just forty words and a pair of thumbs, compromise she believed should not be the answer. If the target of destruction is a complete family, and if the thumbs become a pair of hands aiming an arrow or any other weapon, swift punishment should be the response. No mercy. No forgiveness.

She knew that words and labels could be weapons, as well, aiming at the destruction of people, beliefs, character, and ideas, often from the lips of the ignorant or the innocent promulgated by factions eager to control or confine freedoms. She believed neither fiction nor fact should be used to pre-judge an individual's innocence. Nor should they be used to deliberately destroy life or reputation without benefit of judge and jury. In Susanna's eyes, those actions were tantamount to murder.

She could be moderate and conservative. She believed in justice, but not when it was modified or redefined simply to benefit one or a few to promote a cabal at the expense of many. She was not an activist, but she was indeed prone to acting when she saw injustice and evil.

"Archer, en guarde."

Chapter Eighty-Three

Emma Meets A Different Peter

The invitation to meet Peter and Larry Leven didn't surprise Emma Patric when Alena delivered their request to her. She had been expecting it—Redfeather told her they were talking to everyone from the agency. After finishing her glass of wine, she headed upstairs.

She was about to knock on the closed door to the office when it suddenly opened to a smiling Peter Dumas. "Emma, thank you for coming to speak with us."

"I didn't have much choice, did I?" She asked, relaxed, her poker face devoid of concern or anxiety.

"Oh, you indeed have choices. You may choose to speak to us with an attorney present or choose to speak to us at the sheriff's office. Or course..."

She interrupted Peter. "Never mind. I'll answer your questions. I want this over; besides, I have nothing to hide."

Peter directed her to a seat across from him and Larry Leven. "I believe you've met Larry. Detective Leven is here from Fort Lauderdale investigating the murder of your father."

Patric's face froze for an instant. "How did you know?"

"We know a great deal, Emma."

Leven broke his silence and asked, "When did you learn Marvin Widdicomb was your father?"

"Before my adopted mother died. Carol Nelson told her. And my mother told me."

"Have you any idea how long Carol knew?"

Peter observed her as she answered Larry's questions.

"No."

"Did Carol ever discuss your birth parents with you?"

"No, as far as I was concerned, Carol was just my aunt. I had no idea she knew my mother or that she was sleeping with my father."

Peter caught the sudden tightness around her eyes, as well as her left hand rubbing her fisted right as if to hide the tension at her knuckles.

Then Peter took the stage. "It must have been difficult for you to see Carol's attachment to Widdicomb?"

Her jaw firm, eyes wide in control, she looked at Dumas and smiled. "She wasn't a true blood relative to me. Besides, what he did happened over twenty-five years ago to a drug addict."

"Time can heal, and sometimes it simply won't," Peter offered. He looked at some notes then asked, "When did Carol decide to give Redfeather handmade arrows for Christmas?"

"Probably before she asked me to check out some sources in Chilton in late September. She told me that she and Redfeather drove up to Wisconsin earlier in the year, and she went with him to see an old Native American who made arrows for Hank. All she remembered was Chilton."

"Were they shipped to the office?"

"I don't know. They were in her office the week before we came up here. She asked me to get wrapping paper for them."

"How many were there?" Leven asked.

"There were six, as I recall."

"Have you ever met your birth mother's parents?"

"No. My adopted mom said they wanted absolutely no contact with me, and any requests for financial aid would be refused."

"When was the first time Widdicomb tried to force sex on you?"

She stood suddenly, anger flashing across her face. "How dare you insinuate my father tried to abuse me sexually?"

"I doubt Widdicomb thought you were his daughter, and based on his history, it is not an unfair question."

"I don't have to answer your questions or accept your rudeness." She turned, slamming the door as she left the room.

"She's holding a lot inside," Leven said thoughtfully.

"There is so much more here than what meets the eye. Did you get her fingerprints or DNA, Larry?".

I think David got the prints on those wine glasses we gave to Sheriff Bush. But to be safe, I asked Alena to pick up Patric's wine glass and carefully put it in a plastic evidence bag I gave her."

Chapter Eighty-Four

The Family Is Home For Christmas

David didn't expect the sequence of events that unraveled in the last four days. When he watched the snow falling during the limo trip to the lake house, his eyes only saw the wonders of a welcoming weekend, a celebration of the season with a group of people he knew and loved, as well as people he'd never met. Widdicomb was just a name, a name of someone at the Ryerson agency, murdered in Fort Lauderdale. Little did he realize what damage that name could do. It led to a family in crisis…to a Native American murdered because of his relationship with Widdicomb and the ancestral art he performed, hundreds of years old, replicating Comanche warrior arrows. And, it was a name that almost led to the death of a woman who had captured Arnstein's heart.

He sat in the driver's seat, occasionally looking back at Susanna, who was leaning protectively against her father, his hands resting in hers. He drove slowly over the snow-covered road, not wanting to give the Ryersons any more motion than necessary. Again, they met no other traffic en route to the lake house. The flat area resembled a vast white wasteland in David's eyes. "Hard to believe this is the Midwest; looks more like the tundra," he said softly to his friend in the passenger seat. "At least this stretch does."

Peter agreed. "Yes, but as soon as we reach the top of this hill, we're back in a Hansel and Gretel photo opportunity."

David laughed. "Funny thing though, winter or summer, those trees probably look the same. Same bark. Same dark green needles. Same everything except in the summer, all of that snow is photoshopped out. Hmmph. Wouldn't it be interesting if cities in warm climates could photoshop snow over everything? Just for Christmas Eve and Christmas—including the temperature, of course. They could then hit undo in the morning."

"You have given me an idea, David."

Before Arnstein could ask about the idea, the turnoff appeared for the lake house driveway.

≈≈≈

Alerted by Peter's text, Leven and two security guards waited at the entrance when David pulled up. The two guards helped Arthur; David helped Susanna.

They entered the house to a series of "What happened?", "Are you okay, Arthur?", "Was there an accident?" While Leven attempted to answer the questions as briefly as possible, he recognized that the time had come to lay it all out. He nodded to David, pointing to the Octagon Room.

David agreed and turned to Susanna, "Do you want to head up, or would you rather come with me?"

"I'll stay with you." But first, she walked to her father, hugged and kissed him, then watched as Peter and the guards helped Arthur to his room.

Chris appeared just as Susanna and David headed to the Octagon Room. "I'm going up to see Gramps, Mom."

"Good. Stay with him a bit, would you? He's pretty down."

"I know. Is this going to end, Mom?"

"Of course, it's going to end. Isn't it, David?"

"Most likely, tomorrow."

"Seriously?" Chris asked, his eyes wide in anticipation. "Do you know who killed my dad and tried to kill us?"

"We're pretty sure. DNA and prints will give us the final proof."

Chapter Eighty-Five

Peter Talks Chess

Chris was leaving just as Peter was about to re-enter his grandfather's room. "Talk to him, Peter. He's furious."

"I will do my best, Christopher."

Peter went to his old friend and suggested he get into bed, but Arthur refused. However, he did agree to settle on the chaise lounge and even managed to pull an alpaca suede throw over himself. "Peter, I'm fine. Just tired. The whole day has been a nightmare. We were lucky we all weren't killed. The truck is a disaster. Guests are all wondering what's going on. And, there's a murderer loose in my house. I don't have much Christmas spirit left."

"It's almost over, Arthur. DNA and print results should be in tomorrow morning to confirm my beliefs."

"Who is it, Peter?"

"I would rather not name anyone. I was wrong when I identified Carol Nelson as Widdicomb's killer."

"She didn't do it?"

"Yes, yes, she did. But I questioned myself. Unfortunately, I failed to search secondary and tertiary interpretations of mind images I received in my attempt to determine a solution. I would have been pre-warned of the attempt on Susanna's life, and I would have expected the attack on the Ford Ranger early enough to foil it possibly."

"Peter, don't punish yourself. If not for the accidents that missed their mark, others might have been delivered with success. Your prediction of an explosion and warning to David and Larry brought us badly needed help. I am ever so grateful. I have my daughter and my grandson. Alive.

"What is your plan to bring this bastard to justice? And do you know his motive?"

"We have had motives by the carload, interacting motives. Different versions of duplicate motives. Have you ever played three-dimensional chess, Arthur?"

"Peter, I'm afraid regular chess is beyond me."

"Bear with me. Imagine that our killer's motive is on a chessboard with three levels of that chessboard beneath it. Since every overlapping square is the same color, the killer, in our game story, has the option to land a piece of his or her motive on any of the four levels. For this reason, two versions of the same motive (or different motives) can occupy the same square on different levels."

"You're making my head hurt."

"I should not be taxing your mind. This is our dilemma — David's, Larry's, and mine. Multiple versions, multiple motives. They inhibit our call for Checkmate. Catch an early episode of StarTrek, and watch Kirk and Spock take on multi-level chess when you feel you are ready."

"I kind of think I know what you're saying, but I'd rather you just told me who the killer is. I'll watch Kirk and Spock another day."

"You must rest. Then I think it would suit you and your guests if you appear at dinner. No conversation, just gifts and tidings of joy. Spend one-half hour and return up here again to rest. I must meet with David and Larry, but I will return to help you join the others."

"Sounds fine. Especially the 'no conversation' part."

~~~

Peter joined David, Larry, and Susanna in the Octagon Room. Christmas carols softly filled the air. Four guests were involved in a game of bridge at the far side of the room. According to Alena, several guests were in the library reading, drinking, and chatting.

Larry spoke first. "Peter, we've been talking. Let's tell everyone what's been happening. A lot of them are worried about Arthur. We've been fielding questions, and they're not satisfied with our answers."

"I agree with Larry, Peter. Besides, we might get something we can use. Several people have said they plan to leave in the morning, and we can't let that happen."

"I, too, feel we must make everyone aware of the situation. I recommend we do so after dinner. Arthur will be joining us for a short time, and he can appeal for patience, cooperation, and help. We can reveal the attempt on Susanna's life, Chief Blackhawk's murder, and the accident. And we should include Carol Nelson's death without suggesting it was cold-blooded murder. Nothing about any of our evidence, suspicions, or assumptions, though."

"Who do you think is behind it all, Peter."

"Your father asked that of me as well, Susanna. All I will say is that one of the motives is jealousy tinged with revenge. I'm going to ask Alena to announce the time dinner will be served and mention that gifts and cocktails will be here afterward. They'll have just enough time to dress."

"Dad planned to distribute those gifts to everyone. Chris should take care of that. Where is he?"

Leven answered. "He's with Abigail in your father's office. I told him to camp out there with one of the security guards, so we didn't have to worry about them."

"David, why not take Susanna up to the office, then let us discuss this evening's reveal. I'll send up a couple of the guards to escort them to their rooms to dress for dinner."

"You got it, Peter."

Chapter Eighty-Six

Girls Talk; Boys Plan

"Jody, did you catch Mr. Ryerson when he came in?' Emma whispered.

"I saw him heading up the stairs. He didn't look too great."

"Maybe that accident was more serious than they let on."

"I wouldn't be surprised at anything after this last week."

"What do you mean?"

"Come on, Emma, you know they're not telling the whole story. It's not like they want any of us not to be disturbed. They haven't brought up Widdicomb's murder or the arrow. They didn't admit Susanna's injury was an accident by arrow. They told some of us, but not all of us. They think one of us is the murderer."

"Yes, but they don't have a clue. During my 3rd degree, Peter Dumas tried to get me to admit Widdicomb sexually assaulted me—I guess to give me a motive. He and his buddies must think we're all stupid. They have no idea who killed him or who missed killing Susanna."

'Or why," Jody whispered. "By the way, have you seen Chris?"

"Earlier. He came in with Detective Leven. Haven't seen him since."

"Think they're keeping him under wraps to protect him?"

"You have a devious mind, Jody."

"No more devious than yours."

Their tete a tete was interrupted by Alena's dinner time announcement.

While David was upstairs, Larry opted to check with the first pair of guards taking dinner breaks in the kitchen.

Peter sat quietly, taking long, deep breaths, his eyes closed.
> He watched the images flash rapidly in his subconscious, a kaleidoscope of colors and shapes until two black steeds began spinning to center stage. Nostrils

flaring, eyes, a bright red, both animals leaping forward with each rider holding one black candle, aflame.

As Peter decoded the message, guests headed up to dress for dinner.

≈≈≈

When Larry and David rejoined Peter, they prepared to discuss the approach to take after Chris distributed the gifts later that evening.

"I think I should start with a recap of Widdicomb's murder."

"That's where everything started," David added. "I can take it from there and explain the attempt on Susanna's life."

"Yes," Peter agreed, "but I think you should describe Chief Blackhawk's murder. His death is integral to our story. And I believe you should introduce Abigail. I will describe the attack on the Ford Ranger, as well as Carol's accident.

"I have a suggestion as well. I think it would be wise to identify the guilty, the perpetrators of all the drama we have witnessed."

Both David and Larry raised voices to object. "What would that achieve? We have nothing to prove without the DNA and print reports," Larry said defensively.

"Wait a sec, Larry. I think I see where Peter's heading. If there's an arrest tonight, we could avoid another attack that may jeopardize the other guests. Right, Peter?"

"I fear the explosion in my mind image may represent not one, but two episodes. More images have invaded my mind. Enough have died. What's more, an early morning escape might well be in the planning stage."

After further discussion, the three men agreed, and David called Sheriff Bush to confirm their concerns and arrange for the arrest.

Chapter Eighty-Seven

Dinner Is Served

One by one, they reconvened in the family room, all dressed to the nines.

There is something rather beautiful when guests appear in formal wear on a holiday. No jeans, no t-shirts, no gym shoes, no workout wear. Dressing up becomes an expression of respect, first for the day's celebration; next as a tribute to the host's generous invitation. And last but not least, it honors the chef and the formal presentation of delectable and traditional bounties cooked to perfection, waiting to be served with sweet and savory scents.

Mordecai served drinks in tumblers, wine glasses, and champagne flutes. Under the din of conversation, Manheim Steamroller, with their familiar sound, suggested guests prepare to listen as they asked, *Do You Hear What I Hear*.

A sudden laugh, a voice raised, a quiet thought whispered, it was a festive crowd bent on celebrating in style, some with secrets held close to their hearts. Others, engendering jealousy and hatred behind warm and welcoming smiles on innocent-looking faces. Still others, smooth in manner, touching a shoulder, a hand in friendliness with furtive glances concealing anticipation of something dark and unexpected.

When Alena entered the room to announce dinner, everyone began to move in singles and pairs to the dining room, where Arthur Ryerson waited in his place at the head of the table. The room was even more opulent than it was on Christmas Eve. Silver stars sprinkled across the pewter table-top joined crystal ornaments, ribboned with red adorning each place setting. Under the upside-down Christmas tree was the antithesis of pewter, crystal, and silver: a simple wooden creche with hand-painted figures from the Bethlehem scene familiar to Christians worldwide. Delicate lambs, donkeys, and straw. Mary and Joseph and the babe Jesus asleep in a rough wooden cradle.

Three kings with gifts of gold, frankincense, and myrrh. In some ways, it speaks some of our reality: a mom, a dad, a baby — sans the raiment of the rich, opulent gifts, and the potential recognized by leaders of countries.

Food was served as Arthur Ryerson raised his water glass to toast his family, friends, and guests with a special note of thanks to Alena, Mordecai, and the missing Hezekiah. A few people asked about the accident, but Arthur brushed it aside, saying, "All's well that ends well."

Peter smiled, hearing Arthur's response. In some respect, he thought *Shakespeare had expressed the effect but not the cause of our motive dilemmas.*

It was a traditional dinner, the kind Arthur came to love when his Annie entered his life so many years ago. A beautifully browned bird with all the trimmings from homemade sage dressing to candied yams and his favorite cranberry sauce with strawberries, raspberries, candied oranges, and pecans. For those non-turkey lovers or guests preferring a duality of entre, a standing rib roast stood waiting with Yorkshire pudding and a wonderfully cheese-filled broccoli, cauliflower, and onion casserole. Music filled the room, a soft breath of fresh air under conversations recalling other times and places that filled minds and souls with long-ago memories of Christmas.

When apple, pecan, and pumpkin pies were ready to serve. Arthur tapped his spoon to his glass. "My doctor prefers I rest to wipe away remnants of the accident earlier today, so I must return to my room. My grandson, Christopher, and his newly found stepsister, Abigail, will assume the role of Santa Claus and helper for the evening's gift exchange. I wish each of you a most blessed Christmas. May the wonder and love of this holy day become the star on the path of your life. Merry Christmas."

A round of Merry Christmas's echoed as Arthur left the room with two security guards at his side helping him.

Christine Cabot turned to Jody Marks sitting at her side and asked, "What did Arthur mean about Chris having a stepsister named Abigail. Isn't she the girl who was serving dinner the other night? Flo. That was her name, wasn't it? She had dark hair, though."

Marks stared quietly at Abigail, sitting across the table next to Susanna.

"Is she one of Marvin's bastards?" Christine probed.

Jody Marks sat silent, ignoring her rude comments.

≈≈≈

After a goodly number of guests cautiously opted for just a "taste" of each of the pies, a series of oohs and ahhs trembled ever so quietly throughout the room.

Redfeather was the first to acknowledge his satisfaction. "You've outdone yourself once again, Alena. I love 'em all, but the apple is the apple of my taste buds. Would you save me a piece for breakfast?"

Alena laughed. "Of course, Mr. Redfeather." He smiled as Phil Conroy and Mr. Gala seconded his request. One for apple and one for pecan. Peter's eyes twinkled. There was no need for him to make that breakfast order; he was fully aware that Alena had baked one of her apple pies exclusively for him.

A few minutes later, Peter nodded to Chris, who rose and invited all the guests to the family room for brandy, coffee, and the exchanging of gifts. After everyone retrieved drinks and settled themselves in the sofas now surrounding the tree, Peter joined Chris and Susanna as they assembled wrapped packages for the members of Ryerson, Foot, and Burner.

"My grandfather asked me to tell all of you how much he appreciates your creativity, your incredible work ethic, your loyalty, and above all, your friendship. RFB had an exceptionally profitable year, and Gramps wants you to share in the profits that your work contributed to the mix. Upon leaving this weekend, you will receive a check, personally from my grandfather, that should demonstrate the board's gratitude and appreciation. The wrapped packages are his gifts for his friends."

Susanna and Peter handed a large box to Chris, who called out, "Hank Redfeather." Next came a box for Charlie Cabot, then Phil Conroy, Jody Marks, and Emma Patric.

Hank Redfeather pulled the wrapping off his gift, curious about the contents of such a large and heavy, rectangular box. While the others were tearing wrapping paper, Hank stared at his present with awe.

Framed under glass was a Comanche war bonnet. Its Golden Eagle feathers, predominately white with brown tips, signified the strength of a young eagle. Each feather was attached to a beautifully hand beaded headband with Red-tailed Hawk feathers hanging from medallions at each side of the temple. Had the feathers been mostly brown from an older eagle, their meaning would have been wisdom.

This was a feathered headdress of a Comanche who earned each feather by achieving significant accomplishments marked by personal bravery and courage in battle to benefit the community as a whole. The multiplicity of feathers measured the man— highly accomplished and highly respected. Redfeather was overcome at Arthur's thoughtfulness and understanding.

Charlie Cabot, a mystery buff, found a First Edition "Gold Bug and other tales" by Edgar Allan Poe.

Phil Conroy, a Civil War reenactment participant, found a Confederate officer's uniform jacket complete with authentic buttons and belt buckle.

Jody Marks, a writer/producer of turn-of-the-century plays, found an 1870 Tunbridge inlaid wood sewing box and a lady's shoes circa 1880-1910 with two period dresses for her growing collection of clothing and accessories for her productions.

Emma Patric, a student of genealogy, found memberships in the professional editions of important databases.

Arthur's choice of gifts particularly moved the RFB group. His knowledge of their interests outside of the office was startling, and matching gifts to their creative passions was indicative of a kind, thoughtful and generous man.

Other guests in the group were not forgotten. The Galas were gifted two cases of their favorite champagne. Christine Cabot received a pair of diamond earrings with a note expressing thank you for sharing Charlie with the creative group at RFB.

Alena, Mordecai, and Hezekiah received generous bonuses earlier that morning. Susanna, Chris, David, Peter, and now Abigail would celebrate the gifts' exchange after the guests departed.

As conversation settled down, Peter rose and asked for attention. "This indeed has been a decidedly wonderful Christmas, which I'm confident you all would agree. Unfortunately, some elements have put a veil of discontent upon the festivities. We have tried to shield you from these elements. However, the time has come to reveal all that has occurred. Hopefully, you may even contribute to the solution of the murders and attempted murders perpetrated during the last four days.

They all looked at Peter. Surprise on many faces. Fear on others.

Who wears the mask hiding murder?

Chapter Eighty-Eight

A Reveal. An Attack.

"I know this is a bit out of the ordinary, but there is nothing ordinary about the killing and chaos that has erupted in the past 96 hours. So, we will share the events, hopeful that one or several of you noticed something unusual. It is going to be a long evening. I suggest we take a break and reconvene in fifteen minutes. You may visit your room to refresh or get comfortable," Peter advised.

"I don't think I want to stay," Christine Cabot announced as she stood up to leave.

"I'm afraid you haven't any choice, Mrs. Cabot," Larry Leven said firmly. "The security guards are here to detain you. Everyone in this room is suspect. Including you."

Eyes wide, filled with fear, Christine looked at the others, who carefully avoided returning her angry stare.

"What's more," Leven continued, "the Wisconsin State Police have closed many of the highways leading to Chicago. Sheriff Bush gave us the news in our call, but he will be happy to escort you to a holding cell in Chilton after everyone has given us a statement. Then you can give yours at the Police Station."

Christine Cabot sat down and grabbed onto her husband's arm.

"Why are the roads being closed?" Redfeather asked.

"A major storm from the northwest has dumped more than sixteen inches of snow just south of us, all the way to the northern suburbs of Illinois. And it looks as though it's not finished," David Arnstein answered.

"Let us take our break. Alena and Mordecai will refresh drinks when you return," Peter added. Eight guests rose slowly and headed to the doors with six security guards close behind. Susanna's guard remained at the back of the room.

"Think we'll smoke 'em out," Leven asked Peter.

"There is no question about it. We must." Then turning to David, he gave instructions to check three rooms after the guests returned. "Look for anything that can create a dangerous situation here."

"You're convinced there's a possibility?"

"Not a possibility, a certainty."

Susanna listened to the conversation. "I don't know if I want to hear everything. Perhaps I'll stay in my room." She looked at David and asked if he would come up and check with her when it was over.

Chris and Abigail each took a seat near Peter as Susanna sidled toward the kitchen entrance when Larry Leven asked for everyone's attention. When she was sure no one was watching, she quietly closed the doors behind her and asked Alena for hot cocoa and a few cookies to take upstairs.

Arnstein left the room before the kitchen doors closed. A security guard accompanied him, running up the stairs as David unlocked the first room. The two men searched for anything that could foster a fire or an explosion based on Peter's instructions. They checked wiring at outlets, cabinets for flammable liquids, lit candles in the adjoining bath, extinguishing them, and removing anything close by that could accidentally burn should the candles be re-lit. They checked luggage and briefcases and every piece of furniture. Room No.1 was clean — bath, bedroom, and closets.

The second and third suites were equally free of anything that could become the mainspring for a fire.

A few doors away, Susanna was sitting in a wingback chair next to the gas fireplace in her room. Her cocoa and two cookies rested on a side table. She was barely awake. Her book had fallen from her fingers. Her eyes were fluttering on the fringe of deep sleep. She failed to acknowledge the knock at the door.

David knocked several times. He wanted to learn if Susanna needed him to bring anything when he came back later with news from the meeting. He was surprised she wasn't answering. After a minute or two, he became concerned — one more knock. No response. He took the key marked 'S' from the master key ring.

The smell of gas hit him like a wall when he opened the door. He saw Susanna in the chair next to the fireplace. Unconscious. He ran to pull her into the hallway while the security guard rushed to open every window in the room.

David yelled out as he began chest compressions to get her breathing, "Check the gas turnoff in the fireplace."

"It's a half turn on," he yelled back as he twisted the handle to close it. "I'll call for help. She needs oxygen. Fire department might be quicker than an ambulance."

After a few minutes, Susanna began to move, but David told her to keep still. He explained what happened and said help was on the way as he rested her head in his arm.

"Jack, get to Peter and tell him about the fireplace and Susanna. Get him to pause the meeting and come up here."

"You got it, Mr. A."

≈≈≈

Peter whispered the news he got to Larry and asked him to continue about the evidence the Fort Lauderdale team discovered. As he approached the stairway, he heard the wail of the emergency van and waited to get the EMTs upstairs.

When he opened the door, one of the EMTs looked at Peter and said, "You guys are having a real run of bad luck."

"One could certainly say that," answered Peter.

The smell of gas lingered in the room, but with none of the oppressiveness that greeted David when he opened the door. He kept thinking if I hadn't stopped to ask if she needed anything…she would be dead.

The oxygen administered by the EMTs was the primary treatment for inhalation injuries, and it was working. Susanna started to get her color back. "She's one lucky lady," the EMT said. "Didn't she get hit by an arrow before that car accident?" he asked.

Peter sighed and responded. "She is, indeed, a lucky lady. Let us pray her luck does not run out."

Susanna sat up. "I wasn't in my room that long. I just started drinking my cocoa. My eyes started to hurt. I smelled something. It wasn't very strong. I've got a cold…that's probably why I didn't think anything of it."

"We think you should come to the hospital for observation. Six to twelve hours, that's it."

"No, absolutely not," she said adamantly. Alena or one of the girls can stay with me. Just tell me what I have to watch for and what

I have to do. Dr. Spenser is coming here in the morning. I just want to be home. I want to find out who's the bastard trying to kill me. And why?"

"I think it best Susanna remains home. We'll watch over her. Give me a list of any symptoms or reactions which should be of concern," Peter acknowledged and left with the EMTs.

David's eyes poured over Susanna. "I think you should stay in my room. That gas smell will be around for a while, even with the windows wide open."

"Why, David? Why now? In the house?"

"Most likely, it was killing two birds with one stone. Hatred for you and an opportunity to create bedlam for an escape."

"I'll wait until Alena or one of the girls gets here. You are not to move from my room. Understood?"

"Of course, how could I ignore the man who saved my life twice."

"Isn't there an old saying that when you save a life, it belongs to you?"

"There may be truth in that adage," she smiled and walked toward his room.

Chapter Eighty-Nine

Peter Ignites The Room

Leven gave the guests much to comprehend when he detailed how Widdicomb was murdered. He explained the timetable. He identified the evidence found at the scene and in Widdicomb's suite. He informed them of Carol Nelson's secret trip. He spoke of arrows and earrings, then finally confessed that Carol Nelson murdered Marvin P. Widdicomb

"But she loved him," Redfeather interrupted. "She had a kid with him, for Christ's sake."

"It is a pity, Hank, that you failed to tell us. Carol might still be alive if you had," Peter responded.

"I don't buy that. I don't buy that she killed him, either. Why?"

"It is all about the children. Widdicomb's children. Birthing them. Adopting them. Acknowledging them. And, most importantly, discovering them." Peter's anger flashed in his eyes. His lithe body seemed to harden head to toe. "It is about legitimacy. Responsibility. Recognition. Carol became enmeshed with the needs of the children, and finally, despite her love, her intolerance of Widdicomb's insouciance sparked her violence. She may not have shared that rage with others, but it was real, refined. She planned her expression of judgment."

Jody Marks twisted in her seat, unable to look at anyone, convinced they all knew Carol was her mother. The woman who murdered her father. A father who she believed never accepted her and would never acknowledge her. She closed her eyes tight and tried to collapse into the sofa.

Christine Cabot rose and headed toward Mordecai, her empty glass searching for a refill. Was her child the fruit of adultery? Did she resent Marvin's legitimate wives and children?

"It was not enough that Widdicomb was killed; his first marital partner became the next target," Peter continued.

Then David stood and announced the arrow attack on Susanna. He explained that the archer used a deer blind to target her on the cross-country trails. "We found the blind. And the evidence left behind. The attempt on Susanna's life was meant to eradicate a legal spouse. And Carol didn't do it. The attempt was to implicate Carol for murdering Widdicomb."

Emma Patric sat very still, listening. Calm. Relaxed. She watched others in the room, a soft smile on her face. Was she Widdicomb's by-blow? Did this mild-mannered, illegitimate daughter send the poem with the drawing? Did she aim the arrow? Was she the redhead spying on Widdicomb in Fort Lauderdale? Did she call Chris?

Charlie Cabot looked uncomfortable. He watched his wife with searching eyes. Christine told him that blue eyes were a dominant trait in her family, though her eyes were big and brown. There were no blue eyes in Charlie's family that he knew. Was he Charlie Junior's father? Or was Marvin the father? Did he find the doctored videotape, or did he doctor the digital footage?

"Chief Blackhawk was an innocent victim this weekend," David continued. "We believe he made the arrows that killed him and Widdicomb, as well as the one that wounded Susanna Ryerson. We'll have confirmation tomorrow of his DNA is on the arrow's sinew binding at the arrowhead and fletching. Someone didn't want us to know anything about those arrows or the calls to learn about Widdicomb. Fortunately, we found the Chief's phone and the evidence on it. Voice ID analysis will tell us the caller who knew about the chief and the arrows."

Blank stares of shock covered the faces of the Galas and Phil Conroy. Henrietta couldn't hold her tongue. "This has been going on while we've been laughing, eating, and dancing?" she asked, her voice rising with each word. "This isn't one of those mystery games, is it?"

"No, Henrietta. Unfortunately, no one expected the intrigue and violence we've experienced," Peter answered, his voice short.

"Continue, David."

"Widdicomb married a second time. His wife was a Native American, and her child, Abigail, is Marvin's legitimate daughter. Blackhawk was raising her. The killer wanted to silence him. He knew too much. Marvin's marriage, his daughter, the arrows, he knew Carol Nelson, as well—Marvin introduced them. Someone copycatted Widdicomb's murder. They stabbed Blackhawk with one of his handmade arrows."

"So, we've been cavorting with a killer," Henrietta exclaimed. "Is the killer in this room?"

"Peter's certain of it," David said quietly.

She sat down suddenly, afraid to look at anyone.

Peter walked to Henrietta and placed his arm around her shoulder. "Fear not, Henrietta. An adage attributed to Confucius should provide solace to you—and to the guilty, confirmation of the reality of justice: *When embarking on a journey of revenge, first dig two graves.*

"Revenge was the motive for Carol Nelson's death. How could a child be legitimatized if the supposed sperm contributor is dead despite a supposed biological relationship? Where is the personal recognition, acceptance, verbal acknowledgment? Carol removed all of that."

"But why the attack on Susanna," Phil Conroy asked.

Before answering, Peter sat himself down in one of the wingback chairs, rested his head against its back, steepling his hands just beneath eyes that challenged the group. "A duality of motive, it would appear. Perhaps anger, even rage that a document could create a legal relationship, and its absence deny legal credence to a biological seed.

"Of course, that anger evolved from its focus on Susanna to all the Ryersons, as well as Widdicomb's progeny evidenced by the arrow attack on the family in the Ford Ranger. Two arrows targeting two tires resulting in a fiery explosion meant to wipe the family out: Susanna, her father, Widdicomb's two legitimate children, and an innocent bystander, Hezekiah. Malcolm X said it best, "You can't hate the roots of a tree and not hate the tree.

"But hating the tree is insufficient when hatred continues to evolve. Why not destroy the family's possessions? The family's friends? Crush them. Annihilate them. Erase them. Our killer tried.

And failed. Once again. A gas leak, discovered before a spark could touch off a fire, prevented an explosion in this house. Today.

"Jody, did you plan to feign a sudden illness to escape before the gas fumes exploded, or was your choice of seating near the kitchen doors a propitious one for a speedy exit free from accusation?"

"Are you nuts? Carol was my mother."

"A mother who chose not to raise you."

"She couldn't."

"Could not or would not?"

"She always checked on me."

"Yet, she never acknowledged you publicly."

Jody's face became hard; her eyes turned black. "Things were different when she had me."

"What about Marvin. Was he willing to acknowledge you publicly when you asked?"

Her eyes locked on Peter's.

"You asked him in Florida, didn't you?"

Tears began to flood her eyes. "He said Carol was sleeping with other guys, too. Said she wanted to marry him and tried to use me to get a ring."

"That must have hurt."

"He practically called her a whore."

"You called Carol and told her?"

"Yes, I did. She already planned to come down."

"You knew she killed him, didn't you?"

"I gave her the idea. Told her about his Comanche-Mohican wife and daughter. Told her he bragged about both of them. After she did it, she got mad at me. Said it was my fault she lost the only man she ever loved. Love? It was lust; love had nothing to do with it. She was stupid. And selfish. She didn't want anyone at the agency to know I was her daughter. She didn't want the competition."

It was as though the room were empty—Jody and Peter calmly discussing murder and mayhem.

"You talked Carol into ordering arrows for Redfeather?"

"It was easy. I planned to kill Widdicomb. I brought one of the arrows to Florida. When I told her what he called her, she lost it. I told her he tried to sleep with me, too. I gave her the arrow that morning and told her he didn't deserve her. She was on a mission."

"Did Redfeather teach you to shoot?"

"My stepfather taught me. We'd hunt rabbits together. Redfeather taught me how to target and judge distance. If Arnstein hadn't turned, Susanna would have been dead."

"You pushed Carol down the stairs. You killed the chief, and Larry almost caught you returning. You caused the collision. And you rigged the gas turn-off in Susanna's room."

"Busy lady, wasn't I?"

"Yes, but unsuccessful with the Ryersons. I have but one question, were you with Carol when she killed Marvin?",

"I taped it."

David walked behind Jody Marks, and with a guard, ushered her into the hall where Sheriff Bush was waiting to arrest her. He arrived earlier in time to hear Peter's questions and Jody's answers.

The silence in the room was deafening. When Peter began to speak, it was as if someone had turned up the volume. One after another, they stepped into each other's comments.

"I can't believe it."

"She was so sweet."

"I thought it was Redfeather."

"No way."

"I thought it was Emma."

"She's really smart."

"I thought they were accidents."

"I thought you doctored the footage."

"There is much to consider," Peter sighed. "If you would like to ask questions, David and Larry will provide answers. I must make Arthur and Susanna aware that our killer has confessed."

≈≈≈

After he met with Arthur and Susanna, he rejoined David and Larry, suggesting they reconvene in the morning to assess the DNA results and all the other evidence. Aside from Redfeather, the other guests had returned to their rooms. Chris and Abigail sat quietly, seemingly stunned by what they heard.

"It's tough for me to come to terms with Jody's confession," Redfeather admitted. "I still can't believe it. It's like she's another person."

"Jody is a psychopath, Hank," Peter explained. "She has no

conscience. No empathy. She can observe other personalities and copy their actions. She's the ultimate performer— charming, believable, pretending she is interested in you when she could care less. People are objects, resources to use for her benefit.

"She's cold and calculating and most likely planned every step of her actions—anything or anyone in her way was expendable. Whether Widdicomb is or is not her biological father, she believes it, and she wanted everything that his familial relationship could provide"

David interrupted. "Peter, you look exhausted. I know you haven't had much sleep. Let's call it a night. We all need to rest our "grey cells."

Peter smiled. "Yes, my friend. The "grey cells" do indeed require rest and restoration."

The Day After Christmas
Tuesday, December 26, 2006

Chapter Ninety

The Irony Of It All

Peter revisited images with his mind consort most of the night, recognizing the complexities of signs with multitudes of meaning.

> *The two black knights. You missed that one, Peter. Her dual personalities. But you clicked on the candles – the collision and the potential gas explosion in Susanna's room. And most likely, you didn't really believe Marks' poor-me act. Bravo, Peter.*

This was a difficult one. Violent actions perpetrated against dear friends, almost family, are incredibly complex. Emotions can cloud images that ordinarily would be so very clear. Till next time, dearest Peter.

When Peter finally went downstairs, David and Larry greeted him.

"Well, you look a little better, Peter," Larry offered. "But you're going to perk up when you taste Alena's asparagus omelet, positively oozing with Gruyere and freshly baked sourdough bread."

"Food for my famished body," Peter responded as Alena put a bowl of fresh strawberries and raspberries next to his omelet.

"We got all the results. The earring at the Fort Lauderdale scene matches the earring from Widdicomb's suite — both with Nelson's DNA. Jody's DNA matches the granola wrappers from the blind and the red hair on Widdicomb's body. Maybe Carol didn't do it? Maybe Jody planted the earring in the park."

"Carol did it," Peter answered, "manipulated by her daughter. She stabbed Marvin and ran. And I believe Jody administered the final death knoll smashing Marvin's head on the ground. And yes, Jody most likely planted the earring to make certain Carol would be caught. Just as she chose to use arrows tied to Redfeather to implicate him as a back-up should she need one."

"We may never be able to prove that. But we did find other matching arrows and a bow wrapped in a white coverall under Marks' car in the barn where it was parked," David offered.

"Yeh, but the real news is that Widdicomb wasn't Jody's father."

"Murder for naught," Peter sighed. "Murder built on misunderstanding, misinterpretations. A lie shared can become a life lost."

Just then, Arthur and Susanna entered the kitchen, followed by Hezekiah and Dr. Spensor. "The prognosis? A full recovery," chimed the doctor. Turning to his patients, he said, "Arthur, I recommend taking some time off, ease back into work slowly. Susanna? You need a vacation and a chance to rewind. I suggest somewhere warm with sun, blue water and blossoms. And as for our miracle man, Hezekiah, I prescribe at least two weeks doing absolutely nothing. Read, walk, get thee to a sunny place."

"The doctor speaks, and my task is to listen," Arthur exclaimed. "My home in Florida is not as elaborate as the lake house, but there are no shadows of evil inside. Friends and family join me there. Let's celebrate the New Year with freshness of thought, mind, and spirit."

Chris and Abigail walked in as Arthur spoke. "Sounds great, Gramps. I'm going to need some time to decide what I'm doing for the rest of my life. I'm quitting the paper. I want more of a challenge."

"Well, pumpkin, I, for one, am glad to hear that bit of news. We all have something to consider for the rest of our lives. Almost losing a life brings new priorities to head and heart." Susanna turned to David and asked, "Will you join me?"

"I thought you'd never ask."

The Final Word...

Jody Marks attempted to retract her confession, but despite her attorney's insanity claim, she was eventually convicted of murder. Not the murder of Carol Nelson, nor the murder of Sam Blackhawk. No real evidence at the scene tied her to their deaths. Only her words to Peter Dumas.

However, digital footage used to re-edit the Cycle, Inc 30-second spot was discovered in her condo — footage she shot of Marvin P. Widdicomb's before losing his life as he fell, grabbing the arrow embedded in his chest. Along with the footage was the original VHS version of the 30-second spot before the re-edit — it was never found in the production room at the agency's lower level.

Further, unidentified skin cells found on Widdicomb's shirt and neck were matched to Marks, no doubt shed when she repeatedly bashed his head on the stone beneath it.

CCTV also caught her entering the park at 7 AM dressed in khaki pants with a yellow vest pushing a trash cart. Forensics was able to magnify and clean up the image enough to show a strong resemblance between Marks' ear and the CCTV figure's ear.

The ear is fully formed when you're born. Some computer scientists who've initiated research on the ear's biometrical uniqueness suggest that ear IDs could rival fingerprints. Granted, it's still pie-in-the-sky, but...Marks' ear lobe suggests she was in the park at the right time to leave her skin cells on Widdicomb's body.

She hated Widdicomb, as well as his legal relationships and the resulting progeny. Her fingerprints were on Granola wrappers in the deer blind, where an aimed arrow followed a path to Susanna Ryerson's arm, almost killing the first Widdicomb wife. In her condo, a burner phone saw Chris Ryerson's number indicated on the day and time when a threatening call announced the existence of a step-sister.

It didn't take long for the jury to convict after she screamed a curse at the name of Marvin Widdicomb, whom she refused to believe was not her father.

The End

ACKNOWLEDGMENTS

Thank you.

Erika, Toni, Dana, Marti, Wendy, Dolores, Phyllis, and Doug for your encouragement, patience, suggestions, and time so generously given. But mostly, thank you for your friendship.

A special thanks to Eileen at the Barrington Library for providing extraordinary research help and direction, and reading my manuscript with a keen and questioning eye.

To my beta readers: a very special thank you for your diligence, honesty, and outstanding creative critiques — Dorothy, Joan, Jane, and David.

For Victim Investigation and Autopsy Procedures: Dr. Howard I Cooper, Lake County Coroner in Waukegan, Il and Dr. Anne Majewski, McHenry County Coroner in Woodstock, Il, who were generous with their time introducing me to the initial examination of a victim and the aspects of the autopsy.

For Investigative Procedures and Homicide Scene Specifics: PIOs Lee Cowart, Miami Dade Police Department, Officer Balsa, Miami Police Department, and Casey Liening, Fort Lauderdale Police Department. Plus, the MiamiDade.gov site with detailed information regarding State support for crime scene investigation from digital imaging, odontology, forensics, toxicology, and other departmental services. DNA: Illinois State Police

Southern Florida Flora: Florida Native Plant Society, Broward County Chapter President, Richard Brownscome, Dade County Chapter President Kurt Birchenough, and Professor Walter Taylor, University of Central Florida, author of Florida Wildflowers, guided me with suggestions of plants and descriptions growing in Fort Lauderdale during the winter.

Patrick Tracey, Appleton International Airport, explained why the snow crews help make it The airport that never closes.

Medical protocol: Staff members at the Calumet Health Department and the critical access hospital, Ascension Calumet Hospital (known as Chilton Memorial, before 2006).

Chuck Palella at A&L Auto Body in Palatine, Illinois, auto collision professional who helped me understand how an arrow targeting a vehicle can start a complicated chain reaction resulting in a major explosion.

Larry Madden (Mohican name—"Muskweenow"— meaning Bear Man/Running Bear), Language Project Manager at the Arvid E. Miller Library Museum and Cultural Affairs Department in Bowler, Wisconsin, who gave me valuable insight into the Stockbridge-Munsee Community and Mohican and Comanche history and rituals.

Michael G. Harris of the Cassidy Tire Company in Addison, Il, who explained verbally and visually the "how, where, and why" an arrow traveling at the right speed could penetrate a tire and cause a crash.

Shawn Woods video (https://www.youtube.com/watch?v=LBE589mbcdU) demonstrating how to make a Comanche style arrow inspired by the Billy Berger article, Treasures of the Smithsonian Part 3 in the June/July 2010 issue of Primitive Archery magazine. Berger's website is PrimitivePathways.com.

Various websites that gave me background information on a variety of topics I've mentioned/introduced in this Peter Dumas mystery— war bonnets, Native American migration; safety measures, death rituals, tribal assimilation, and naming ceremonies: TexasHistory.com, NativeLanguages.org, Mohican.com, WisconsonHistory.com, Wikipedia.com, warpathstopeacepipes.com, NicorGas.com.

And a special thanks to my family, friends, and former colleagues, for their encouragement and optimism.

About the Author

L.C. Blackwell began a writing/producing career in premier Chicago ad agencies, creating Radio-TV and print advertising for Fashion, Food, Consumer Products, Retail, as well as Children's shoes and toys.

A growing interest in TV saw her trade advertising for programming as an independent writer-producer developing creative for a select group of projects. Among them: "Belleza Latina", daily short-form beauty programs licensed to the Spanish Entertainment Network; A bull-riding documentary airing on ABC and Univision affiliates in Phoenix, Arizona; Multimedia promotion, including a jingle titled "Pass It On" for the National Fitness Foundation presidential appointee, George Allen; And, creative and production for TV pilots, radio spots, and jingles for a national Hispanic food producer; plus, a video production site for Realtors®.

LC wrote two children's books before turning her thoughts to murder in the first Peter Dumas novel, *For Sale MURDER*. *Ready Aim MURDER* is Book 2 in the series. Book 3 is gathering momentum in LC's mind.

Too Young To Be This Old was written in memory of two close and dear friends who motivated LC to begin writing fiction.

Other Books

by
L.C. Blackwell

The Peter Dumas Series
For Sale Murder Book 1

Children's Books
For Sale: The North Pole
A Very Special Truck

Women's Fiction
Too Young To Be This Old (March 2021)

CPSIA information can be obtained
at www.ICGtesting.com
Printed in the USA
LVHW050849281121
704654LV00008B/704